Real Riders Never Die
A Novel By:
A'Zayler

Text LEOSULLIVAN to
22828 to join our mailing
list!

To submit a manuscript for our review,
email us at leosullivanpresents@gmail.com

© 2015

Published by Leo Sullivan Presents

www.leolsullivan.com

All rights reserved.

Author's Notes

This is a re-release of the series Real Riders Never Die now under the publishing company of Leo Sullivan Productions

Dedication

December 2014...Then

I would like to dedicate this book to my beautiful friend Ananius Luckey. We've been friends for almost eleven years now and she's been loyal since day one. We may not talk every day, or every week but your place in my heart remains the same. From the moment I met you you've been yourself. You've never changed or been anything less than genuine. You're a very strong and amazing person. I love you, and remember God gives his toughest battles, to his strongest soldiers!

October 2015...Now

It's crazy how not even a year ago I dedicated this exact same book to you. Oh how things have changed since then. When I wrote that dedication last year I had no idea of what was to come. All I knew was that you were one of my best friends and I loved you. I knew I wanted you to survive. I knew I wanted you to fight until you kicked Cancer's ass. I knew I wanted you to get well so we could continue having our long conversations about nothing, fighting about everything, and watch the cooking channel talking about food we were never going to make for real. I just want you back here so I can hear your voice again. I miss you so much. A lot of times when you cross my mind I can laugh, and others all I can do is cry. It seems like I'm crying more days than laughing but it's for a good reason. You're free now friend, from all the pain, all the suffering, and all the trials you had to endure during your last days here. Thinking back on the day when you first told me you were sick, I wasn't even worried because you were so strong. I knew if anybody could handle that, you could and you did. You did an outstanding job! You fought hard sis and I'm so proud of you. The week before you died when we were in your hospital room I knew it was coming and I thought I could handle it but when your day actually came I wasn't so sure anymore. Some days I'm still not. Like now, I'm typing this and I can hardly catch my breath. I know if you were here you would be making fun of me for crying and although that should make me laugh it doesn't. It only makes me wish you were here even more. Your spiritual healing finally came and you deserved it. You were my sister and I'll love and miss you forever. Rest peacefully baby and I'll see you again someday.

Oh and I bet you look so pretty with your wings ☺ I miss your smile like crazy Anna!!

Chapter 1

Winter

2014

"*Even though I'm in the streets, you know exactly
what I do, when I chase this paper you ain't gotta wait
for me to bring back home to you, cuz I ride or die girl
we gon be good, and if you ride or die, we gon make it
out this hood"* blasted through her speakers as she
walked back into her closet. Taryn-Lee sang along to the
song as tears ran down her face. How could she have
gotten to this point? Where had she gone wrong? She had
been alone basically her entire life, and the one time she
found true love it's taken away. She had given all the
love she could, been loyal from day one, and where did it
get her? Nowhere! Only place it had gotten her was in her
apartment with a broken heart, and a closet full of his
clothes to pack. She knew exactly how Ace Hood felt;
they were supposed to always be good. She was his ride
or die.

Taryn was so out of her mind that she tripped over
a shoe in the middle of her floor. As she fell into her
closet, she hit her head on the doorknob. While lying flat
on the floor, she lifted her head a few inches and came
face-to-face with the black safe beneath her shoeboxes.
At that moment, she figured there was no way her life
could get any worse. Either hitting her head on the door
magnified her pain, or the amount of self-pity she was
feeling had consumed her. She reached for the case and
opened it. The small pink Cobra .22 felt heavy in her

hand. As she leaned back against the wall, she stared at the gun for a long moment; she had nothing else to lose, and nothing to look forward to. The only person she had was in a big church with a suit on, waiting to be eulogized. Shaking back her tears, she raised the gun to her mouth and stuck it inside. *Lord please forgive me* she prayed in her mind before pulling the trigger…

Nine months earlier…

"Taryn, hurry up!" Todd yelled from outside of the bathroom door. Todd was one of her five foster siblings.

"I'm coming Todd! I just got in, give me a minute please!" she yelled back as she washed the shampoo from her hair. Because there were so many of them that lived there, the shower was one of the things they fought about the most. She should have taken a shower last night, but she had to wash her hair and by this morning, it would have been a dry tangled mess. Leaning under the water, she rinsed her body and stepped out of the tub. She didn't even bother to turn the water off, being that Todd was about to get right in behind her. After wrapping her pink towel around her body, she retrieved her clothes from the floor and walked out.

"It's about time Princess Taryn."

"Oh shut up," she said, pushing her door closed. Inside her room that she shared with her foster sister Reese, she began getting dressed. Today was her first day at her new school. It was her senior year in high school, and she had just been placed in this new foster home. The Turners were the seventh foster family she'd been with since she was two, and prayerfully the last. Being that she would be eighteen in less than a week, she would officially be grown and no longer a ward of the state. She had been through a lot in her life, and she was ready for it to end. When she was two, her mother and Father, Erin and Terrence Lee Alvarez, were killed in a car accident. She had been placed in foster homes immediately after that because she had no other family. Her parents' families had disconnected with them long before she was born, so all she knew was them. All of her foster homes thus far had been terrible except the one right before her current one. The Jones' were some of the best people she had ever known. They treated her like she was their real daughter. She hated that she had to leave in order to make room for the younger kids. Her current home in Columbus, Georgia only housed children that were nearing or already 18.

"You nervous T?" Reece asked as she sat on her bed watching Taryn get ready for school. Her and Taryn had gotten close over the last couple of months, but that was about to come to an end as well. Reece was already eighteen and was leaving for the Army at the end of the week.

"Kind of, but not because it's a new school with new people, but because you're not going to be there with me."

"It's okay lil sis, I'll be here when you get home. You'll be fine. As long as you don't get in any fights for taking somebody ma." Taryn laughed as she pinned her hair back

"Girl that ain't even what I'm on and you know it."

"Yes! I already know." Reece couldn't understand for the life of her why Taryn downplayed her beauty. She was one of the prettiest girls she had ever seen. She was so exotic and rare looking. Taryn was 6'0 with a very shapely body, almost like the Australian rapper Iggy Azalea, but a little thicker. She had bright black eyes that were round and slanted in the corner, cute lips, and she had the prettiest dark skin ever. Their foster mother always made fun of her because she was so dark, but in reality that was her best quality. She wasn't your ordinary dark skin girl. Her dark was smooth and odd, assumingly from her Ethiopian mother. Her hair was a long, black, thick, and silky mix because her father was black. On most days, she wore it big and wavy. She was absolutely gorgeous; her beauty was intimidating, but you'd never know because she was such a sweetheart. She knew she would draw attention off her looks alone, not to mention it was the middle of the semester, so she chose a casual outfit for today.

After she got dressed, she grabbed her backpack and left for school. She left an hour early because she had to walk. Her foster mother hated her, and her foster father loved her. He was the main reason her mother didn't like her. He always made nasty comments to her or touched her inappropriately. She despised it, but she needed somewhere to live. She tried her best to avoid him. Taryn really hated that she had to walk because it was April in Georgia, which meant it was hot as hell outside; not to mention, she would probably be sweating by the time she made it to school. She tried to make it there as fast as she could without busting a sweat. Aside from walking in the heat, she had to deal with the various cars of men offering her rides, which she continuously declined. She pulled out her phone and called Reece so she wouldn't look or feel crazy walking alone. This was nothing new. She and Reece had made this a habit because they were always walking. She talked to Reece until she walked into the parking lot of Carver High School. She got a sick feeling in her stomach upon seeing how big the school was. She wasn't a fan of too many people.

"Alright sis, I'll call you when I'm on my way home."

"Nah don't call me. Find you one of them fine men up there and make him drive you home." Reece laughed as she hung up the phone. Taryn was happy once she finally walked into the school. She was so happy she had worn her two French braids today. Neither her hair nor her clothes were sweated out. Because she had so much hair, her braids were both thick and long. After getting her schedule from her counselor, she stopped by the bathroom before heading to class. She had to check and be sure she still looked as cute as she did when she left the house.

While walking to her class, she fixed her big gold hoops and applied some more lip gloss. She could already tell dressing up was a big deal here. Taryn had always loved to shop and dress cute but being that her money was limited, she shopped on a budget. Her foster parents made her get a job to buy everything she needed, from clothes to food. It didn't bother her though; she had been making her own way her whole life. The moment she got into her classroom, all eyes were on her. Both males and females were watching her. She didn't know if it was because she was new, tall, or pretty. Maybe it was all three. Either way, she didn't care; she got this everywhere she went.

"Class, this is Taryn-Lee; introduce yourselves and make her feel comfortable." Taryn rolled her eyes. She couldn't believe her teacher had just put her on the spot like this was still elementary school or something. On top of that, she had said her name wrong.

"It's *Taryn*, like Aaron with a T," she said, correcting her.

"Oh I'm sorry sweetheart, you can sit right back there in that desk next to Kia; Kia raise your hand," her teacher said. Noticing the girl raise her hand, she made her way to her seat with all eyes still on her. Although she loved school, she hated it at the same time. She loved to learn, but she was definitely not a people person. The rest of the day went by in a blur; after her third block, she was ready to go home. After she walked into her last class of the day, which was PE, she got her class uniform and went to change. Even though she didn't mind PE, she hated that she had to change, especially since the shorts they gave her magnified her curves. The little jersey shorts made her butt appear larger than it was and she hated it. She wasn't like normal girls with big butts; she couldn't stand when people made a big deal out of it. Once she got back to the gym, the boys' basketball team had gotten in there and were shooting around the gym.

"Aw hell," she mumbled to herself, noticing she had to past them to get to where her class was sitting. She had almost made it by the group when one of them said something.

"Aye Pocahontas!" he yelled. Stopping in her tracks because she knew he was talking to her, she turned around.

"What?" she asked, looking at him like he was crazy.

"You new?"

"Nah I'm not new, I'm old, what kind of question is that?" she asked, obviously annoyed by the dumb question.

"Damn you got an attitude problem little girl" he said, making his friends laugh.

"No I don't, that was just a dumb question. You know you have never seen me before today."

"You right because you would definitely be impossible to miss," another boy with a thick accent said. Looking at the boy, she thought she would faint. He was fine as hell to say the least. He was tall and brown-skinned with the cutest little freckles on his face. He had long blonde dreads and green eyes. The thing she liked the most was that he looked to be about 6'7; because she was tall, she didn't pay men under six feet any attention. His shoulders were wide, and he stood on a pair of the sexiest bow legs she'd ever seen. His presence was commanding; it was like he oozed confidence. He was medium-build and muscular in a pair of basketball shorts and a **Carver Basketball** t-shirt. She wasn't sure if he made that statement because he thought she was pretty, or because she was almost as tall as he was. Not knowing

14

what to say, she just smiled at him and turned to walk away.

"Hold up girl, what's your name?" the loud boy asked her again. She could tell he didn't mean any harm; he just talked a lot, so she dropped her attitude.

"It's Taryn-Lee."

"That's your whole name or just your first name?" he asked.

"It's just my first name, it's hyphenated. What's your name since you're all in my business?" she asked, crossing her arms over her chest.

"It's Courtney"

"Oh okay, well nice meeting you Courtney but I got to go," she smiled and walked away.

By the end of the day, she was past ready to get home. This feeling was short lived because her foster dad Terry was home. Breathing hard, she walked into the house and into her room. After locking the door, she began her homework. Halfway through, she heard a faint knock at the door; she knew who it was automatically because they were the only two home.

"I'm busy!" she yelled, not moving to open the door.

"Taryn-Lee, open up this damn door," he said. She already knew he was about to start some mess today. He only acted mad when he was doing shit he wasn't supposed to be doing. Opening the door, she stood back so he could enter.

"You don't pay no fucking bills in here, don't be locking no damn doors," he said, blatantly staring at her breasts in her fitted shirt.

"Sorry Terry."

"What did I tell you about calling me that shit?" he asked, getting in her face.

Looking to the side so his mouth wouldn't accidentally touch hers, she said, "Sorry daddy." She knew he wanted her to call him this in more of a perverted way than a daddy daughter way- but whatever.

"That's better. You gaining some weight ain't you?" he asked, palming her butt. Not even bothering to answer, she stood silent, hoping he would hurry up and leave. Pressing her against the wall, she could feel his tiny hard on against her thigh. She was a lot taller than Terry, so his advances were somewhat in vein.

"Taryn you feel this big dick?" he asked. She tried not to, but she couldn't help it and burst into a laugh so hard her eyes watered. Terry's penis was anything but big. Knowing why she was laughing, he got mad and slapped her face so hard her head snapped to one side.

"Laugh at me again you big bitch, and you'll be fucking homeless," he snarled. Taryn held the side of her face as she willed herself not to cry. Terry was too weak for her tears. He grabbed her butt again and started grinding on her thigh. Seconds later, her bedroom door pushed open and in walked her foster mother Tammy.

"What the fuck are you doing, Terry?" she yelled, like she didn't know what was going on. She had caught the looks Terry gave Taryn all the time, but acted as if she didn't. She was tired of it now. Just like Taryn figured they would, he lied, and Tammy believed him. Taryn tried explaining her side because she had nowhere else to go, but Tammy wasn't trying to hear it. After arguing with them for another ten minutes, Tammy got fed up and put her out. Taryn refused to beg anybody for anything, so she nodded her head and got ready to pack. She grabbed her two orange duffel bags from under her bed and started in her closet first. Midway through packing her stuff, Tammy and Terry had left the room. Only then did she let a tear escape, but she cleaned it as quick as it fell. After packing all of her belongings in both bags, she sat down and wrote Reece a note explaining what happened. Close to an hour later, she had her bags and backpack and stood on the front porch to wait for her cab. She stashed her clothes at her job in their storage room and got back in the cab. They'd had been riding around aimlessly for the last two hours. She knew the cabby felt sorry for her by the way he kept looking at her in the rear view mirror.

"Have you decided where you want me to take you yet ma'am?" She shook her head no, and looked out the window.

"There's a women's shelter ten minutes from here if you would like me to take you there," he offered. She knew she had nowhere to go, but she wasn't sure she wanted anybody to know yet. She told him no and asked to be dropped off at lake bottom park down the street. He did as he was told, but slid her a card with the women's shelter address and number on it before pulling off. She sat on the swing with her head down, crying for a few minutes before her phone rang; it was Reece. She talked to Reece until it got dark. She lied about being at the women's shelter so she wouldn't worry. Moving to the bench under the streetlight, Taryn racked her brain trying to figure out what she was going to do. She had put an extra pair of clothes in her backpack for school tomorrow, but that was as far as she had gotten. She tried to stay off her phone so it would have some juice for the night being that she had nowhere to charge it, but she was getting scared. Fighting the urge to call Reece, she closed it and looked up at the stars. She was in deep thought when she heard two voices behind her at the basketball court. She turned to look and see who it was, and saw a short dark-skinned girl with the tall cutie from her school. She could tell they couldn't see her from where she was sitting, but she could see them. The way they were hugging and playing, she knew the girl had to be his girlfriend. Even though she was inwardly hoping he was single, she had to admit they were cute. Getting up from where she was sitting on the bench, she walked around the slide and sat on the bench that wasn't under the street light. She would hate for them to see her sitting there all by herself for no reason. She watched as he shot the ball a few times, while the girl stood next to the goal talking to him. By the time they left, it had been another hour and a half, and it was almost ten o clock at night. Lazily putting her feet up on the bench, she wrapped her arms around her legs and laid her head on her knees. She could imagine everybody in their houses getting ready for school and work the next day. Here she was seventeen and homeless, with no family except Reece, who was leaving her soon too. She began crying again thinking about how different her life might be if her parents were

18

alive. All she wanted was to be normal, have a normal family with a mom and dad that loved her, and her siblings. Sadly, that would never be the case; she had no siblings, and she had no real parents.

"Pocahontas," she heard a deep voice say. Looking up, she met eyes with the sexy dread head from earlier. She tried to hurry and wipe her eyes on her jeans before he could tell she was crying, but it was too late.

"How did you know it was me?" she asked, trying to distract him from her crying.

"I saw your braids. What you doing out here this late, you waiting for somebody?" he said before taking a seat next to her.

"No, I just needed a quiet place to think."

"I feel you; your folks don't care about you being out this late?" She looked away and shook her head no. He sensed something was wrong with her, so he waited a minute before saying anything else. He just sat there with her in silence, looking at the stars. He had noticed her earlier when he was at the court with Alicia but he didn't want to be rude, so he walked Alicia home first then came back. The silence was interrupted when she started asking questions.

"Where you from?" She had to ask, because his accent was sexy as hell.

"I'm from Cameroon Africa." The moment he said that, her mouth dropped open; she would have never in a million years guessed that. He laughed at her reaction; anytime he told people he was African, they would give the craziest responses. Surprisingly, she thought it was cool. He reciprocated the question.

"Where are you from? Because you don't look American at all."

"I actually am American, I was born here. My mother was Ethiopian and my father was black."

"Why you keep saying was like they ain't no more?" After she disclosed they were dead, he wanted to kick himself. He didn't mean to pour salt on an already open wound. The water in her eyes made him feel worse, so he apologized. She normally didn't get choked up talking about her parents because they had been dead for so long, but after the day she'd had she couldn't help it.

"Well who do you live with?"

"I live in a foster home." she figured there wasn't a reason to tell him the truth; for one, she didn't know him and even if she did, he couldn't do anything about it anyway. To change the subject, she started telling him about her birthday. Once she turned eighteen, she would no longer be a ward of the state, which made her happy. He listened so intently that she had to smile. He was so cute to her that she couldn't help but stare.

"Yo lil mama, why you looking at me like that?"

"You're just different from anybody I've ever seen before. I never saw an African that looks like you. Especially not one that sounds so country," she said as they shared a laugh. The moment he opened his mouth you could tell he was from somewhere else, but he still sounded country like he was from the south.

"That's a good thing. At least now I know you'll remember me, like I'll remember you."

"Why will you remember me?" she asked with a confused look.

"You act like you don't look different. You look exotic as shit."

"No I don't, I look like a regular ole black girl," she laughed, taking her feet down off the bench and placing them on the ground.

"I'm just a regular old African," he laughed. *Lawd he fine!* she thought as she watched his face light up from laughing. Then it hit her, she still didn't know his name, so she asked.

"Demoto?" she asked, making sure she said it right.

"Yeah, like Dee-Mo-toe," he said, breaking it down in syllables for her, before telling her his last name.

"Well Demoto Youngblood, I'm Taryn-Lee Alvarez," she said, sticking her hand out so he could shake it. Her hand was so soft and she smelled so good; he had to get up and head home before she made him rethink committing to Alicia.

"How long you plan on sitting out here?" That question brought her back to reality. He watched as her mood went down, which brought him back to her crying earlier. Because it was so late, he offered to walk her home. He wanted to believe it was because it was dark, and not because he wasn't ready to leave her yet. She turned him down as soon as he asked her. She made up some lame excuse about his parents, so he had to burst her bubble. He lived here with his older brother; their parents were still in Cameroon.

She hated herself for not going to the shelter earlier; now she had to find a way to get rid of him. There was an issue with her and going home, so he sat back down on the bench.

"Come, on let's talk about it."

"Talk about what?" she said, trying to avoid the obvious.

"Why you don't want to take your ass home." Looking at him, he seemed like he could be trusted, so she decided to tell him a little bit.

"Does he hurt you?" he asked after she was finished. He wanted to know did he ever molest her, but didn't want to outright ask it. Her head shook subtly as she looked back at the ground. His chest loosened a little upon hearing they weren't having sex, but for some reason he was angry about her situation. The way he was sitting and listening made her feel comfortable enough to talk, so she kept going. She was so busy venting she hadn't noticed the sudden change in his mood; his nostrils had flared, and his green eyes had turned a dark auburn color.

"Yo what the fuck? You want me to beat that nigga ass?" Hearing she'd been slapped by her stepfather blew him up. She was momentarily caught off guard by his anger, because he didn't know her well enough to care. She dismissed the offer and made jokes about Terry's size to ease some of the tension. She smiled at him and lay her head back on her knees. She had sat down a minute ago so they could finish talking. She thought he would let it go, but he hadn't. He probed her for information about what would happen when she got home tonight. Truth be told, she was too embarrassed to be saying this out loud, and it felt even worse saying it to Demoto.

"Is that why you don't want me to walk you home?" Instead of answering, she just nodded her head. *Looking at this girl, you would never know*, he thought as he scooted closer to her on the bench.

"Do you want to go home tonight?" he asked her.

"Not much of a choice, Demoto."

"You do got a fucking choice, you can come to my crib," he said like she should have already known. After she continuously turned down his offer, he became more forceful.

"Nah fuck that, you ain't got no choice no more, you coming with me," his voice filled with finality. In her mind, she knew this was crazy but where else did she have to go? It was either his house or the shelter. He stood and reached out his hand for her to take. Looking up at him for a long time, she finally took his hand and got up. They walked in silence the entire way to his house. When they got to the front of an apartment

complex called Greystone Summit, they walked until
they reached the fourth building and went up the stairs.

"You sure your brother won't mind?" she asked,
grabbing his shirt before he unlocked the door.

"Man Taryn chill, my brother cool, and if it make
you feel better he probably sleep by now anyway."
Turning back around, he unlocked the door and stood to
the side for her to walk in. Once inside, she waited for
him to lead the way. The apartment was dark except for
the small light over the stove. When they reached the
back bedroom, they walked in and he closed the door
behind them. She sat her backpack down and asked for
directions to the restroom so she could take a shower.

"It's down the hall to the left; you want me to
come with you?"

"Nah I think I can find it." She took a shower and
put on her pajamas. After unbraiding her hair, she ran her
hands through it and brushed her teeth before exiting.

"Shit girl," Demoto said, eyeing her body as she
walked back into his room.

"What?" she asked a bit nervous.

"Jeune fille que vous avez assez d'enfer," he
rattled off in perfect French. If she'd had on panties at
that moment, they would have been soaked. She thought
his country accent was sexy, but when he started
speaking in another language she almost lost it.

"What did you just say to me?"

24

"Girl you pretty as hell," he filled her in while still eyeing her lustfully. He had saw how rare of a beauty she was at school today, but looking at her up close with all her hair out was even better. She had so much fucking hair, but it was sexy as hell.

"In what language were you speaking?" she asked, still trying to gain her composure.

"It was French baby girl, I speak French." Turning around to place her book bag on the floor, she had to fan herself.

"Whew lord!" she mumbled. This was about to be a long night; this boy was past fine.

Chapter 2

Demoto stood behind her and watched her every move; she was so tall and pretty; he wasn't lying when he said she looked exotic. On top of her being pretty, her body was banging; he didn't know how he was about to lay in a bed with her and keep himself under control. Pulling his shirt from his body, he grabbed his old spice bear glove body wash and left the room. He needed a cold shower ASAP! In the shower, he wondered to himself was he doing the right thing letting her stay with him tonight. He knew this wasn't a permanent solution, but he wouldn't have been able to sleep thinking about her being in the house with her foster dad. She seemed cool and trustworthy, so he would see how tonight went and help her figure out something for tomorrow. If Alicia found out about this, there would definitely be trouble.

With her phone on the charger, Taryn texted Reece to let her know her change of plans, and promised to call and explain everything tomorrow. Although Demoto looked like he could be trusted, she didn't know him or his brother and somebody needed to know where she was. She had just put her phone down when he walked in his room in a towel. *Now why he do that?* To distract herself, Taryn got up and brushed her hair into a messy bun at the top of her head, and walked back to his bed. She wanted to tie her hair up but she didn't want him to see her scarf, so she would just skip tonight.

"Aye T, you gon' be comfortable sleeping in the bed with me?" he asked, sliding on his basketball shorts.

"Yeah I'm good, living in foster homes you get use to sharing beds," she said as she kneeled on the side of the bed and said her prayers. Demoto stood on the opposite side watching her; he hadn't prayed since he left Cameroon. As a child his parents always made them pray, but since he'd been older he didn't bother. She looked so pretty, even with her hair all balled up. He rolled his eyes and grabbed a rubber band off the dresser. Demoto tied his dreads in a ponytail at the back of his neck and pulled the covers back. Once she finished, she stole a glance at him before getting into bed. He asked her was she hungry before cutting off the lights, but once again she declined. It hadn't even crossed her mind that she hadn't eaten since earlier that morning before school, but she didn't want to bother him. After flipping the switch for the lights and cutting the fan on, he got into bed with her. For a long time, there was an awkward silence that filled the room, neither of them sleeping, but neither knew what to say.

"I'm glad you decided to stay with me tonight."

"Me too, thanks for letting me," she said quietly. Turning on her side, she scooted to the edge of the bed, careful to give him his space as she tried falling asleep. She wasn't quite sure how long she had been sleeping when she heard him on his phone. She heard him say Alicia, so it was probably the girl from earlier.

"Taryn, you sleep?"

"I was, what's up?"

"Nothing, I just didn't know whether I had woke you up or not." It was evident he wanted to say something but didn't know how, so she helped him.

"What's going on?"

"Nothing, I was just going to ask is it okay if I lay by you." Against her better judgment, she said yes. She knew as sexually attracted to him as she was, he didn't need to be near her, but oh well. He scooted to the middle of the bed and pulled her up against him, her back to his front and left his hand around her waist. She had never been this close to any other man in her life except Terry, and surprisingly it felt completely different. Being all up on her like this wasn't the smartest decision, but he couldn't help it. He kept smelling her peach body wash, and knowing she was in his bed he just had to. If he thought not touching her was torture, having her ass right in his lap was even worse. *What was I thinking*, he wondered to himself as he smelled her hair and neck. Out of nowhere, she asked was Alicia his girlfriend. He thought about lying, but there was no reason to so he said yes. Although they had nothing going on, for some reason he didn't really want to talk about Alicia with Taryn; it felt wrong. Of course, he flipped her question back on her.

"Nope, I don't do boyfriends."

"What you mean you don't do boyfriends? What kind of shit is that?"

"I've just never really had one. I like boys and everything, but it's hard for me to be with a person that doesn't understand me, and most men usually don't."

"You must be complicated."

"A little." she smiled.

28

"We'll see about that," he said, scooting closer to her and tightening his grip around her waist. Before long, they were both sleep. Halfway through the night, Demoto woke up with a massive hard on and a need to piss; leaning up, he made sure Taryn was still asleep before sliding out of bed. She looked so peaceful that he didn't want to accidentally wake her. Once out of bed, he stared at her for a few minutes before exiting his room. If she didn't look like she had already been through enough, he would have made her wake up and handle his morning wood, but in the back of his mind he already knew she wasn't that type. Just as he flushed the toilet and pulled his shorts up, he heard somebody behind him. As soon as he turned around, her saw her standing in the doorway rubbing her eyes. Not only was one side of her tank top rolled up, exposing her flat stomach, but her hair had fallen out of the bun and was in a big bushy ponytail.

"Did I wake you up?"

"Yeah, I'm a light sleeper. Why you peeing with the door open?" she asked, giving him a lazy smirk.

"I left it open in case you wanted to come in." She smiled, walking into the bathroom with him. She didn't know whether the bathroom was just little or if both of them were just big, because it seemed as if the space in there got smaller that fast.

"You must plan on watching me pee or something?" she asked, noticing he was still standing against the sink.

"Yeah I did, but I see you don't want me to," he laughed and walked out of the bathroom. Once she was finished, she was headed back to his room until she saw him in the kitchen. He was sitting on the kitchen counter drinking a bottle of water when she entered. Looking her up and down, Demoto noticed for her to be as tall as she was she walked with ease. She walked so light you wouldn't even know she was coming if you didn't see her.

"This is a nice place y'all got," she said, leaning on the counter in front of him. Demoto was so lost in her body that he had totally disregarded what she was saying.

"How long have you had your nipples pierced?" he asked. Forgetting that she didn't have a bra on, she crossed her arms over her breasts before answering. She never really liked wearing bras to bed; they were uncomfortable, so she'd woke up a few hours ago while he was asleep and taken it off.

"For about two months; me and my foster sister Reece got them done together."

"I don't know what you trying to hide 'em for now, I already seen 'em,'" he smiled.

"I'm not hiding them. I just forgot I didn't have a bra on," she said looking down. He could tell from how embarrassed she looked that she was definitely inexperienced when it came to men. Every time he would look at her, she would smile and look away or fidget a little. Demoto thought her innocence was kind of cute.

"If it was up to me, you would never wear a bra," he said, blatantly starting at her breasts through her thin shirt. She had to be at least a size C; they were big but not too big, and they definitely weren't small.

"Now why you got to be so nasty Demoto?"

"I can't help it girl, they right in my damn face," he laughed, hopping off the counter. After sitting his bottle of water down, he walked up to her and leaned his body against hers. He could tell he had caught her off guard, but he didn't care. He untied the drawstrings on her shorts and slid his hands down the back of her shorts, palming her butt.

"You so soft T, and you smell so good." Nuzzling her neck, he sniffed a little more before kissing it. He hadn't planned on doing this with her, but he couldn't help it; his dick got hard the moment she walked into the kitchen.

"You want me to stop?" he asked as he leaned back to look at her face. She was too nervous to talk, so she just shook her head no instead. It took her a minute to get with it after he kissed her, but she eventually began kissing him back. He was so glad that she was tall like him, because he didn't have to do the most just to kiss her. He thought he liked short girls, but Taryn was making that a distant thought. Her mind was going a mile a minute; she didn't want to have sex with Demoto yet, but she was too scared to make him stop. Her body was yearning for his touch; every time he put his hand on her, she shivered.

Just as she got into their kiss good, he picked her up and sat her on the counter top. In a swift motion, he grabbed her thighs he pulled her to the edge of the counter so she could feel how hard he had gotten. The moment he pressed himself against her shorts, he could feel the heat coming from her body. She released a quiet moan. Demoto had her body on fire; she couldn't even think straight. After locking her legs around his waist, she started running her hands through his hair. She loved his blonde dreads; she had been thinking about touching them since she had first saw him at school.

"Damn baby," he said as he lightly bit her nipples through her shirt. He was in the middle of pulling her shorts down when his brother came out of his room. Taryn leaped from the counter and stood behind Demoto's back.

"Damn, my fault Moto," he said, going back into his room. Taryn was so busy hiding behind Demoto she didn't even get a chance to see what he looked like. His accent was just as thick as Demoto's. Taryn was big, but Demoto was bigger so it was safe to say with her standing behind him, his brother hadn't gotten a good look at her either. Demoto reached and pulled her from behind him.

"Come on, let's go in my room then with your scary ass," he said, pulling her by her hand. By the time they had gotten in his room, it had given her enough time to get herself together. He apparently felt the same way, because he got right into bed.

"Now T, don't be grinding all up on me like you was doing the first time."

"I was not grinding on you."

"Yes you were! I woke up and my dick was hard as hell, so don't do that shit no more," he said as he slapped her butt before getting into bed. She didn't know what it was, but when he hit her butt she got wet all over again. For her sake, she hoped he had enough self-control for the both of them. Scooting close to her in bed, Demoto made sure to put his dick right on her butt before wrapping his free arm back around her waist. He didn't know when, but in the back of his mind he knew he had to get a piece of Taryn, and he would. Exchanging goodnight's they fell asleep almost instantly.

*****

The next day at school, Kia and Taryn were on their way to lunch but had made a pit stop at the bathroom. Taryn didn't see why Kia was making such a big deal out of the lunch they had. Yeah, the basketball team was in there, but that was none of her concern. Taryn didn't pay boys her age any attention; they either liked her or they didn't. Honestly, she really didn't care who she had lunch with; she had too much other stuff on her mind. Today was a new day, but at the end of it she was still homeless. She had thanked Demoto a million times this morning for letting her stay with him last night, but she already knew that wasn't permanent. Taryn watched Kia fix her hair and lip gloss in the mirror. She didn't care either way; she already knew she was fly. Her clothes weren't the most expensive, but the way she styled them you'd never know. Today she wore a pair of dark blue distressed high waist jeans and a thin white racer back top, with a couple of gold chains and her gold hoops. Because she was pushed for time this morning, she didn't braid her hair down again; instead, she wore it big and all down with a part on the side. She loved her hair when it acted right; it reminded her a lot of the actress Lashontae Heckard's. Demoto had joked with her the whole ride to school about her looking exotic, but that was after she caught him staring a few times.

After they left the bathroom, Taryn took her eos out and coated her full lips with the chapstick. They walked into the lunchroom, and it was like a party. She had missed lunch yesterday fixing her schedule, so today she was a tad bit nervous. Now she saw why Kia wanted to check herself out in the restroom first. This cafeteria was packed as hell. They walked past the line and a few tables, and headed straight to the back. There were about six tables in the corner, where obviously the popular people sat. She noticed the boys from the basketball team taking up four of them, while a few groups of girls sat at the other two. Initially she felt nervous, but that went out the window the moment she saw the girls at the table with their faces screwed up. She had dealt with jealousy from girls her entire life, so she paid them no mind and followed Kia to sit down. Just as she pulled out a chair to sit down, she heard Courtney's voice calling her Pocahontas. She turned around and waved.

"What's up girl, I ain't know you had this lunch, I didn't see you in here yesterday."

"I didn't come yesterday I had some stuff to do," she said.

"Oh okay, you wearing the fuck out of those jeans too," he said, drawing a few comments from the rest of the boys at the table.

34

"Thank you," she said dryly as she rolled her eyes and sat down.

Their conversation was completely over; if it was one thing she couldn't stand, it was a man talking about her body. Especially in public! That was the fastest way to piss her off. Reece had told her she needed to chill with the attitude because people couldn't help it. Reece tried explaining to her too many times that her ass was big and people were going to notice; some would even say something about it, but it still made her mad. After picking up on her attitude, Kia tried to sympathize with Taryn, although she didn't understand. If she had a body and a face like Taryn's, she would be the biggest hoe in the country. Kia was pretty too; she was 5'7 and brown-skinned, with a short haircut and a nice body. She wasn't built like Taryn, but she wasn't lacking very much in the necessary areas.

"I just hate when people do that; them little bitches over there already looking at me crazy," she fumed.

"Girl so! Fuck them hoes, they're only hating because you look better than them." This made Taryn laugh. She had just met Kia yesterday, but she knew after talking with her in class she would like her.

"What up T!" hearing Demoto's voice made the butterflies in her stomach take flight. She tried to suppress the smile that was creeping on her face before she turned around. When she looked up, she saw him standing next to Courtney. He had to have just gotten there because she hadn't seen him when she first walked in. Right after she spoke, he got onto her about not eating. She claimed she wasn't hungry, but that had to be a lie.

She'd said the same thing last night and they hadn't stopped for breakfast on their way to school this morning. With her being in her current situation, he knew she had to be stressing.

"You better stop trying to be cute and go eat," he smiled as he pushed some of his dreads over his shoulder.

"Hell, she ain't even got to try that hard," another dude sitting at the table with Courtney said. Looking to see who it was, she noticed a dark-skinned boy with a low fade, big eyes, and damn was he fine! How she had missed him a second ago she didn't know, but he could definitely get the business. Blushing, she said thank you and turned her head. Demoto had noticed her reaction to his friend Jeremiah's statement, and for some reason it made him feel some type of way.

"Come on T, let's get you a salad or something," Demoto said, grabbing her hand and pulling her from her chair. Standing to her feet, she fixed her belt before moving. Either her butt was too big, or that thin ass belt wasn't for her. It had been getting on her nerves all day.

"You killing the game Pocahontas," Courtney said again in pure lust. The high waist jeans were hugging her hips just right, and because of the high back her ass looked enormous. Smiling and shaking her head, she linked her arm through Demoto's and walked to the salad bar.

"You got these niggas out here thirsty, T."

"That's just Courtney's mannish ass," she frowned.

"You must just don't like Courtney, because you ain't frown up like that when my boy Jeremiah said something." Smiling, Taryn just looked at the ground. Demoto had caught her.

"Nah, it just wasn't anything wrong with what Jeremiah said. Courtney is just rude. I don't like when people talk about my body like that." This was news to Demoto, because most girls liked attention, and here it was somebody that deserved it didn't want it.

"Well I don't mean to sound like a pervert or no shit like that, but Taryn you got to know niggas are going to look. Any man that don't is either gay or blind, and Courtney ain't either," he said, making her laugh. Hearing her small giggle made him smile; the first time he heard it last night, he wanted to keep hearing it. Taryn had to explain to Demoto that it wasn't that he said it, more so the way he said it. Had he said it quietly or just to her, she probably wouldn't have gotten mad.

"Well in that case, Taryn you look good as fuck today. I like your hair, I like your ass in them jeans, and I like your nipple rings," he said, smiling down at her.

"Oh my gosh Demoto, shut up," she blushed in embarrassment. Hearing him say those words had her dark skin turning red. He could tell he had embarrassed her, but he could also tell she liked it.

"What? You said I just couldn't say it out loud."

"I know, but I ain't know you was about to say all that, with your nasty ass," she laughed, taking her food from the lunch lady.

"Nah, I would be nasty if I told you I wanted to taste you last night but we fell asleep. Now that would be nasty." Shocked by his comment, she just looked at him, then at the ground. He was really showing out right now. He smiled as they walked back to their table.

"Well if we're being honest, would I be nasty if I told you I would have let you?" she asked as they reached her table. Not expecting her comment, he just stood there silent for a second before telling her

"Vous ne savez simplement pas." (you just don't know) He knew it would catch her off guard. She watched him with a longing look in her eyes; she had to hurry and close her mouth before someone saw her.

"Oooh bitch, you better do that! Got Demoto fine ass walking you to get food and shit," Kia said the moment Taryn sat down. They laughed and made jokes as they ate their food.

Chapter 3

After lunch, the rest of the day seemed to fly by and before Taryn knew it, it was time to go home. She hated this because she had nowhere to go. She decided she'd just walk to her foster parent's house and call a cab from there, so no one from school would see her. She needed to go by her job, get her clothes, and check in at the women's shelter before it got too late. In the front of the school, she saw Demoto, Courtney, Jeremiah, Alicia, and one other girl leaning against his black Audi. She tried calling Reece so she didn't have to walk past all of them looking crazy, but she didn't answer. Sucking it up, she kept her pace and continued walking. She threw her hand up and waved to the group and kept walking, but was stopped by Demoto calling her name. She hated he'd called her to him. He wanted to know where she was headed. She felt Alicia and her friend's eyes on her, so she glanced their way for a second before turning her attention back to Demoto. She was glad she had already put her sunglasses; on because she almost couldn't stop her eyes from rolling. She could tell Alicia was feeling a certain kind of way about her talking to Demoto but she didn't care; hell, he had called her name. Once they figured out she was about to walk, Jeremiah offered to take her. She declined because she didn't want anyone in her business. As bad as she wanted to take the ride, she didn't trust him enough. As she finished saying everything she had to say, she turned to leave.

"Aye T, you want me to take you?" Demoto asked. He had planned on taking her home anyway, but didn't want to seem pressed in front of Alicia.

"Nah you good Demoto; thanks, I'll see you tomorrow," she said as she continued to walk. She was halfway across the parking lot when she heard someone running behind her.

"Yo T slow down, let me take you home, it's too hot out here to be walking," Demoto said.

"Boy what is wrong with you? You better take your ass back over there before I have to slap Alicia." He laughed because she looked just like she would slap Alicia. They went back and forth a few more times before he convinced her to let Jeremiah take her. She insisted on not starting trouble with Alicia and continuously denied his ride. After turning back around, they walked back to his friends.

"Aye Miah, take T home before her chocolate ass melt out here in this heat," he laughed.

Cutting her eyes at him, she shot him a bird before following Jeremiah to his truck. He opened the door for her as she got in. His truck was so nice and clean, and smelled just like him–it was intoxicating. Once he was in, they pulled off and headed towards her foster home. The ride was smooth with a limited amount of small talk. Jeremiah was so cute and sweet that she had given him her number before she got out. Walking towards the front porch, she was so happy he hadn't waited for her to get in the house. The moment he pulled off, she took off walking in the other direction. She had called a cab and was waiting for them up the street from her old house. Once she got her clothes from work, she went to the shelter and did everything she needed to do to check in. Once given a room, she did her homework and changed clothes. The building was brand new, with at least thirty rooms and sixty beds. She didn't mind all of the people, because she had practically lived her whole life like that. After checking to see what time she had to be back, she grabbed her phone, sunglasses, and left. She didn't want to just sit in the room, so she decided to walk around for a little while. Surprisingly, the shelter wasn't far from her foster house, or Demoto's apartment complex. She was just about to pass the park she was at last night when she heard Gyptian and Nicki Minaj singing *Hold Yuh* from somebody's car. Her head turned and she locked eyes with Demoto. His black Audi was so clean she couldn't help but stare. Slowing to a stop, he waved her over and told her to get in. Once she was in, he drove off.

"You won't be happy until I'm beating the shit out of Alicia, will you?" she asked, smiling at him as he laughed.

"Man T, what you talking about girl? I told you she straight."

"Um huh, if you say so–even though I don't know one woman that would be okay with her man driving another female around. I know I wouldn't."

"I thought you didn't do boyfriends though."

"I don't, but let me put it this way, Demoto. If you was my boyfriend, which you wouldn't be because I don't do boyfriends, you wouldn't have no other bitch up in your ride, *especially* one that looked better than me. I would fuck this Audi up," she said, looking at him with a smirk on her face. He laughed at her for a minute before he could respond.

"Man T, you look like you crazy as shit for real, and how you just gon' call my girl ugly?"

"I'm really not Demoto. I'm just talking to make you laugh. I didn't say she was ugly, I just said I look better," she said, turning back around to look out the window. Truth be told, she really was just talking. She was so sensitive sometimes it made her sick. If Demoto was her man and she saw another girl in his car, she would probably just cry or some weak shit like that. He could tell she had never been in love before; she probably hadn't even been in any serious relationships. Taryn had this innocence about her that drew him. All the slick shit she was talking, he could tell was a front.

"All girls can be a little crazy."

"Your fine ass would know! You probably got these girls going crazy," she laughed. He dismissed her with a laugh, and turned the music back up. They had been riding for a few minutes, and she hadn't even asked where they were going. Truth be told, she really didn't care. She was off for the next two days, and it wasn't like she had a home to go to. Feeling her phone vibrate, she looked down and noticed she had a text from a number she didn't know.

7063930768: *This Jeremiah lock my number in beautiful*

Her: *I sure will* ☺

She was blushing so hard from being called beautiful that she didn't notice Demoto staring at her until he started talking.

"Who got you smiling that hard?" Leaving her thoughts, she laughed a little.

"Jeremiah." That caught Demoto off guard; he knew Jeremiah was checking for her, but what he didn't know was that she was interested.

"Word? My boy got you cheesing like that after one ride home?" Balling her fist up, she punched him in the shoulder. Demoto laughed at her a little while longer, because she probably thought her little punch had hurt. "I'm just playing T. Jeremiah my nigga, he cool peoples for real." She nodded her head and put her phone down.

"Good, because I'm thinking about making him my lil boo." He didn't know how to describe this feeling of possessiveness he was feeling. He hadn't known Taryn long enough to want to protect her, but in his heart that's all he wanted to do. He didn't think he wanted her as his own; he had Alicia for that, but it was something about her. Chalking it up to him feeling a hint of pity for her, he switched gears and continued up the street.

*****

"What's up my boy?" Jacko said as Jeremiah walked into the building. He and Jeremiah had been long time friends, and had recently started their party promoting business. Jeremiah walked around the counter and to the back, headed towards the storage room.

"Check that brown box; the flyers for the Rich Homie Quan party just got done yesterday." Joining Jeremiah in the storage room, the two proceeded to grab the flyers to pass out around school the next day. Jacko was the lead promoter in Columbus, and he had a few friends around the way in different areas of the city to help him distribute. Jacko was a hustler; if there was a way to make money, he had a hand in it. He lived by the motto *If I want It I get it*, so therefore there was never a time for slacking off. He did everything from promoting parties, stealing cars, selling stolen merchandise, to working at the clothing store in the mall. Jacko was the man to see, and he made sure of that.

"You want me to take some to give to Moto?" Jeremiah said, taking the rubber band off the stack of flyers he was holding.

"Nah I just got off the phone with him, he on his way over here now."

"Oh okay cool, but bruh let me tell you! I think ya boy in love," Jeremiah smiled as the two walked back to the front and out of the building.

"In love? Nigga with who?" After listening to Jeremiah talk about this girl, Jacko had to see her. Jeremiah was a lady's man; if a woman had his nose open like that, she had to be special.

"Aw man, my nigga turning into a groupie," Jacko said, dramatically wiping his hands across his face. "If she got you like this after a ride home, Ima have to meet her. I might need to steal her for my starting five," Jacko joked just as Demoto pulled up.

*****

"Where are we?" Taryn asked as they came to a stop. When she looked out of the window, she saw Jeremiah and another dude. He was a short brown-skinned boy with tattoos everywhere. He had shoulder length dreads that were pushed back with a band, and he looked to be about 19 at the oldest.

"This my boy Jacko spot, we promote parties. I had to come get the flyers for the Rich Homie joint this weekend," Demoto said as he killed the engine and opened the door. He told Taryn to come with him as he got out. After blowing out a nervous breath, she checked her face and got out. The moment she got out the car, she pulled her shorts down around her thighs and fixed her shirt. She met eyes with Jeremiah the moment she looked up. His face was filled with a mix of lust and adoration. He leaned against the window with one foot kicked up against the wall. With her hand in his, he leaned down to kiss it.

"Hey beautiful." Instead of speaking, she just smiled back; it had been forever since a guy made her blush. Demoto spoke, giving both of his friends a pound.

"What's up baby girl, I'm Jacko, the money man." This statement drew a laugh from her.

"How are you, Jacko? I'm Taryn-Lee"

"That's a pretty name for a pretty girl, I'ma call you Pretty Lee."

"Fall back little Jack, this all me right here," Jeremiah said, making her blush again. Demoto tried to mask his envy as best as he could. He was happy with

Alicia and not necessarily interested in Taryn, but he still didn't want to watch her with another man.

"Y'all boys trying to handle business or what?" Demoto said in a clipped tone. Taryn had caught the shortness, but obviously Jeremiah and Jacko hadn't; they were still laughing and joking. She didn't know what Demoto's problem was. He was fine in the car, so she hung back and asked him after Jeremiah and Jacko had entered the building.

"You alright Moto?" She grabbed his arm to keep him from going inside. He stood speechless for a moment, because even though pretty much everybody he knew called him Moto, when she said it, it sounded different. A good different! He turned around and gave her a slight smile before reassuring her he was fine. She reminded him that they were having a good time, so he lost the attitude. Once they got inside, Jeremiah was coming back to the front with a small brown box that housed flyers for the party. He gave it to Demoto and returned to the back to get his own. Coming back to the front, Jeremiah stopped in front of Taryn and grabbed her hand

"What you doing with this nigga? Didn't I already take you home one time today?"

"I found her ole lonely ass walking down the street looking crazy, so I scooped her and made her come ride with me," Demoto said as he and Jeremiah started laughing at her.

"I don't know why y'all laughing because ain't nothing funny. I was bored at home so I decided to take a walk, dang," she said, pulling her hand away.

"Oh so you mad T?" Demoto asked Taryn once she rolled her eyes. Jeremiah apologized, trying to ease her attitude. She gave them her back as she walked outside with Jacko. Back in the front of the building, she stood against the wall next to Jacko

"What's up Pretty Lee, you from around here?" he said as he offered her the blunt he was smoking. Declining, she shook her head and pushed his hand back towards him.

"Nah, I'm not really from anywhere specific." When he looked at her, he saw her staring off in a daze.

"So you want to tell me what that mean or not?" She declined and complimented his tattoos instead. She used her finger to trace the face of the little girl on his arm, which she later found out was his niece. She was his deceased twin brother's daughter. Jacko took over responsibilities for her after his brother died. With the exception of Jeremiah and Demoto, he rode solo.

"I feel you on that one, Jacky boy. I like to keep my circle pretty small too." Just as Jacko was about to ask, Demoto cut him off.

"Jacky boy? What the fuck kind of name is that for a grown man, T?"

"Well he gave me a nickname so I gave him one," she laughed as she dapped Jacko up.

"It's cool Pretty Lee, I think I kind of like it," he smiled, showcasing a mouth full of gold. Demoto gave both men another pound before he and Taryn got ready to leave.

"Yo Taryn, hold up real quick shawty." Jeremiah followed her down the sidewalk to the car, checking to see did she have any plans for later. Taryn was so lost in his smooth chocolate skin, big eyes, and perfect teeth that she couldn't help but smile.

"Yeah, I have some stuff to take care of at the house"

"Well how about you call me when you finish, maybe we can link up or something," he said, stepping closer to her. They set a time for him to call before she retreated to the car.

Once inside and buckled up, they were back on their way. It took a good ten minutes before she got up the nerve to say anything. Demoto was back in the same little mood he had been in at Jacko's spot. For a second, she allowed herself to think that maybe he was jealous of the attention Jeremiah was giving her, but she quickly dismissed that idea. Why would he be jealous, they barely knew one another? She was almost sure he wasn't checking for her like that. Yeah they had joked and kissed last night, and again today in the cafeteria, but who wouldn't? He and her both were very attractive people; the lust between them was a given. She was most definitely not confusing it with him liking her enough to be jealous. Watching him rapping along with Yo Gotti made her stomach do flips; he was so handsome, and watching him drive was making matters much worse. The way his dreads were hanging down all over his back and around his chest had her so far in a daze that she didn't even see him looking at her. Her eyes were trained on the way his muscles bulged as he shifted gears.

"T, you good baby girl?" Shaking her head, she stuttered a little.

"Ye...yeah I'm straight, why you ask that?"

"Because you staring a hole in the side of my head." She hurried to apologize before turning to look out of the window. Although he wasn't saying anything, he was always aware of his surroundings. He had felt her looking at him for the last couple of minutes, just like he had caught her biting her nails, obviously in deep thought about something. He had always been good at reading people, and Taryn didn't prove to be much different. Her presence was overwhelming, he could almost feel whatever it was she was thinking–that's how open she was.

"You want to talk about it?" he asked, looking over at her again.

"What? NO!" she exclaimed until she noticed the confused expression he wore. It was then she realized he must have been talking about her problems at home.

"Oh I'm sorry Demoto, you're talking about me being homeless?" she said in a joking matter. She wanted to throw his mind away from her initial reaction when she thought he was asking her about the dirty things she was thinking about him in her head.

"Wait what? Since when did you become homeless? They put you out?" Noticing she had just let the cat out of the bag, she paused for a second before answering. *Now how did I do that*, she wondered to herself.

"Umm…yeah, but it's cool"

"Taryn, what the fuck you mean it's cool? No it ain't! Where the fuck you supposed to stay?" he asked, practically yelling. Taryn tried to hurry and convince him that she'd been staying with her friend. A friend she'd just made up. Demoto probably didn't believe her, but he didn't say anything about it. He looked at her sideways because he could tell she was lying, but chose to ignore it for now. It was obvious she didn't want to talk about it. The muscle in his jaw was moving like crazy, a clear sign of anger. She placed her hand on top of his to calm him. The feeling of her hand on him quickly mellowed his mood; he was far from content with her situation, but he was relaxing a little. He decided to let the conversation go for now. He knew she would tell the truth when she was ready to.

Chapter 4

Back at the women's shelter, Taryn had just
gotten out of the shower and was ironing her clothes for
school the next day. Everyone there was so nice and
made her feel welcomed. There were women from all
over the place for various reasons, majority of them being
either battered women with their children, or teenage
girls that were pregnant and had gotten kicked out of their
homes. It was semi-crowded, but that didn't bother her
one bit; she had been living in these types of
arrangements her entire life. This wasn't her permanent
home anyway; she needed one week, two at the most to
get things lined up for her own apartment. Once she'd
finished ironing and braiding her hair down into two long
French braids, she slid on her pink Adidas flip flops and
walked down the hall to the lounge. They were holding a
mandatory meeting for the newcomers to explain the
rules. She hadn't wanted to come, but she needed
somewhere to sleep so she had no other choice. She made
herself comfortable in a seat in the back corner of the
room. As she glanced around at the other people, she
observed their individual situations. After a few minutes,
a small-framed lady came in with a heavier set one and
stood at the front. The smaller framed woman was light-
skinned with shoulder length hair, small round eyes, and
a soft voice. She wasn't the prettiest, but she was far from
ugly and looked to be around 27 or 28; the bigger lady
looked to be the same age.

"Hello everyone, I'm Janay Richards and I'm the
center's social worker. I'd like to welcome you on behalf
of the entire staff here and let you know that anything
you may need, don't hesitate to ask," she finished as she

smiled at everyone in the room. The discussion went on for another twenty minutes before everyone was released. The meeting had gone surprisingly well. The women had gone around the room explaining their situations, and playing icebreaker games. This eventually helped everyone warm up to each other. Just as she was about to walk back to her room, she felt someone grab her arm from behind. Turning around, she saw Janay.

"Hey Taryn, I was just trying to catch you before you walked back to your room. You didn't seem very interested in anything we had going on tonight; are you okay?" she asked with genuine concern.

"Yeah I'm fine, I'm just not much of a people person, that's all."

"Well I can understand that, but when you're here we're all family, and if you look at it that way you may actually enjoy your stay."

"I'll try," Taryn smiled before walking away. Truth be told, she didn't want to make friends because she didn't like people in her business; the more you kept private, the less you had to explain.

*****

"Babe you good?" Alicia asked, turning Demoto's head so he was facing her.

"Yeah boo I'm straight," he lied. All that night, he had been worried about Taryn. He had dropped her off at work earlier that day, and he hadn't been able to stop thinking about her since. He knew she was lying about where she was staying; he could tell by the way she told the story. She sounded as if she was making things up as she went, but he had no way to prove it so he left it alone. She was obviously a private person because she hadn't even bothered to tell him last night that she had actually gotten kicked out of her house. She'd accidentally let it slip today and tried her best to cover it up. There wasn't much he could do, but he at least wanted to make sure she was somewhere safe and wasn't back outside at the park again. In order to give himself a peace of mind, he'd walked back down there before coming home to make sure she wasn't there; luckily for him, and her she wasn't.

"Demoto, you're not paying me any attention," Alicia said as she climbed on his lap.

"Yes I am baby, I'm just really tired, that's all," he lied.

"Well let's go lay down then," she smiled as she leaned in and started biting on his neck. Looking at Alicia, he could tell she wanted the D, so he was about to give it to her. He picked her up and headed for his room, pushing all thoughts of Taryn out of his mind and focusing on Alicia.

*****

The next day at school, Taryn tried her hardest to concentrate on her work, but she was too busy daydreaming. Once she got back to her room after the welcome meeting, she'd called Jeremiah and they talked for hours. He was so sweet, and for some reason knew all the right things to say. They'd talked about everything, from their favorite colors and movies to his family and background. She had chosen not to disclose any of her personal information. She didn't know him well enough yet. Yes, he was nice and she enjoyed talking to him, but she wasn't the type to trust easily.

Keeping her personal life private not only kept people out of her business, but it also kept them at a distance, and that's how she liked it. He had asked a few times about her parents and where she'd just come from, but she'd given very vague answers if any at all. Anytime the conversation got to her, she would flip it back on him, which was very easy to do. Jeremiah wasn't conceited but he was confident, so he didn't really mind talking about himself. He was the second oldest of four boys, worked as a part time party promoter, and had plans of joining the marines after high school. Thinking about how he was going to look in a marine uniform had her mind everywhere except the math lesson her teacher was giving.

Just as her thoughts were about to go off the deep end, she was startled by the desk behind her pushing slightly into her back. Someone had sat down. Shaking her head lightly, she tried to focus on the board but she couldn't; the cologne that the boy who had just sat behind her was wearing was captivating–it was mesmerizing even, and it was definitely one she was familiar with. As she turned in her seat, she saw a smile so bright and infectious she couldn't help but smile one of her own.

"What's up gorgeous?" It seemed as if her smile made his grow wider. The light brown freckles adorning his nose caught her attention first, then she made eye contact and almost got lost in his emerald green eyes.

"Nothing handsome, what you doing in here?"

"My coach pulled some strings and got me in here, because I need it for graduation."

"Umm huh, let me find out you stalking me," she whispered before turning around in her seat. She couldn't bear to look at his beautiful face or the way his long blonde dreads fell over his shoulders another second. That sexy southern African accent was turning her on. He was so beautiful to her. His brown skin and blonde hair with those green eyes were a hell of a combination, but she'd be lying if she said it wasn't a fascinating one.

"Aye T, why you turn around?" she heard him whisper.

"Because we're in class, crazy boy."

"Oh so you one of those smart girls that be acting stuck up huh?" he said, making both of them snicker a little. Instead of answering, she shot him a bird over her shoulder and tried to zone back in on their teacher. Leaning to one side, she felt a hand slither up the side of her body and stop right beneath her left breast. She tried her best to ignore him, but when he started massaging her ribs through her shirt, it was almost impossible.

"Boy get your hand off me."

"Here," he said, causing her to look down and notice the folded piece of paper he was holding in his hand. She took the note, opened it, and laughed. He had asked her was she serious about fucking him, check yes or no. Leave it to that fool to take her shooting a bird at him as something sexual; he was such a clown. With her pen in hand, she checked no and threw it over her shoulder. The moment she heard him suck his teeth, she knew he'd read it. She laughed quietly to herself while she resumed taking her notes. Sitting behind Taryn was already proving to be fun. Upon hearing his classes had been changed to a more advance course, he was a little angered at first until he had walked in and saw her sitting damn near at the front of the class.   Happy that there were two empty desks behind her, he sat in the one closest to her. He loved picking with her; she was so fun and easy to enjoy. Just like with the note, she could have easily gotten offended by it or the fact that he had been purposely feeling on her when he slid it to her, but she wasn't. She laughed and played along, like she had been doing since he'd met her. Her personality was consuming and he didn't understand their situation one bit. Here he was playing and flirting with her, and on other occasions he felt protective over her, almost like a big brother. Being that he had Alicia and she was obviously feeling Jeremiah, it was safe to say sticking with the brother sister feeling was more appropriate. Once the bell rang, they grabbed their things and were headed out the door when the teacher called him back. Since it was her last class of the day before gym, Taryn decided to wait on him. She fixed her books in her arm and leaned against the wall until she saw him coming out of the door.

"Took you long enough," she said, walking up next to him.

"I know right, that was her nosey ass all in my business."

"Teachers are always like that when you first come; I've been new enough times to know," she said, stopping at her locker.

"I was hoping you were gon' wait on me. I thought maybe you left as long as her ass took to put me in the computer."

"Now you know I wasn't about to leave you," she said, putting her books up and grabbing her bag with her gym clothes out.

"I know, that's why you my nigga T," he said, taking her bag from her and wrapping his free arm around her shoulder. To everyone around them, the gesture looked to be innocent as a sibling embrace, but the feeling that shot between the both of them was anything but. She could tell by the way he moved his arm that he'd felt it too, but this feeling wasn't as new to her as it was to him. Anytime he came around, touched her, looked at her, anything with the slightest touch of intimacy, she felt all tingly inside. They walked and talked the rest of the way to the gym for PE until she spotted Jeremiah coming out of the locker room.

"I'll be right back Moto," she said as she walked off and wrapped her arm around Jeremiah's waist. When he turned and saw who it was, he smiled and grabbed her into a hug. He said something to her while releasing her from the hug, because she was blushing like crazy. Watching the exchange brought back up the confusing emotions Demoto had been thinking about earlier. Here he was getting jealous about her being with Jeremiah. He had to get a hold of himself, and quick. He gave Jeremiah a handshake as they began to joke about who could lift the most weights. They were deep into making fun of each other when Taryn told them they were both weak. Taryn laughed as she walked between the two and headed towards the female locker room.

"Taryn-Lee, don't make me fuck you up shawty," Demoto laughed as Jeremiah bent down and picked her up over his shoulder.

"Now what's all that weak shit you was talking," he said as he slapped her hard on her butt.

"Jeremiah stooooop put me down," she squealed.

"Nope! I want to hear all that fly shit you was just on," he said, slapping her butt again.

"Demoto make him stop please!" she yelled. Jeremiah had her head down, with her butt straight in the air for everyone to see. To say she was embarrassed would have been an understatement. Although embarrassed, she was still having a good time. Taryn was laughing so hard tears were starting to leak from her eyes.

"DEMOTO!" she yelled again.

"Man y'all wild," Demoto laughed. "That's what you get T," he said again, walking past. He had almost made it by her when she reached out and pulled the bottom of his shirt to stop him.

"Demoto, if you don't make Jeremiah put me down, I'm not speaking to either one of y'all again," she said, trying to sound serious.

"Oh I know that's a lie," Jeremiah said, slapping her butt again. By now their classmates were standing around, laughing and smiling at them.

"Jeremiah, put that girl down!" Coach Sims said as he came out of the locker room and into the hallway. Thanking God for the coach; Taryn slid down the front of Jeremiah's body slowly as he placed her back onto the ground. She knew he could have sat her down faster with a lot less body contact, but she had enjoyed it. Looking her in her eyes, he kissed her nose before turning around to face his coach. He instantly tried to plead his case. Demoto had seen their coach coming out of the locker room, but didn't say anything. Anybody that went to Carver High School knew Coach Sims. He was a tall bald man that wore glasses, and he didn't play. If he wasn't making jokes about you, he was cussing you out; everybody loved him. He talked rough, but everybody knew it was all in love.

"Boy I don't care if you was playing or not, that girl don't want your nasty hands on her," he said, drawing laughs from everybody in earshot.

"Man coach, that's my girlfriend" At that moment, Taryn was glad his back was to her because she would have hated for him to see her face when he'd said that. Her eyes bulged out of her head at the same time she pushed her head forward a little. *What in the world?* she thought. She liked Jeremiah and wouldn't mind being his girlfriend, but he was definitely jumping the gun with that one. Finally looking up, her eyes immediately went to Demoto; for some reason she wanted to see what he thought of the statement, but his face was straight and void of any emotion. Not saying a word, she grabbed her bag from Demoto's hand and turned to walk away.

"Young lady, you don't let these lil knuckleheads put they broke hands all over you like that. If he is your boyfriend, I sure do feel sorry for you," he said before she could make it around the corner.

"I won't sir, that was him," she laughed as she hurried off.

"Y'all get y'all behinds in here," Coach Sims said, ushering the boys into the locker room.

*****

School had just gotten out and Taryn was past ready to go. She had to go to work today, and on top of that she wanted to see Reece before she left for basic training. She pulled her cell phone from her small red backpack and dialed Reece. It rung three times before she finally answered.

"Hey baby!" Reece screamed.

"Hey sister!" she yelled back, drawing a few stares from the girls walking in front of her.

"I'm so glad you called. I was just begging my recruiter to bring me by your school to see you before I leave. We out here now, do you see this big white van by the entrance?" As she looked out across the parking lot, she spotted the van and speed walked towards it. The front passenger side door opened, and out hopped Reece. She was a few inches shorter than Taryn with long black hair that she had pulled back in a bun today. She was dressed casually in a pair of cotton shorts, a tank top, and some white converse. She didn't know what had come over her, but the moment she saw Reece water came to her eyes, and she took off in a full speed run. Once Reece noticed her, she did the same thing and they ran until they met in a parking space. The moment they were close enough, they grabbed one another in one of the tightest embraces they could muster.

"Reece I'ma miss you sis!" she said through a tear broke voice.

"It's only for a little while, T; we'll be back together soon."

"I know, but what I'ma do without you?"

"We can write letters and I'll call you whenever I can sis, don't be sad," Reece said, fighting back her own tears. She was trying her hardest to keep it together. She loved Taryn like no other. Over the few months they had known each other, they had formed a bond that was unbreakable; there was nothing or nobody in the world that she loved more. Taryn was the only family she had; she was close with her other foster siblings, but it was nothing like what she shared with Taryn. Taryn was there whenever she needed her; whatever went on with one went on with the other. They faced anything together. She was not only her sister, but her best friend as well. The same thing went for Taryn; blood couldn't have made them closer.

"You're going to be great Reece, I love you," Taryn said, breaking their embrace. Standing back, she looked at her sister and smiled.

"Man go ahead Reece before I start crying again."

"Alright, let me go because this is too much for me. You want me to cry the whole way to South Carolina," she joked. Grabbing each other in another quick hug, they kissed each other's cheek. Reece got back into the van and it pulled away.

Watching them drive off, Taryn got even sadder. Reece had been her rock when things got hard; she was serious when she asked what she was going to do now. Maybe she was making a big deal out of it; after all, basic training was only a few months, but after that there was no telling where she would be sent. Taryn wiped the tears that kept falling and went to find Kia; she had agreed to give her a ride to work.

Walking down the empty hallway, she stopped short when she saw Demoto and Alicia leaning against the wall kissing. She was standing on her tip toes holding him around the waist. She couldn't hate if she wanted to; the whole scene was cute. She decided to avoid them, so she bent the corner and headed towards Kia's locker to see what the holdup was. Kia wasn't there either, so she decided to just call her. She told her she was doing some make up work for class and she'd be ready in a minute. When she walked back past, she expected to see Demoto and Alicia still standing there but she didn't; it was just him. When he looked up to see who was coming, Demoto shut his red cell phone off and closed his locker. The moment he laid eyes on her, he knew something was wrong.

"What's up baby girl, what's wrong?" he asked, grabbing her by her elbow and pulling her to him. Her eyes were big and red, like she'd been crying. She thought for a moment whether she should make

62

something up or tell the truth. In a weird way she wanted him to care, and if it was serious he might. Deciding that was lame, she just told the truth.

"Nothing for real, my big sister left for basic training a minute ago; she came by here to see me and now I'm all in my feelings. She all I had," she said as her eyes started watering again.

"It's okay T," he pulled her into his arms and squeezed her tight. He was holding her so tight it was as if he was pulling all of her feelings into his body. As each minute passed, she started to feel better but she wasn't ready to let him go yet; he smelled too good! She gave a weak smile as she pulled away. At home was fine, but she didn't want anyone to come and see her all hugged up with Alicia's man; that would most definitely not be a good look.

"It's only a few months, she'll be back soon," he smiled as he pushed some hair behind her ear.

"I know, it's just she's the only person I really had; now it's just me. I'll be cool soon enough; it's just still real fresh right now."

"If it makes you feel better, I'm still here. I'll take care of your big head ass," he smiled and pinched her cheek.

"I guess I'll take that as sympathy coming from you." He could see she was genuinely hurt, and he hated that for her but eventually it would get easier. Once he and his brother Adisa had moved from Cameroon, it was hard at first but over time it became the norm.

"I'm serious T, anything you need I got you," he said, looking intently into her eyes. He wanted to make sure she knew he meant what he was saying. "No matter what it is, I'm here."

"What if I need some sex, you got me?" she asked with a straight face.

"Hell yeah I got you, especially if it's sex!" She couldn't hold her laughter in after hearing that. She laughed along with him.

"Boy you are a fool, Alicia would break your neck."

"Mannnnn, whatever," he laughed.

"Speaking of neck, I seen you and her over here a few minutes ago all down each other's throat, y'all so nasty." He knew he had heard someone walking earlier, but he didn't bother to check and see who; now he wished he had have.

"Yeah, just like I ain't know you was in a relationship now," he said with a raised eyebrow.

"Man I don't know why Jeremiah said that. I think he was just playing for real though; besides, you know I don't do boyfriends."

"Yeah I hear you talking, but why you ain't say nothing earlier? You just stood there watching us kiss?" he smirked.

"I didn't just stand there, first of all, and secondly what was I supposed to say?" she challenged. They stood there for a moment staring each other down until he reached out and grabbed her by both of her arms and pushed her backwards into the boy's bathroom. After he kicked the door closed behind them, he locked it and pinned her against the wall with his body. He could tell she was nervous, because her breathing had sped up but she maintained eye contact, which gave him the reassurance he needed. He pulled the band from her ponytail and let her hair fall loosely around her shoulders. He loved her hair; she had so much of it and it drove him wild. With her hair down, she looked like a goddess.

"Vous êtes tellement belle." (you are so beautiful) Clenching her legs tightly together, she let her head fall against the wall. She loved the way he talked, especially when he spoke French.

"You with me, Taryn?" he asked, leaning his head back to look into her eyes.

"Always," she whispered back.

"I'll always take care of you. You'll never have to want for anything as long as I'm around. I promise, anything you need, all you have to do is ask," he rattled off in perfect French. She didn't have a clue what he was saying, but she could tell he was serious about whatever it was. She wanted to ask what he'd just said, but she didn't want to ruin the moment.

She would never get used to seeing him; he was rare in every aspect of the word. He looked like your average street thug, minus the brown skin and blonde hair–that part was unique. His appearance alone made her melt. She wrapped her arms around his body, pulling him tighter to her, and placed three soft kisses on his lips. She was a little hesitant at first, but that changed quickly when he kissed her back. The kiss was soft and intimate in the beginning, but the pace changed drastically when she released a small moan. Hearing the sensual sounds she made, made him want to hear more. After that night at his house, he wanted to hear them again, over and over, while he was deep inside her. There hadn't been the right time up until now. He kissed her with such an extreme ferocity that it made his knees weak. He was hungry for her; it was as if he was a lion and she was his prey. He had to have her, had to hear the sounds of struggle from her lips. A struggle between love and lust, the struggle to stop or keep going, to kiss or to devour; so he gave it all to her. In his mind, she was his; had been since the first day he saw her in the gym. He didn't care that he was already involved, or that one of his best friends liked her; Taryn-Lee was his.

She didn't know what had gotten into Demoto, but whatever it was she was thankful for it. He was kissing her like he was crazy. His kiss was filled with an abundance of aggression; the way he was touching her was almost animal like. He was grabbing and squeezing every part of her body; the guttural moans escaping him had her in a frenzy. She moaned his name as she ran her hands through his dreads. He was leaned so far on her that his hair was laying all over the top of her shoulders, shielding their faces.

"Sshh baby girl, just let it happen," he spoke in between kissing and picking her up off the floor. He turned around so now his back was against the wall; he slid down and sat on the floor with her on his lap. Lifting his hips up a little, he nudged at her warmth through their clothing. She followed his lead and began to grind harder onto him. They had gotten so caught up in their kiss that Taryn had totally forgotten about meeting Kia out front until her phone started ringing. She broke from their kiss as he begged her to ignore it.

"I can't, it's Kia; she's taking me to work today. I have to go," she said, leaning her forehead against his. They sat there for a moment, invading each other's space with their breathing until he spoke.

"Taryn, you confuse the hell out of me girl."

"No Demoto, you confuse yourself. One minute you acting like my brother, and the next you tongue kissing me in the bathroom."

"Man I know, I just can't help it! I got to do something about this though," he said, lifting them both up off the floor.

"Yeah you do," she backed away and fixed her clothes.

"Come give me a hug before you leave." Walking slowly into his arms, she laid her head on his chest and closed her eyes. After a few minutes they let go, and she was about to open the door until he stopped her.

"Aye, find out what's going on with you and Miah." Looking at his face, she couldn't deny the attraction so she nodded her head and left. He waited a few minutes so if someone was in the hallway they wouldn't see them come out together. Walking to the mirror, he tied his dreads back at the base of his neck and stood their eyeing his reflection. He had to figure out what he wanted with Taryn, and fast. It was selfish to want her all to himself given their situations, but he didn't care. Demoto was a man that knew what he wanted, and made sure he got it no matter what.

Chapter 5

As Young Thug's song Lifestyle blared from his speakers, Jacko cruised down Manchester Expressway headed to the mall. He had a busy weekend ahead of him and needed to make sure he had stuff to wear. He was the only person out of all his friends that had to buy something new any time he stepped out. He had so many clothes and shoes he had to move from his one bedroom apartment and into a two bedroom so that one room could house his wardrobe. He made money, so it was nothing to spend it. He was twenty years old with no real responsibility, besides his car note. He had a 2014 charcoal gray Corvette Stingray with red interior and Blackhawk rims. His car fit him perfectly; he was flashy yet low key, and he loved attention but only if it was for good reason. More often than not, he stayed to himself and kept a low profile. Everyone knew who he was, so he had to make sure he was surpassing their expectations of him. Aside from his mother and niece, he had no one to spend his money on so he shopped. Ever since his twin brother had been killed, he had taken over responsibility of his daughter; he made sure her mother had everything she needed. Sometimes he went overboard but he loved his niece, she had just turned two and looked just like his brother. Of course because they were identical twins, she looked exactly like him as well, which is why a lot of people had mistaken her for his. He looked back at her on his backseat waving her arms in the air. Her happy face made him smile. She was so pretty; his brother would have been proud. He pulled his car to a stop and went around to the other side, got her, and proceeded into the mall. He didn't plan on being in there long, but he knew nine times out of ten he would see people he knew and have to stop and talk.

"You want Uncle Jack to get you some shoes?"

"Yes I want Dora."

"Okay well let's go see if we can find you some Dora," he said as he walked into Kids Footlocker.

"Ooooh Jack-Jack!!" she yelled as she ran to the wall and picked up a pair of pink and purple Air Max.

"Izzy, those are not Dora," he smiled as she handed him the shoes.

"Yes they are Jack-Jack look, it has pink and purple just like Dora." He couldn't do anything but smile. He had been paying for her to go to private school since she first turned two five months ago. It was really paying off. She was smart and talked better than kids twice her age. He grabbed her little hand in his and walked to the front of the store to get help.

"Excuse me," he said to the girl leaning over the counter with her head down reading receipts. Her head came up, and a smile came to her face.

"Heyy Jacky boy."

"Man I ain't know that was you pretty Lee," he dapped over to the counter. He had never seen her in here before. She explained to him they'd switched her stores a few days ago before leaning down to talk to the baby. She knew that had to be his niece; she looked exactly like him.

70

"This my girl right here, say hey to Miss Lee Izzy," he said, pushing her towards Taryn.

"Hi, I'm Isabelle."

"Well hi Isabelle, that's such a pretty name, I love it. My name is Taryn Lee, but you can call me Lee," she said as she shook the little girl's small hand.

"I like your name too. It's pretty. My uncle Jack-Jack told me I can get the Dora shoes." Smiling, Taryn stood from the floor and looked at Jacko.

"Why are you trying to fool this baby? This is not a Dora shoe."

"Them the ones she picked out; she said they pink and purple like Dora, so whatever," he laughed. Taryn got her size from Jacko before coming back with two boxes. She'd bought the same show in different colors so he could pick. Jacko loved Izzy, so he bought her both pair without even trying them on. It was always like that when she accompanied him at the mall. While she Taryn was gone, Isabelle expressed her like for her. She told Jacko she was pretty with long hair, like her Barbie doll. He laughed at Isabelle; she was truly his pride and joy.

Once she finished talking, she grabbed one of his dreads and rubbed it. Ever since she had been born, whenever she was around him she would play in his hair. She lay her head on his chest and continued to play in his hair. He put her over his shoulder and met Taryn at the counter. Just as he was pulling his money from his pocket, his phone rang. Taryn watched Jacko as he talked on the phone; she had to admit he was a real cutie. He wasn't her type, but he was definitely a ten; his dreads and tats along with that cool demeanor that oozed from him was everything. His voice and smile was immaculate; she could tell he probably had women everywhere. Fine as he was, there was something that just screamed the word *brother*. From the moment they had met, she had gotten that brotherly vibe from him.

"Yeah bruh, I stopped by the mall for a minute. I'm in here with your girl now," he said as he turned his attention to Taryn. She gave him a quizzical look. "Here Pretty Lee, my boy want to holla at you real quick," he grinned, showing his mouth full of gold.

"Umm who is that?"

"Answer and see." Grabbing his phone, she answered.

"Who is this?" she didn't even bother with the pleasantries

"Damn baby, hey to you too," Jeremiah said. Hearing his voice instantly made her face light up.

"Hey Jeremiah."

"Can I see you when you get off?" he asked, making her smile again. The thought of seeing him had her stomach in knots. She agreed before handing Jacko his phone back. They talked for a few more seconds before he hung up.

"Man Jacky, you could have told me who that was."

"Who else was it supposed to be Lee? Demoto?" When he said that, it felt like she had lost all the air in her lungs. She tried to play clueless, but Jacko was far from dumb. He wouldn't be where he was now if he didn't pay attention. That day at the shop, he could tell Demoto felt a certain type of way when Taryn and Jeremiah were talking, but he didn't say anything. Both men were his friends, and Taryn didn't belong to anybody so she was free to do what she wanted. He had acted like he wasn't paying attention, but he had saw them outside talking after he and Jeremiah had gone in.

"Don't worry about it Lee, your secret is safe with me," he pinched her cheek and turned to leave. "Oh yeah, Izzy said she likes you and you're pretty with hair like her Barbie," he winked and left. She shook her head and smiled as she watched him walk out of the store. She liked Jacko; he was a true sweetheart. She didn't know him well, but she could tell he was as real as they came. If there was one thing she could respect, it was being in the presence of a real nigga. You could just look at him and tell he wasn't anything to play with. Along with his genuine sweet spirit, you had to love him. She didn't get that vibe from everyone, so she knew without even asking him not to that he wasn't going to tell Jeremiah or Demoto anything.

*****

Kia (bestie): *We going to the block party tonight right?*

Taryn: *You know it!*

Kia (bestie): *Let's get dressed at my house*

Taryn: K! I'll be there after work

Tonight was the annual Stop the Violence Block Party, and Taryn and Kia were past excited. Kia told her that this function brought the city out every year. It would be Taryn's first time going, but she was ready. After looking at the clock, she noticed she had fifteen minutes until closing time so she started straightening the shoes along the wall. Once she finished and had started folding the shirts, she heard somebody come in.

"Welcome to Kid's Foot Locker," she said without even turning around. If they needed something, they would ask. She was almost done fixing all the shirts when she smelled cologne. Whoever was behind her smelled good as hell but more importantly, they were very close to her. If she could smell his cologne, he was in her personal space. When she turned around, she almost ran right into him. Demoto was standing there looking so beautiful that the only thing Taryn could think about was sex. *Lord help me!* She backed up some, putting some space between them.

"What are you doing here?"

"I came to see you. I've been thinking about our bathroom rendezvous all day."

"Bathroom rendezvous? Cute," she smiled as she walked back to the register. Demoto followed her and leaned against the counter.

"You coming to the block party tonight?"

"Yeah, me and Kia." She was nervous and could barely hide it. Demoto watched as her hands shook nervously while she counted the receipts. He could tell she was out of her element at the moment, so he decided to leave her alone. It was obvious she was still on her bullshit, so he would let her have it. If she wanted to act like a scared child, then he would let her.

"Well alright T, I guess I'll see you later then." She looked up with wild eyes.

"Why? You might as well wait and walk me to my car." He checked his watch; he had a few minutes to spare, so he stayed. He sat on the bench while her and the other boy that worked there handled everything for closing. When she'd clocked out, she grabbed her backpack and headed to the front to get Demoto. When she got out there, he was texting on his phone. She tried to peep the name as she sat down next to him, but he moved it.

"Fall back T," he said with a hint of an attitude. His reaction caught her by surprise. After rolling her eyes, she stood up and waited by the gate until he was ready. He followed her immediately as they exited the back of the store. The walk down the hallway was a quiet one; she on one side of the hallway, and he was on the other. It was almost dark when they reached the door. Demoto hadn't parked back here, so she would have to drop him off to his car in the front. Mr. Buck had given her his truck to drive today, and she was glad. She would have hated for him to take her home. Her and Kia had stopped by one of his traps on her way to work earlier, and he'd given her his keys. Taryn tried sneaking glances at him, but every time she did he wasn't paying her any attention.

"Demoto, what is your problem?"

"I ain't the one with the problem."

"Please just say what's on your mind. I don't have time to play these little kid games."

"Obviously you do, that's all you play!" He didn't mean to snap, but he was irritated. He had been texting Jeremiah and found out he and Taryn were supposed to be hooking up later that night, and it made him mad. He thought he and her were on the same page. Here she was playing simple games with him, but making plans with the next nigga. If she wanted to do it like that, he would stick with Alicia. He looked at her and turned his head. He didn't even want to look at her. Jeremiah had made it seem as if they would be sleeping together tonight, and that's what made him the angriest. If anybody was getting it, it should have been him. He was seated in the front seat of her car, and she still hadn't said anything else to him.

"So you supposed to be meeting up with Miah tonight?"

"No, I told you I'm going to the block party with Kia."

"That ain't what I heard."

"Fuck what you heard, Moto. I just told you what I'm doing!" Demoto looked at her as she wrapped her hair into a ball on the top of her head before pulling off. He hated that her beauty was distracting him. Her smooth chocolate skin was so beautiful. He'd always had a thing for darker skinned women, and looking at her he could see why. When she pulled next to his car, she killed the engine and just sat there. She turned in her seat to face him.

"If I see Alicia tonight, I might slap her."

"You better not!"

"Watch and see," she said with finality. If he wanted to act sour about Jeremiah, then she would be the same way with Alicia.

"Taryn, don't make me fuck you up. Don't open your mouth to Alicia, that's not your place." His words cut deeply. She thought they had a better connection than that. He was sitting in her car taking up for another woman; she couldn't tolerate the disrespect. She wanted to punch him in the side of his head, but instead she cranked her car up.

"Get out!" He looked at her before moving. She looked straight ahead as he got out. She didn't even wait until he was all the way out of the car before she pulled off. She wasn't even paying attention that she'd almost run over his foot.

The whole ride to Kia's house, she fumed. She couldn't believe the nerve of him. She walked into Kia's house and right to her room. She was in her mirror wrapped in a towel. Her hair was freshly done, and she was putting on her makeup. She looked up when she heard her door open. She knew it had to be Taryn, because no one was allowed in her room without knocking. Buck would kill anybody that invaded her privacy. Taryn was the only one allowed to just bust in like that.

"Damn, who pissed in your cereal?"

"Demoto Youngblood! Pissed all in my fucking corn flakes! I want to break his neck, he so stupid! Uggh I hate him." Kia laughed at her as she walked around the room ranting.

"What he do girl?" Taryn went on to tell Kia the whole story, from Jeremiah calling Jacko's phone to Demoto checking her about Alicia. Kia was listening and could understand why her friend was mad. Instead of pumping her up and adding fuel to the fire, she decided to change the subject all together.

"Why you ain't tell me Jacko was up there? You know that's my husband!"

"Bitch Jacko is not your damn husband! He's my brother, get your life," Taryn laughed as Kia threw her lotion at her. Taryn knew Kia had a crush on Jacko, so they joked about it on the regular. She had been meaning to try and hook them up for a while, but she kept forgetting. She would do it tonight at the block party. If anybody was going to be there, it would be Jacko.

The girls sat and talked for another two hours before they were completely dressed and ready to go. They still had Buck's truck, so that's what they drove. The ride was smooth; they got there about fifteen minutes later. It was packed already, and had only started an hour ago. Kia wanted to stunt, so she drove through the crowd behind the other cars before parking. Men were whistling

78

and yelling at them through the window as they cruised down the street. Her and Taryn had the music up so loud that people turned their heads before they even got close to them. Once they got to the end of the line, Kia parked in the lot and they got out. They checked their outfits to make sure they looked good before walking back down the hill. Her and Taryn both decided to dress simple in shorts, fitted shirts, and sneakers. Taryn had her big wavy hair pulled up into a ponytail with a gold watch and 14kt gold bangles. Her necklace was a simple gold cross. Kia's hair was spiked in the top, with her sides laying down. They were both looking pretty without being overdressed. Taryn topped her attire with her black rimless shield chained Chanel shades. It was dark, but she didn't care.

"Taryn, take them damn shades off, it ain't even no sun out."

"Nope! I don't want nobody looking all in my face."

"Correction, you don't want Demoto looking all in your face! You ain't fooling me!" Taryn laughed and wrapped her arm through Kia's. She was her best friend for a reason. Once they got down the hill, the music was blaring and you could smell the food a mile away. There were people everywhere. The atmosphere was live! There were people playing basketball, cooking, playing dice, cards, and some just standing around. The further down they got, they saw people dancing and rapping. The whole scene was relaxed and safe. Taryn wasn't big on crowds, but this was cool. Kia had told her to stop being so scary, but she still didn't trust too many people in one place at once. Her and Kia had just passed a group of men rapping when two of them started following her. He was still rapping, but he was now free styling about Taryn. He talked about everything from her hair to her long legs. She turned around and smiled at him once she realized what he was doing. Her and Kia stood still and listened as the two boys rapped. The other friend had begun to drop lyrics about Kia. They stood smiling and blushing like crazy. When the boys had finished, they leaned in to get hugs from both girls.

"What's your name baby?" rapper number one asked Taryn. She answered and they conversed for a while as Kia talked to his friend. She was so caught up in conversation she didn't even feel eyes on her.

*****

Demoto stood there watching Taryn laugh and talk with some dude as he held her hand. He, Jacko, and Jeremiah were all standing next to the basketball court when he'd spotted them coming down the hill. He had made sure to stand where he could see the entire park. He needed to watch his back at all times. He'd watched the boys follow them and it pissed him off. He knew he shouldn't be mad because of the way he'd treated her earlier. He hadn't wanted to be mean; he was just angry. Making her mad was the only way he could get her to feel how he felt about her and Jeremiah. He knew she wouldn't understand his logic any other way.

"There go your girl," Jacko whispered to him. When he looked at Jacko, he had a large smile plastered across his face.

"Bruh chill with that shit, you know that's Miah."

"From the way you standing there watching her, it looks more like she's you." Demoto shook his head. He should have known Jacko hadn't missed him and Taryn's little exchanges. Jacko nudged his shoulder before walking over to the girls. He hadn't even waited on Demoto or Jeremiah to come with him. Demoto watched as the men walked away, and Taryn and Kia started talking to Jacko. Jeremiah walked closer to him and noticed the girls. His face lit up upon spotting Taryn. She, Jack, and Kia were walking towards them. He wrapped her in his arms the moment she was close enough. He squeezed her tight and left his arms around her waist.

"You looking really pretty."

"Thank you Miah. How long you been here?" she asked.

"Not long. I'm glad you're finally here though."

"Why is that?"

"Because I've missed you." She smiled as she took in his beautiful features. She continued talking to him for a while before stepping out of his embrace. She walked over and nodded her head what's up to Demoto. He grabbed her arm before she could walk past.

"You ain't speaking today T?" *No he didn't*, she thought.

"I said what's up Moto."

"Nah lil girl, you nodded your head. Give me a hug," he said, pulling her into him. She gave him a quick hug before pulling away. He looked like he wanted to object, but didn't. He didn't want to be too obvious in front of Jeremiah. He was glad he'd too worn his shades, because he would have hated for Jeremiah to see the way he watched her as she walked away. Just as they'd walked off, Jacko ran up and whispered in her ear about her and Demoto's awkward exchange before laughing and walking away.

The rest of the block party went by pretty cool. She'd caught Demoto's eye on her a few times, but she never maintained eye contact. She picked with him on purpose. She knew he was watching her, so she would stop and converse with men along the way. She'd even gone as far as to stop and talk to Alicia. She didn't really care for her, but she knew it would make him mad. The next time he thought about checking her, he would think twice about it. When they'd walked around and ate enough, her and Kia headed back towards the truck. They had just stopped at a gas station when Taryn's phone beeped with a text. It beeped twice, one from Moto, one from Miah.

Demoto: *I need to talk to you*

Sure you do

Miah: *Can I still see you tonight?*

She told Kia about their messages, and all she did was laugh.

"Go ahead then with your hot ass. You just got all the men!"

"Shut up Kia. I ain't stun neither one of them."

"Dang, what Miah do?"

82

"Moto had an attitude for something, Kia. Jeremiah probably said some slick shit about me or something. It ain't no telling what he told that darn boy." She had been thinking about it since earlier, and there was no reason for Demoto to be mad unless Jeremiah had told him something wrong. She knew how boys could be, so she wouldn't have been surprised if that was the case. She closed her phone and decided not to respond to either one of them.

*****

Demoto sat in his car with his boys, waiting for Taryn to text him back. He figured she probably was mad and that's why she hadn't responded. He knew she had to have gotten his message and was just ignoring him. He couldn't let her do that; they needed to see where they stood. He was confused and he hated it. He decided to call, but she let it ring to the voicemail. She could ignore a call, but she would read a text so he sent her a message.

Demoto: *I'm sorry for talking to you like that today. U forgive me? I'm just confused T, I don't know what to do. I like you but so does one of my best friends. I have a girl, and shit is just all fucked up. You don't have to talk to me, but at least let me know how you're feeling.*

It took her a few minutes to respond, but he heard his phone beep a little while later.

T: *It's cool Moto. I'm good, we're good. Let's just be friends. If it's meant to be, we'll be together at a more appropriate time.* ☺

Demoto: *Cool, u still mad at me?*

T: *Nope! Goodnight Mr. Youngblood*

Demoto smiled and drove away. He was good with that. They'd figure this crazy relationship out one day.

*****

"Man Alicia what you doing, suck that shit right!" Demoto said with a handful of Alicia's hair. He had been at her house since leaving the barbershop earlier that day, and she was starting to piss him off.

"I am Moto damn," she spat, heated. She didn't know what his problem was, but she was tired of his attitude. He had been in a pissy mood all day, and she was two minutes from putting him out.

"Man, just stop!" he said as he pulled her off her knees, until she was standing upright in front of him. Her parents had gone out of town for the weekend, and he was staying the night with her.

"Demoto what is wrong with you?" she asked, clearly upset. Looking at her pretty face in anguish, he knew he was wrong for being salty all day but he couldn't help it. His brother had brought him up to speed with some shit earlier, and he had been aggravated ever since. Pulling her down on his lap, she straddled him and began kissing all over his face.

"I'm sorry, I just have a lot on my mind." She leaned back and smiled at him.

"I can make you feel better." She stood back up and removed all of her clothing. They went at it for another hour or two before falling asleep. Demoto awakened to his phone vibrating across the dresser. It was Jacko. They discussed a few details concerning the night's events before deciding to meet at Jacko's apartment. After hanging up the phone, Demoto lay there in complete silence. He was past tired, but tonight was the Rich Homie Quan show that he'd been promoting for all week. Before getting the call from his brother, he had been hype about going; now he wasn't. It had been a while since something like this had come up. He hadn't decided how he was going to handle it yet; all he knew was that he had to.

*****

Taryn had just gotten back to the shelter from work, and was changing her clothes when someone knocked on her room door. Earlier that week, the girl she had been sharing the room with had moved out, so she had it to herself. She was busy and didn't feel like being bothered, so she waited a moment before opening it. Once she opened the door, there stood Janay. Janay was nice and had a genuinely sweet personality, so Taryn lost the attitude.

Ever since the night of the meet and greet, they had been keeping in touch. If Janay was there for work, she would always check on her before leaving. She eyed Taryn up and down, admiring her beauty along with her wardrobe. She told Janay she had plans to go to the Rich Homie concert tonight. Janay was ecstatic to find out because her brother in law was going too. She had wanted to hook them up for the longest, but hadn't yet. Janay smiled at her; she really liked Taryn. She even offered to drop her off at Kia's house since that's where she was staying that night. Kia had talked Taryn into staying the night with her after the show. It didn't take much convincing being that she wouldn't have had anywhere else to go anyway. She and Janay talked until she finished getting dressed.

Once she got inside Kia's house, she immediately felt uncomfortable. It was dark and there was loud music playing. There was obviously a party of some sort going on. She had texted Kia the moment she pulled up, and she met her at the door. There were people everywhere, mainly men and a few women. Taryn eyed everyone as they walked through the living room

"Why you didn't tell me y'all was having a party?"

"It's always a party at my house. My daddy sell drugs." Kia kept walking though all of the people like it was nothing. Taryn hadn't known about Kia's father, but she could have guessed. He was a fat man with a baldhead and a gold tooth. He was handsome and clean cut. The men surrounding him were watching his every move and listening intently. You could tell they respected him. Taryn looked at herself again in Kia's full size mirror. She wore a pair of black satin shorts, a black and white crop top, and a cute red member's only jacket. She wore a pair of black and white Jordan 10's to compliment her outfit. She couldn't decide whether to wear heels or flats, but decided at the last minute to go with the sneakers. She had washed and conditioned her hair, so it was big and wavy. Her lips were painted red with her favorite KA'OIR's Show off lipstick. She wore big gold earrings and bracelets with two gold rope chains around her neck. She wanted to make sure she was cute without looking overdressed. Kia had on a pair of multicolored high waist tights, and a lime green crop top and wedges. Her short hair was spiked with blonde highlights. Kia was looking past cute. Taryn smiled to herself; her and her girl were about to have a good time. They had just gotten out of the car at the concert when one of Kia's father's young runners got their attention, letting them know to call when it was over and he'd be back to get them. They closed the door and headed towards the entrance.

*****

The show was going good so far; they just had to make sure they kept it that way. Demoto, Jeremiah, and Jacko were all leaning against the wall backstage listening to the crowd. They had been working on the show for the past three months, and it had turned out to be a success. Jeremiah and Jacko were laughing and having a good time, while Demoto stood silent. He had been mapping his plan out in his head for the last few hours. He had an important situation to handle, and he couldn't afford to make any mistakes. Jacko looked over, noticed how quiet he was, and instantly knew what was up. He had known Demoto long enough to know when he had things on his mind. He wanted his friend to relax and have fun, so he got ready for the surprise even they had planned. Jacko walked to the side of the stage and looked out in the crowd towards the section Taryn and her friend were supposed to be in, and found her.

"Y'all ready to surprise our girl?" Jacko asked as he turned around smiling.

"You know it!" Jeremiah said, walking to dim the lights as Demoto headed for the stage. The three hadn't known Taryn long, but she had this innocence about her that drew them. She was cool people and a real sweetheart. Tomorrow was her birthday, so they all wanted to do something for her. Jeremiah had already disclosed the little information he knew about her family life with them. Demoto knew more than Jeremiah did, but he chose not to speak on it. He trusted Jeremiah and Jacko, but that wasn't his business to tell. Rich Homie had just finished his last song when Demoto walked onto the stage. They dapped each other up before Demoto leaned in and whispered something to him. They spoke a few more words before Rich Homie Quan came back on the mic.

"Taryn-Lee where you at girl?" he scanned the crowd, just as Jacko had the spotlight centered on her and Kia. Her face popped up on the two large screens in the front of the arena. The look on her face was priceless. She looked shocked to say the least. Kia stood up and pulled her arm so that she too was standing. Looking around obviously embarrassed, Taryn smiled and waved towards the stage. She was about to take her seat when Jeremiah walked up behind her and grabbed her hand, leading her to the stage. The entire concert sung happy birthday to her before it was over. Demoto and his friends were glad everything had turned out the way they planned. Taryn enjoyed her surprise, and was truly grateful. Demoto hung up his red phone and walked outside, where everyone was to wait for Taryn and Kia. He had a present for Taryn in his car. He was standing there texting when Alicia walked up smiling. Demoto smiled from ear to ear; she was bad! Alicia was flawless, from her smooth skin to her perfect body; he couldn't help but to love her. She had just finished asking him to stop by Waffle House on his way to her house when three boys came out of nowhere and stopped next to them. He could tell by the way they approached them that it was bad blood. Demoto had noticed the men approaching, but continued to play it cool. Once they were close enough, he turned to face them. He pushed Alicia behind him just as the tallest one of the crew stole on him. His fist hit Demoto's face so hard his head went to the side. That one punch started it all. The other two men jumped in, and together they jumped him. Even though there were three of them, Demoto was holding his own. A small crowd had gathered around to watch. Alicia's screams for someone to help fell on death ears. Everybody wanted to see, but nobody wanted to help.

*****

Taryn and Kia had just exited the building when they heard a lot of commotion coming from their left side. They looked around for the guys first, but when they didn't see them they walked towards the crowd. Taryn wasn't the one for drama, so she was hesitant about getting closer to the large group of people. Kia, on the other hand lived and breathed drama. She was from the hood; this was what she was accustomed to. Finally reaching the crowd, Taryn looked over people to see what was going on. Once her eyes finally registered the scene, her entire body got hot. She immediately pushed her way through the onlookers; she was past heated.

Once she made it to the front, she saw Alicia standing there screaming like a lunatic. She snatched her jacket off and quickly wrapped her hair in a bun. Taryn was moving at record speed. Kia was about to say something, but it was too late. Taryn had just punched the dude that was kicking Demoto. Realizing he had been hit, the man turned around and got hit two more times. Growing up in foster care had her ready; she had been fighting since she was small. Boys, girls–she didn't care. When it was time to handle business, that's what she did. The men were stronger than her, but she was holding it down.

Having one of the men's full attention on her gave Demoto the leverage he needed, and he was beating the shit out of the other two men. The man was getting pissed because every time he could get a lick in, the girl was hitting him with two. She had caught him off guard jumping in the fight from the beginning, so now she was about to get it. He lunged towards her, and they fell off the sidewalk. The moment her back hit the cement the wind was knocked out of her, but she kept swinging. She was raining punches on his head nonstop until he picked her up and body slammed her on the ground again. This time, she lay there for a few seconds unable to move. Taryn knew he was a coward the moment he started to kick her. He was kicking her any and everywhere. She thought about balling up in the fetal position and just taking the blows, but it wasn't in her. There was no way she was going to sit still and take a beat down. If she was going to go down, it was going to be with a fight.

*****

Demoto hadn't been in a fight in so long that it took him a minute to get with it. Three men had been jumping him for what seemed like forever. After a while, somebody jumped in and began helping him. This was exactly what he needed; three was a stretch, but two he could handle. He was beating the shit out of the two dudes. He was so busy fighting he didn't notice who it was helping him until he heard someone say her name. It was then that he glanced over quickly to see the other dude stomping Taryn out. It was as if his body had transformed. His adrenaline was pumping so hard that he could feel it. His anger maximized in those few seconds. He was trying his hardest to get to her, but the two men he was fighting wouldn't let up–but neither was he. He gathered all the strength he had and punched one of the assailants in the back of the head, knocking him unconscious.

The size difference between Demoto and the second dude was massive. Demoto was big, and this man was like a shrimp. Demoto picked him up and slammed his head against the ground. He wasn't unconscious like his friend, but by the way his head was leaking blood, you could tell he was out. With them laid out, he ran to Taryn's rescue but it was too late. Her girl Kia was hitting hard! Taryn had gotten off the ground and both girls were on the man, putting in major work. After a short while, the police came and broke everything up.
Demoto didn't know who the men were or why they had come for him, but he was going to find out. He noticed a black van pull off just before the police had come. He thought he recognized that van from somewhere, but he couldn't place it. He was heading to check on Taryn and Kia when Taryn brushed past him like a raging bull. He looked to

see where she was going, and she was heading straight for Alicia. The moment she was in close enough range, she drew back and slapped the taste from Alicia's mouth. She hit her so hard it could have been heard across the parking lot.

"Bitch why the fuck you didn't help him? Taryn yelled. "You just stood your ass right there and let him get jumped! What kind of woman are you?" Demoto hurried towards the girls. From the looks of things, Taryn was ready for round 2.

Chapter 6

Taryn stood there waiting for Alicia to answer her. There was no excuse as to why that little bitch had stood by and watched him get jumped. If she was his girl, she was supposed to help him.

"What the fuck was I supposed to do?" Hearing her act helpless only pissed Taryn off more.

"What the fuck you mean? What were you supposed to do? You his girl–he swing, your ass fucking swing!" Taryn drew back to slap her again, but Jacko stopped her. He and Jeremiah had just walked up. They'd been so busy wrapping up everything with the concert they had missed the entire fight.

"Chill Pretty Lee, what the fuck is going on?" Jacko asked, turning her around and not noticing her face was scratched and bruised

"I don't even know Jacky. Some niggas was jumping Moto when me and Kia came out, and all this bitch did was stand there!" she was fuming. She didn't really care for Alicia already; this just made her hate her. Hearing that, Jacko immediately got angry. He was flying off the hook when Demoto walked up. He had been talking to the police when he saw Taryn slap Alicia.

"Yo T, you good babygirl?" he asked. Her eye was swollen almost shut on one side and her lip had burst, but other than that she was fine. She had a couple of scrapes on her knees and elbows, but she was good.

"Yeah Moto I'm straight. You good?"

"Yeah I'm straight, I appreciate you having my back, but don't do that shit again," he said as he grabbed her into a hug. Being in Demoto's embrace made everything on her body feel better. She didn't care how long she had known him; she would always be in his corner. He had been there when she needed him, so she would do the same.

"Moto you need to get you another bitch, this hoe ain't shit!" Taryn was glaring at Alicia; she didn't understand why she hadn't helped. Kia had even jumped in.

"She stood right there screaming and shit instead of helping!" Taryn could tell Alicia felt bad about it now, but it was too late. Alicia walked towards Demoto trying to explain herself, which only made Taryn madder so she turned to walk away.

"Yo T, chill right here for a minute," Demoto called out to her. Taryn stopped and looked over at Kia, who was explaining the situation to Jacko and Jeremiah. Both men were deeply engaged in what Kia was saying. She didn't know what Kia had just said, but Jeremiah rushed towards her at the same time as Jacko turned to look at her. They had obviously just realized her and Kia were in the fight as well. Taryn wasn't a weak female by far, but it was something about Jeremiah's presence that broke her down. As soon as he touched her, she melted. She cried silent tears while hugging him tightly around his waist.

"I'm sorry I wasn't here to help you baby. The niggas are dead when I see them." He was running his hands through her hair. It had fallen out of her bun while she was fighting. Jeremiah was holding her tight and whispering in her ear everything would be fine. Taryn leaned back so she could look in his face. His smooth dark skin and full lips turned her on every time. He examined her face before leaning down to kiss her. They kissed for a few minutes before Jacko walked over to them.

"Pretty Lee you okay?"

"Yeah I'll be fine. I'm not new to this fighting shit. I'm a beast my nigga," she said, drawing a laugh from the whole group. Demoto didn't know what to say because he didn't want either of the girls getting hurt, but had Taryn never jumped in things probably would have been a lot worse. He knew Alicia and she wasn't built for this type of stuff, but Taryn was different. Alicia was born with a silver spoon, whereas Taryn had to fight for what she wanted. He couldn't lay the blame on Alicia, but he could definitely feel where Taryn was coming from.

He hugged Alicia and sent her home to try to diffuse the situation between her and Taryn. Taryn was angry and he didn't want her to kill Alicia. After walking Alicia to the car, he returned to his friends. They were all standing off to the side of the building waiting for him. Taryn was leaning against Jeremiah, watching him walk up. They made eye contact and held it. The look on her face was intense; he could tell she was trying to read his feelings. She needed to make sure he was ok. She may have been wrapped in another man's arm, but he could tell her heart was with him. He looked at her face, and it pissed him off how swollen it was on one side. From this day forward, he vowed to himself he was going to take care of her. She was a real ass female, and that was rare.

She saw he needed help and she was there–no questions asked. Demoto wrapped his arms around Kia and hugged her tight.

"Thank you for helping me Kia. I appreciate that shit."

"It's all good Moto, that's what friends are for."

"Man Moto what the fuck happened bruh?" Jacko was all ears. He was a known hot head; he was going to handle this shit.

"I'm not sure honestly. Three men approached me when I was talking to Alicia; the next thing I know we were hitting. We fought for a while before Taryn came to help me out." He looked over at her and smiled.

"When T and I came out everybody was just standing around watching. That's when she snatched her stuff off and got to it. She ain't waste no time after she saw it was Moto. My bitch was going hard for her boy. She was working that nigga until he slammed her on the ground and started kicking her." Demoto laughed at how hype Kia was getting as she told the story.

"So ain't none of the niggas out here try to break that shit up?" Jacko yelled.

"Nope! They ain't have to, I helped her! I wasn't about to stand there and let my friend get beat up, especially not by a nigga!" Demoto had always known Kia was a real tough chick, but he hadn't known to what extent until tonight. She hadn't known Taryn long, but she was already looking out for her. He was happy Taryn had someone as loyal as Kia on her team. Jacko on other hand was in love! Kia was his type of woman. From her size and style, to the way she would ride for her people when it was time. He was going to need Taryn to do some matchmaking on his behalf. Taryn smiled at Kia as she broke from Jeremiah's embrace and hugged her. The group went on talking for a little longer before deciding it was time to go. Kia retrieved her and Taryn's things from behind the trash can. She had thrown it back there before engaging in the fight.

"Dang T, with all this mess going on I forgot to call our ride."

"That's cool, I'll get Jeremiah to take us home." Taryn pulled out her phone and called him; he answered on the first ring. The next thing you know, he was pulling around to the front. Taryn really liked Jeremiah; he was so cute and sweet.

The ride to Kia's house was pretty quiet, except for the music Jeremiah had playing. All three of them were lost in their own thoughts. Taryn and Kia were so tired from fighting; all they wanted to do was go home and lay down. When they pulled up to Kia's house, Jeremiah killed the engine and waited for the girls to get out. Kia figured he probably wanted to talk to Taryn alone, so she headed for the house without her. Taryn leaned over the console to give him a kiss before opening the door. She wasn't out of the car all the way before he grabbed her arm, pausing her.

"You want to go home with me?"

"What about you parents?"

"My mom is out of town and my dad doesn't care." Taryn thought about pretending she didn't want to, but changed her mind. After the night she'd just had, going to sleep in his arms would be heaven. She told him to wait on her while she went to tell Kia. Kia had left the door open, so she walked right in. The living room was empty besides Mr. Buck's young soldier that had dropped them off. He was asleep on the couch. Taryn walked quietly past him to Kia's room. When she got in there, Kia had clothes in one arm and body wash in the other. Her hair was already tied up and her shoes were gone. Taryn told her she was going to spend the night with Jeremiah, and she'd be over in the morning.

"Okay well take my keys so you can let yourself back in when you get here in the morning. Or tonight, you never know how niggas will act."

"Jeremiah seem cool."

"I hope he stay that way when he realize you ain't giving up that butt. They start acting brand new once you deny they ass." Taryn hadn't thought about that, so she took Kia's keys. Kia was right; she didn't know how Jeremiah was going to behave. She hugged Kia real quick before grabbing her things and leaving.

*****

The inside of Jeremiah's house was so nice, and smelled like cinnamon apples. It was spacious, and so elegantly decorated. There were pictures hung all over the walls of his family. His mom had decorative pillows on the couch, with vases filled with flowers on the tables.

It felt so warm and inviting. It felt like a home. Taryn wasn't used to seeing houses as nice as this, so it took her a moment to take it all in. She wanted to stay and look at the family portraits to see what his family looked like, but Jeremiah was pulling her up the stairs.

The hallway was dark as they passed two rooms with closed doors. Jeremiah's room was a burnt orange and gray. You could tell his mom had decorated it, because everything matched. It looked nothing like something a boy would pick out. Aside from his clothes and various football and marine posters on the wall, it looked interiorly decorated. He had clothes on his bed, the floor, and a chair in the corner. He tried to pick some of them up and place them in the closet. She caught a glimpse of the shoe-filled closet. There were boxes stacked to the ceiling. Jeremiah always appeared to be spoiled, but she didn't know it was this bad. She watched him as he stirred around the room trying to clean up. Once he was finished, he turned around to face her.

He removed his jacket and shoes, then sat on the floor next to the bed and began taking off hers. With her feet free of her sneakers, he removed her socks and reached for her jacket. He stored all of her things in the chair next to his dresser.

"You want to take a shower?"

"What? What if somebody see me?"

"I already told you my daddy don't care, and my brothers are already asleep. Come on, I'll go in with you if you want me to," Taryn smiled at his last comment. Jeremiah must have thought she was a fool if he thought he was about to watch her take a shower. He must have read her thoughts.

"I'm not going to watch you, our bathroom has two sides. Get your stuff and come on, I'll show you." Taryn was skeptical, but she followed him anyway.

The restroom was just like he'd said. It had a shower, bathtub, and toilet on one side, with two sinks and a linen closet on the other. It was connected by a small walkway that had a long bench along the wall. Jeremiah turned the water on and gave her a towel and washcloth before retreating to the other side. By the time she had gotten done showering, Jeremiah was dressed in nothing but a towel. He'd removed his clothes and was on the bench waiting for her to finish. His appearance caught her off guard momentarily, but she tried to keep her focus. When he walked past her, she had to take a deep breath. He didn't even wait on her to leave before he dropped the towel and got into the shower.

"Jeremiah you ain't slick!"

"What you talking about girl?"

"You just want me to see you naked."

"Nah, that's where you're wrong. What I want is for you to be in this shower with me," he smiled devilishly before sliding the glass door closed. Since he was being so bold, she decided to do the same. Instead of walking to the other side, she sat on the side of the tub and watched him. Jeremiah was so silly as he turned towards her, displaying his wet body. Taryn crossed her legs tighter, trying to suppress the feeling in her panties. Their eyes remained connected the entire time he bathed. He motioned for her to come to him, so she did. After she slid the door open again, she stepped back a little to avoid getting wet. He grabbed her hand and guided it to his manhood. Taryn pulled back a little, but he kept going until it rested in her hand. He guided her hand up and down the shaft until his breathing got ragged. Taryn felt her body getting the best of her, so she pulled away and returned to the tub. He laughed at her and closed the door back.

"I fuck with you Taryn-Lee," he smiled as he finished washing. Taryn was relieved once they were safely back into his room. She sat on the bed, while he grabbed the lotion. As he kneeled in front of her, he began to rub her feet.

"You know I like you right?"

"Yeah I know. I like you too Jeremiah."

"I was serious about you being my girlfriend. What you think about that?"

"I think it's nice, but let's just give it a little more time first."

"Cool, so tell me about yourself."

Taryn hated the direction this conversation was about to take, so she leaned forward and kissed him. No objections came from him as he leaned her back and lay on top of her. They kissed as he rubbed his hands under her shirt. Taryn wrapped her legs tightly around his waist, trying to feel his hard body on hers. He caught on to what she was doing and began pressing his lower body into her, putting pressure on her already throbbing clit. He grunted at the same time a moan left her lips. The more she grinded against him, the harder he got, so he pulled back. Taryn looked at him like she didn't understand, so he went back to kissing her. This time instead of touching her breasts, he stuck his hands in her shorts and rubbed his hand along the seams of her panties. He rested his hand between her thighs, lightly massaging the wet spot on her panties. Taryn's face twisted in pleasure until she moaned again. Jeremiah was growing bigger by the second. He pulled his body from hers and grabbed a condom from the drawer on his dresser. In that millisecond, her brain started back functioning properly. She scooted up on the bed and closed her legs.

"What's wrong Taryn?"

"Nothing, I just don't think I'm ready for this yet." Jeremiah looked at her and smiled before replacing the condom. *Fuck! We too old for this shit,* he thought but played it cool anyway. He lay down and pulled her to him. They lay under the covers in the quiet room. Taryn could tell he was a little angry, and the only thing she could hear was Kia's voice. She snickered a little, because she couldn't wait to tell her tomorrow.

"What's funny?"

"Nothing. I just thought about something Kia said earlier. I hope you're not mad Jeremiah. I really like you, I just don't want us to move too fast."

"You good baby. Let's just get some rest, I know you got to be tired."

"I am, and my back hurt." Jeremiah wanted to offer a massage but he already knew that would leave him with blue balls, so he decided against it and went to sleep.

*****

Across town, Demoto was lying in Alicia's bed with Taryn on his mind. He'd texted her to make sure she was good and found out she was with Jeremiah. He didn't want to be jealous, but he couldn't mask it. He just hoped Taryn didn't let Jeremiah hit. That should have been the last thing on his mind being that he'd just finished running through Alicia, but it wasn't. All he could think about was Taryn. While inside Alicia, his thoughts were of Taryn. Alicia was on his dick, and Taryn was on his heart. He had given Alicia some of his best work, and she probably thought it was because of her.

In his mind, he was making love to Taryn. It was her thick thighs and ass he pictured when he was hitting Alicia from the back. The whole time she slid up and down his pole, he wished it was Taryn wrapped around him. He was basically making love to Taryn through Alicia. Frustrated with himself and her, he rolled over with his back to Alicia. She probably thought he was mad about her not helping him, so he wouldn't let her think any different. In reality, he was trying to protect her feelings; if he talked, he'd probably say the wrong thing. He had to bite his tongue during sex so he didn't scream out Taryn's name. Demoto blew out a heated breath and tried to find sleep.

*****

6 months later

It had been months since the fight at the civic center, and Demoto still hadn't put his hands on the people that attacked him. He and his boys had their ears to the streets, but nothing came up. He sat back in his seat and thought about everything he had going on. He was stressed to the max, but he tried to remain cool. He and his brother Adisa had a meeting with a man named Cayman Rasheed in thirty minutes, and he was nervous. Cayman was an African businessman; he too was from Cameroon. He was in charge of Official Opportunities, also known as Double O. It was one of the most notorious corporations in the south. He did everything from money laundering, drugs, prostitution rings, to murder. He had everybody on the payroll–small businesses, dirty cops, judges, teachers, car salesmen, anything you named he had a piece in it.

Cayman was a fair guy and worked with everybody, but he wasn't the one to cross. He was ruthless! Everyone knew it was best to stay on his good side. There had been numerous cases in Columbus alone where people had gone missing, or been found dead due to his wrath. Although all of that was impressive, that wasn't the reason Demoto was nervous. He was nervous because Cayman had specifically asked for this meeting with him. He had done small transactions with him before, but he'd never seen him face to face. The only people that saw him were his right hand men; everybody else followed the orders that were given to them. Demoto had been racking his brain for the past two days trying to figure out what Cayman could possibly want with him, but he couldn't come up with anything.

Checking his red cell phone, he noticed he had a message. It was Cayman's 2nd in charge, Dank. He was confirming their meeting. He slid the phone back into his armrest and pulled out his iPhone 6. The red phone was for business only. Cayman ran a strict operation, and anybody that had ever worked for him had the same red phone. He'd had them imported directly to him for his workers. They were all prepaid phones that couldn't be tracked or traced by the government. No matter how big or small the work you did for him was, you could only operate with one of those phones. No one else in the world had those; they were made especially for Double O. Demoto ran his hand over his face and let out a loud sigh. He was scrolling through Instagram when Taryn's picture popped up and Lil John's song *Ms. Chocolate* started playing. He'd given her that ringtone because it fit her perfectly.

"What's up T. Lee!"

"Hey Mr. Youngblood! What you doing?"

"About to handle some business."

"Oh okay, well call me when you done. I need to ask you something." He told her he would before hanging up. He and Taryn had gotten really close, like siblings. They hung out and talked and texted on the regular. It was innocent for the most part, but deep down they both knew it was something there. They'd decided to ignore it for now. Adisa had just pulled up beside him so he got out, locked his car, and joined his brother on the steps of the building.   "You nervous Youngblood?"

"Nah I'm just ready to see what this is about."

The two walked into the office building and took the elevator to the top floor. The doors opened and Adisa walked ahead; he'd been there a few times before, so he knew where he was going. The floor seemed to be empty; only thing you heard was the humming from the air conditioner. The closer they got to the door, the more anxious he got. They turned the corner and walked into a long hallway lined with doors; they went to the second to last one and knocked twice. The door opened immediately.

Inside there were four men standing on each side of Cayman. Two were white and two were black. One of the white men looked extremely familiar to Demoto; he just couldn't place his face at the moment. He and Adisa walked in and stood directly in front of the desk he was sitting at, and waited. Cayman wasn't the arrogant type, so he didn't make them wait for long. He looked up, gave each of them a friendly smile, and motioned for them to sit down.

"Hello my friends, thank you for coming." His accent was so thick it reminded Demoto of a world he once knew. Cameroon was home, but it was a place he definitely wasn't planning to return to. He and Adisa nodded their heads, still not speaking.

"Demoto. How are you my young friend?"

"I'm well, thank you."

"I called you here today because I'm impressed with your work. I haven't had one complaint about anything you've done, so I wanted to offer you something a little better. It's something more imperative to your spot in my organization." This got Demoto's attention. Being acknowledged for his work by Cayman was epic, but he remained cool. He had mastered his poker face a long time ago. There weren't too many times he wanted people to know what was going on in his head. Demoto expressed his gratitude as Cayman turned his attention to Adisa.

"I asked you to accompany him because it's a two man job. Most of the things that need to be done, Demoto can do on his own, but it's always necessary to have backup." He listened intently as Cayman spoke. Adisa was an older version of Demoto, minus the dreads and green eyes. He wore a low cut and his eyes were hazel. Demoto was eager to ask what the job entailed, but he knew that part was coming. He watched Cayman stand up and whisper to the familiar looking white man before he nodded his head and left. He waited for the man to return before speaking.

"Demoto, this is Bradley Marks; he's the Secretary of Double O, and one of my most trusted friends. You will be working with him from here on out; anything you need, no matter what it is, he will see that you get it." Demoto nodded his head towards Bradley and returned his attention to Cayman. He had come around the desk and was sitting directly in front of him.

"I chose you for this position because I trust you. I know that you will do an exceptional job. Here's how this will go. I'm going to present you with this opportunity. You have three days to get back to me with your answer. I'm going to give you all of Bradley's contact information; if you choose to take the job, simply reply YES to his text. If you choose not to, reply DONE."

Demoto could tell the job was serious. Cayman never gave you the option to refuse his offers.

"Okay, what is it?" Demoto looked directly at Cayman and waited for an answer. His father had taught him and Adisa to always look a man directly in the eye when speaking. He explained that your eyes were the gate to your soul. You could tell real or fake, lies or truth, sincere or phony all by looking in a person's eyes. Cayman's eyes were hard and earnest. He was the real deal. Demoto saw no fear or dishonesty in them.

"Demoto I would like for you to be my number 2 assassin." *Assassin?* That was definitely not what he expected to hear, but yet in still he remained cool.

"How will that work? What do I have to do?"

"If you decide to take the job, you'll be provided with various contracts that have been sent to me by either the government, or personal vengeance. Along with the contract, you will be given the name, address, photo, and schedule of the target. Before starting this job, you will attend a mandatory training for two months to learn the necessary skills." Demoto sat back taking it all in and nodding every once in a while, but truth be told, the offer had caught him completely off guard.

"Your payout will vary depending on the person. The minimum for each kill is 20,000, not including your traveling expenses. I will handle everything else; all you do is make the kill." The meeting went on for another twenty minutes. Cayman answered all of his questions in detail before they left.

*****

Taryn had been sitting in her room at the shelter all day. It had been almost six months, and she was ready to go. On top of her having to hide it from all of her friends, she was just ready to move. She was now 18 and old enough to get her own apartment, and that's what she wanted. The only thing holding her back was a co-signer. She needed someone at least 21 years or older to sign her lease, and she had no one. She knew Janay would do it, but she didn't want to ask her. Anything she did, she wanted to do it on her own. She lay back on her bed and looked out of the window. All of her thoughts went to Jeremiah. They had been getting pretty serious lately. They spent a lot of time together but never took it further than kissing, but tonight was different.

Today was Jeremiah's birthday, and she could tell he wanted sex. He wasn't forcing her, but he dropped hints every time they were together. She knew he wouldn't wait forever, but she didn't think she was ready yet. She'd only been that close to one other man willingly, and that was Demoto. She replayed that night in her head over and over to prepare herself for Jeremiah, but it didn't help. Along with the other times she'd spent with Jeremiah, she hadn't gotten far enough with either of them to teach her anything. She discussed it with Kia all the time, but she was still nervous. She took her phone off the charger and texted her best friend.

Taryn: Hey hoe what you doing?

Kia: Nothing, sitting here bored, wyd?

Taryn: I'm about to come over there

Kia: *Okay!*

Come on!

Taryn brushed her hair up into a neat ponytail, grabbed her purse, and left. She threw her purse into the front seat of her dark purple Camaro and drove off. She pulled up into Kia's yard and parked next to her car. Kia's car was identical to hers, except hers was pink. Her dad had bought them both a car for graduation. Being that her and Kia had gotten extremely close, she spent a lot of time at her house. Whenever she was over there, she would laugh and talk with Kia's dad just like he was hers. She loved him and he loved her; he was like the father she never had. He schooled her on everything, from boys to the streets. Anything he got for Kia, he got for her also. She got out the car and walked to the porch, where Kia's dad and one of his young workers were sitting.

"Hey Daddy, hey Dee!"

"Hey Tee-Tee, Kay-Kay didn't tell me you were coming." Kay-Kay and Tee-Tee is what Mr. Buck called them. Taryn loved her nickname because she knew it was out of love. Kia on the other hand acted like she didn't, but Taryn knew she did.

"She didn't know, I just told her."

"I got something for you before you leave."

"Okay Daddy." Taryn turned and entered the house. Once she got to Kia's room, she saw her sprawled out on the bed watching Sons of Anarchy. She kicked her shoes off and climbed on the bed with her. They laid there and talked about Jeremiah for a while before taking pictures on her phone. Taryn had just posted a picture of them on her Instagram when her cell phone rang. She knew when she heard *My Nigga* by YG it was Jacko. Jacko was like her brother. She loved him; he was always calling to check on her or ask her advice on women.

"Hey brother!"

"What's going on pretty Lee? What you doing?"

"Nothing at Kia house chilling." She lay backwards on the bed and looked up at the ceiling. "What you doing?"

"Just got done handling some business, you and Kia feel like taking a ride with me?"

"You know I'm down, come get us from here." As soon as she hung up, she got up and put her shoes back on.

"Come on Kia, Jacko want us to ride somewhere with him real quick." Taryn and Kia fixed their hair and clothes, and went to wait on the porch. A few minutes later, Jacko pulled up. They were almost off the porch when Kia's dad called for them.

"Kay-Kay and Tee-Tee, come here let me holla at y'all real quick." Taryn motioned for Jacko to wait a second.

"What's going on Daddy?" Kia asked, taking a seat on one of his legs while Taryn sat on the other.

Big Buck loved his girls; he'd just met Taryn but after Kia told him about her past, he wanted to help her. She was a sweet girl and needed some guidance, so he

stepped up. He'd always wanted another daughter, so
Taryn fit right in. The fact that Kia loved his and Taryn's
relationship as well made him even happier. Kia was
normally jealous over his affection, but she didn't mind it
when it came to Taryn. Having both of his grown girls sit
on his lap like they were kids warmed his heart. They
were the only two people able to do that. Nobody else got
to him the way they did. He would kill a person just for
breathing too hard, and everyone knew that. Buck had
been the Vice President of Double O for the past fifteen
years, and he was respected.

"I got some money I want y'all to pick up for me.
It's at uptown barbershop. It should be $20,000. When
y'all get it, split it ten and ten and put it in the accounts."
Both girls nodded in understanding before kissing his
cheeks and leaving. He'd opened them both accounts
after graduation and had been putting money in there
every chance he got. Both girls were responsible, so they
hadn't touched any of the money yet. He'd told them to
save it because he wouldn't be around forever. Both girls
hated to hear him talk like that, but it was the truth.

****

"Where we going Jacky boy?" Taryn was looking
out of the window as they breezed down the expressway.
They had been riding for the past fifteen minutes and still
hadn't gotten anywhere. Jacko smiled slowly as he
looked at her.

"I got some money to pick up and I want y'all to
do it for me." Taryn stared at him for a brief second
before looking in the backseat at Kia

"Why you want us to do it? What can't you?"

"Because Pretty Lee, I need to teach these lil hoes a lesson, but I'm not a woman beater."

"So basically you want us to go beat they ass, and take your money?" Kia asked from the backseat. Taryn laughed at her best friend's bluntness. Kia was as hood as she could get. She was one of the realist females Taryn had ever come in contact with.

"That's exactly what I want y'all to do."

"Well you know I'm down, what about you T?"

"I'm with it," Taryn said as she answered her phone for Jeremiah. He had been out of town with his parents all day. They made small talk before making plans to meet up later that night. She had just hung up the phone when Jacko turned into Elizabeth Canty projects. E-Canty, is what the local people called it. It was one of the most popular public housing complexes in Columbus, GA. It was brick buildings with black doors and stairs. The grass needed to be cut, and there was trash everywhere.

Driving down the street, Taryn looked at the group of men standing on the corner. They looked to be in their early twenties; she could bet they were drug dealers. They continued driving, passing by a host of children playing and residents on their porch.

Jacko pulled his Corvette to a stop and turned in his seat so that he was facing both girls.

"Look, it's two girls; they steal cars for me. They were supposed to have brought me forty bands last week but they haven't. I've been calling and they've been dodging me. My lil partner told me they in apartment D, so I need y'all to go get them. I brought y'all because they rowdy as hell; if it gets ugly, I'll handle it." Taryn listened to Jacko without saying anything.

"Alright we got it! Come on Kia!" Kia and Taryn exited the car and walked up the stairs to the door. Taryn knocked first, but when no one answered Kia started to kick it. She was kicking it so hard the windows were rattling.

"Open up this fucking door!" she yelled, still kicking the door. The locks clicked and the front door swung open. A short light-skinned girl with long red weave pushed the screen door open and glared and both girls. She asked who they were with way too much attitude for Taryn's likes. Deciding to forget all the pleasantries, Taryn cut straight to the chase.

"We came to get Jacko money."

"Well I don't have it," she rolled her eyes.

"Listen, I don't have time to play these games. Go get my brother money and bring it out here so we can go." By now, another girl had joined them on the porch. She was tall and chubby, with a low haircut.

"I said, I don't have it!" Kia stood there watching every move the girls were making. She didn't recognize the first one, but the baldhead chubby one used to run dope for her father. He had removed her from his squad a few months ago for stealing, so she knew they were lying. She must have just noticed Kia because she nodded her head and smiled like they were friends.

"What's up Kia?"

"Hey Ace. Where is Jacko's money?" Taryn looked at Kia, then back at the girl. She didn't know her but, Kia knew everybody so she wasn't surprised. Ace walked back into the house and came back with $30,000. Taryn counted it quickly, because they already had it separated.

"Y'all owe him ten more! Stop fucking playing! I don't have time for this shit!" Taryn had barely got the words out of her mouth when Ace lunged at her. Taryn figured they were going to try something like that, so she ducked and Ace slammed into the wall. Kia rushed over to her and pulled her gun from behind her back, and put it in her face.

"Ace, send your friend to get the rest of Jack's money before I blow your bald head off." Ace looked at Kia like she wanted to say something, but changed her mind. Everybody knew Kia was Buck's daughter, so Taryn didn't have to guess why she chose not to say anything.

"Red, go get the other ten!" The whole transaction took about ten minutes before Taryn and Kia were headed back to the car.

Chapter 7

Demoto had just gotten out of the shower when he heard a knock on his front door. He wasn't expecting company, so he looked at his phone for missed calls before checking to see who it was. He slid his shorts on, and headed for the door.

"What you doing here girl?" Demoto smiled as Taryn rushed in the door. She was obviously getting ready to go somewhere, because she was dressed up. Demoto eyed her up and down in her silk black romper and wedges. Her hair was all down with the front pinned up with a gold clip. She wore simple gold jewelry and a small gold clutch. She had so much style. That was one of the things he loved about her. She had walked right past him and into the kitchen. He watched her as she was walked towards him with his Gatorade. He'd just bought it from the gas station on his way home, and here she was drinking it. Demoto let out a small chuckle and shook his head.

"What you think you doing T?"

"I'm thirsty. This all y'all had in the refrigerator, *and* you never called me back earlier." He had totally forgot about calling her once he'd left from seeing Cayman.

"My fault T. I meant to, I just had some serious stuff going on earlier" Her face frowned up immediately.

"What's going on Moto, everything okay?" He had to love Taryn; she was so caring. He wrapped his arm around her shoulder and pulled her to him.

"Don't mess up my hair Moto, I got a date tonight!" she eased away from him and sat down on the couch.

"With who? Miah?"

"Yes! Who else Demoto? But anyway, I need to talk to you about something." He walked around and sat in front of her. He waited for her to start talking, but when she did, it was definitely not what he expected. She explained about her being a virgin and Jeremiah wanting sex. She was scared he wasn't going to want her anymore if she didn't do it, but she wasn't ready. He sighed heavily before responding. He wanted so bad to tell her not to have sex with Jeremiah, but he didn't. He knew he would only be saying it because the thought alone made his blood boil. He wanted her for himself, but he had to push that to the back of his mind. He yearned privately for Taryn; he wanted to be the first man to have her. She hadn't spent the night with him since the first night he saw her in the park, so he hadn't been able to. That hadn't stopped him from wanting her. Every time he saw her the feeling got more intense, especially at moments like this. Jeremiah was his friend, but there was no way he was about to talk her into sleeping with him. It was selfish and petty, but it was how he felt. No man in his right mind would push the woman he loved into the arms of another man. Demoto had realized he loved Taryn about a month ago, but he kept that to himself as well.

"So what should I do Demoto? I mean, I like Jeremiah and everything but this is a big step. He's so sweet to me." The look on her face was one of pure confusion.   "You love him?"

"Yeah, I think so." He remained calm, but he was fuming on the inside. Taryn's beautiful dark skin looked as if it were glowing. Her big hair framed her face with just enough pulled up to amplify her beauty. She was looking at him, pleading with her eyes for an answer. He knew he could give her one, he just wasn't sure if it was the one she wanted. He stared at her.

"Don't just stare at me Demoto, tell me something."

"Don't do it." Demoto's voice was low but firm. He sat there waiting for her to respond.

"Why not?"

"Because I don't want you to," he said with finality. He could tell by the look on her face she was shocked. He hadn't meant to say that, but when he opened his mouth that's what came out.

"Okay I won't," she said in a hurry. Standing, Demoto reached his hand towards her, and she took it. He led her down the hallway and to his room. He closed and locked his door. Taryn stood next to his dresser, biting her nails. He could tell she was nervous. Grabbing his remote, he turned on his music. He pressed play and Silk's *If You* poured through the speakers.

Been checking you for so long and I feel

Girl, you should let me know what the deal

Been peepin' out your life, I think you want to let me slide

So what you need to do right now is keep it real

I know you want me, girl, just like I want you

So stop frontin' like you don't when you do

So if you're feeling naughty, naughty and if you're really 'bout it, 'bout it

And if you get me rowdy, rowdy my love's gonna make you shout it, shout it

"Come over here Taryn-Lee." She moved towards him slowly. Once she got closer, he grabbed her by the front of her romper and pulled her the rest of the way. He wrapped one arm around her waist and rubbed along the inside of her thighs with the other. Taryn's thighs were thick, and her body was warm. Demoto continued to run his hands all over her body until she was relaxed. He leaned forward until their foreheads were touching.

"I want you Taryn." His voice came out in more of a desperate plea than he intended. The burn for her had turned into a full-blown inferno. His need to feel her was surpassing his rational thinking. The way she melted under his touch wasn't making it any better.

Taryn's mind was all over the place. Her panties were wet and her legs were weak. The hold Demoto had on her was exhilarating. When it came to sex with Jeremiah she was skeptical and undecided, but Demoto was different. Her body reacted to his touch in a familiar manner. Every part of her body he'd touched was tingling. She was on fire for him.

"I don't know how Moto." Although she had just told him in the living room she was a virgin, she felt the need to remind him of her inexperience.

"I'll show you." With that, he picked her up and sat down on the bed. She was straddling his lap as he ran his hands up and down her back. Taryn knew in the back of her mind this was wrong, but it felt so right. She loved Jeremiah, but what she felt with him couldn't compare to the way she was feeling right now. She eased back off his lap. He went to reach for her, trying to stop her from moving but she stepped back.

"Taryn please." Taryn could see the desperation in his eyes. He obviously thought she was changing her mind, when in reality she couldn't have if she tried. She stood before him, watching him intently as she removed the clip from her hair, letting it fall around her shoulders. She then removed her shoes and bracelets. Once she'd finished, Demoto pulled her between his legs as he sat on the edge of the bed. He fumbled with her zipper before pulling the romper completely off.

She watched as he trailed kisses from her stomach down to her thighs. She was so nervous that she could barely stand still. He must have sensed her nervousness because he placed both of his hands on her hips, stopping her jittery movement. She glanced over at the clock; she had an hour and half before her date with Jeremiah.

"Demoto stop. This ain't right"

"You really want me to?" She stood silent, unsure of what to say.

"I knew you didn't, so stop talking all that shit." She smiled as he lay back on his elbows. Taryn fidgeted under his stare. His green eyes were almost hypnotic.

"Bring your pretty ass over here T, and stop looking so scared." His accent would never get old to her. The thick country slur in his words turned her on to no end.

"I am scared. I wish you would stop looking at me like that."

"I can't stop Taryn-Lee, you're perfect!" Taryn didn't know what to say, so instead she crawled on top of him. His arms immediately snaked around her, pulling her down onto his hard body. Demoto knew Taryn was inexperienced, so he flipped her over so he was on top. He kissed her all over before unsnapping her bra. He alternated between sucking and biting on her nipples. He twisted and pulled playfully at her nipple rings, bringing vibrant shudders from her body. After blowing lightly down her stomach, he stopped with his head between her thighs. He licked the sides of her thighs, then turned his attention to her warmth. He licked slowly around her essence, teasing her before pushing her panties to the side. Taryn's breasts were rising and falling at a rapid pace due to her breathing. Demoto could tell she'd never felt pleasure to this extent. He ripped the panties from her body in one quick motion. After the first flick of his tongue, she screamed.

"Damn baby," he said as his lips and warm tongue slid up and down her wetness. He sucked and slurped at her juices passionately as she squirmed around the bed.

"You taste so good," he said as he French-kissed her opening. He twirled his tongue in and out of her sweetness, causing her to moan in ecstasy. Demoto sucked on her clit, applying the right amount of pressure to make her cum. She was moaning loudly as she held a hand full of his dreads. Demoto was enjoying pleasing her so much; he hadn't even noticed he too was moaning. With one finger inside of her, he zoned in on her clit. He was enjoying how sweet she was. Demoto could tell she was on the edge, so he went back to French kissing her wetness. Taryn gasped loudly just before screaming. He thought maybe she couldn't catch her breath, but that was all over the moment she exploded all over his face. Demoto eagerly lapped up her juices, making sure he tasted it all. She was pulling his dreads and arching her back as she came.

"That's right T, cum in my mouth baby."

"Oh Moto, that felt so good," she moaned. Taryn lay on his bed looking exhausted. Her hair was sprawled all over his pillows. Taryn-Lee was absolutely stunning. The look of a fresh orgasm adorned her face; she looked satisfied and weak.

Demoto grabbed a condom from his nightstand drawer and got into bed with her. He quickly slid it on and got on top. Taryn was lying extremely still as he guided the tip of his manhood towards her opening. He slid it around in her moist heat, making sure to rub it against her clit. It was obviously still sensitive from her

122

orgasm, because she jumped and let out a small sigh. He checked to make sure she was okay before he continued. She nodded her head and grabbed both of his forearms. Demoto balanced himself on one arm and held his dick with the other. He put the head to her opening and slid it in slowly. Taryn's entire body tensed up. She pushed at Demoto's stomach and scooted back, making him slip out.

"It hurts Moto," she whined.

"I'm sorry baby, I'll go slower." He leaned down and cupped her butt with both hands, pulling her back to him. Once again, he slid only the head in. Taryn winced in pain, but he kept going. He was met with a strong resistance. Taryn was so tight and wet he had to bite down on his bottom lip to keep from moaning. He eased out and pushed in again with a little more force. He did this a few more times until he was all the way in. She gasped loudly, like she'd lost her breath. Taryn's body felt heavenly wrapped around his dick. Taryn had her arms and legs wrapped around him so tight he could hardly move. He pulled back some so he could look at her face. Her eyes were closed, and her face was twisted in pain.

"You want me to stop?"

"No keep going, just go slow."

Demoto picked one of her legs up in the crook of his arm and started grinding. He was trying to go slow, but it was starting to feel too good. The slower he went, the wetter she got. Her pussy was dripping wet, and making all kinds of gushy noises. Demoto loved it! He had slept with a number of girls in his past, but they didn't have shit on Taryn. Alicia was running a close second, but Taryn was in a league of her own. Demoto continued to slide inside her, all the while whispering in her ear how beautiful she was. He spoke in French because he knew she loved it.

"This shit was made for me Taryn. You hear me? Your body was made to be mine! You better not give it to anybody else!" He knew Taryn and she was loyal; if he said not to, then she wouldn't. Yes it was selfish of him to make that decision for her, but so what! After tonight she would forever be his, no matter who she was with.

"Oww Demoto, its hurting me so good."

"It feel good to you baby?" She nodded her head ferociously. Slowly the pain had obviously turned into pleasure, because she was now grinding back against him. *Damn this pussy good.* He stroked her slow a few more minutes before speeding up. He was punishing her and he could tell; she was screaming so loud he was sure Adisa could hear her.

"Be quiet and take this shit T, you a big girl. Take this dick for me." Demoto hit her with deep rough strokes until he climaxed. "Damn Baby!" he yelled as he fell beside her onto the bed.

Taryn pulled the sheet over her body and looked at Demoto. She wanted to know how she'd done. Demoto turned his head and looked at her.

"Excellent. You took this muthafucka like a champ, I'm proud of you." Taryn loved Demoto, but hated this crazy relationship they had. One minute they were friends, and the next he was fucking her brains out. Sex with him was everything she thought it would be. She was in some serious pain, but it was worth it.

"I have to go Demoto." she whispered. He didn't say anything; he just nodded his head in understanding. Taryn stood up still wrapped in the sheet and grabbed her clothes.

"Taryn I don't know why you trying to hide, your body is gorgeous! You're fucking perfect!" She blushed at his comments. She hadn't noticed he was still watching her. Although he had just seen every part of her, she was still shy.

"Close your eyes so I can put my clothes on."

"I wish I would. You better put them damn clothes on." Demoto was laughing at her, which only made her even more nervous. Taryn looked at him with pleading eyes, but he only smirked. Figuring he was going to watch her no matter what, she dropped the sheet. She tried to put her panties on, but had forgotten they were ripped.

"You owe me another pair of panties too sir."

"I got you baby," he laughed. Taryn finished getting dressed and wrapped her hair into a messy bun on the top of her head, and prepared to leave. Demoto slid out of bed and put his shorts on. Taryn tried to act like she wasn't watching him, but she couldn't help it. His body was sexy, and his dick was even better. It was so big and thick; she thought he was going to rip her walls apart. She'd never felt something that hurt so bad and feel so good at the same time.

Breaking her gaze from his body, she followed him out. They walked in silence until they reached his front door. She watched his dreads fall around his chest, as he pulled her to him. He leaned down and took her bottom lip in his mouth, sucking it. He slipped her his tongue for a passionate kiss. Taryn willingly accepted it. They kissed intimately for another five minutes before he slapped her on her booty and watched her leave. Once she'd gotten in her car, she rushed back to the shelter; she had to meet Jeremiah at the movies in twenty minutes. She hurried so she could take a shower and get herself together. Once she got into her room, she sent him a text letting him know she would be late. After he said okay, she sent Demoto one as well.

Taryn: Did you really mean what you said?

Demoto: I said a lot, be specific

Taryn: About being yours, and not giving it to nobody else.

Demoto: hell yeah I meant it! That's my shit, and ain't nobody allowed in it but me!

Taryn: Okay Demoto, I won't

Demoto: Promise?

Taryn: I promise

Taryn smiled at her phone. Demoto made her feel wanted. She hadn't felt like that in a long time. Checking the clock, she rushed to get dressed.

Chapter 8

Today was only his second day of training and he was already tired. Demoto was currently sitting at the gun range waiting for his turn. He'd accepted the job from Cayman and had two months of training to go. Initially he hadn't wanted to accept it, but the money was good and the job was easy. He wasn't a stranger to murder; he'd been killing since he was a kid. His father had groomed he and Adisa from childhood. The thing that bothered him the most wasn't that he was ready to get home, it was his reasoning behind wanting to get home. He wanted to see Taryn. He'd been thinking about her nonstop since he got there. He hadn't made any attempts to contact her since the other night after they'd had sex. He'd texted her once to make sure she'd gotten home from her date safely, and that was it.

"Youngblood, you're up next!" his instructor yelled. Pushing all thoughts of Taryn out of his head, Demoto grabbed his .45 and walked to the target.

*****

"Ewww Miah you are so nasty! I don't want none of that mess!" Taryn leaned her head away from the fork full of food. She and Jeremiah were having lunch at a Japanese steakhouse called Fuji's. They'd been out shopping all day and decided to stop on their way home.

"Stop playing and taste it baby."

"No. I don't like onions," Taryn smiled and pushed his fork back towards him. Jeremiah was truly a sight for sore eyes. Everything about him was relaxing and cool. They had been spending practically all of their free time together since he'd been back. She enjoyed being around him. She'd had one of the best times of her life on their movie date the other night. He was the perfect gentleman. They talked and played all night. Taryn smiled as he eyed her up and down across the table.

"Taryn you need stop playing, and be my girlfriend."

"I will when you're ready for me. But right now you aren't ready."

"What you mean when I'm ready? I am ready!" Jeremiah leaned forward so their faces were only inches apart.

"Jeremiah, I'm a real woman. I'm nothing like what you're used to. Being my man is going to take a lot more than looking good." Jeremiah laughed at her. She watched as he took in the things she said as if they were a joke. The more he laughed, the more annoyed she got. She saw nothing funny about what she'd said. Taryn sat back in her chair and rolled her eyes.

"I don't understand how you can sit here and tell me what I'm used to. You don't even know me for real T." She was really annoyed now. They'd been spending practically all of their free time together since she'd first given him her number at school. To make matters worse, he'd called her T; only Demoto called her that. She couldn't count how many hours they'd spent on the phone talking and sharing personal things, and he had the nerve to say she didn't know him. She was pissed!

"Well since I don't know you, why would you want me to be your girlfriend? I know I wouldn't want to be with a person who had no clue who I really was." She watched his face turn serious, but he wasn't looking at her. He was looking past her. Following his eyes behind her head, she saw the red head girl that had tried to keep Jacko's money.

"You want me to get you some more coke, Taryn?" Jeremiah asked. Taryn was about to say no, but he was already out of his seat and headed for the drink machine. She watched him for a moment in disbelief until she saw the red head walk up to the same machine, pretending to get some soda as well. Taryn figured it was something fishy going on, so she retrieved her compact mirror from her purse and used it to look behind her. If Jeremiah saw her staring at him, then whatever he was about to do with this girl, he wouldn't. She could tell by his body language and hand movement he was fussing. The girl wore a sad expression as she left the restaurant. Taryn replaced her mirror quickly and grabbed her phone. When he walked up, she was on Instagram. The moment he sat down, his forehead was filled with stress lines and he complained of a headache.

"We can get ready to go if you want, I'm full now anyway." After grabbing her purse, Taryn stood and waited for him to pay. Taryn read silently on her phone as they rode back to Kia's house.

"You like working at Foot Locker?" Jeremiah asked her out of nowhere.

"Yeah it's cool. It's enough to pay my little bills."

"You work off commission, right?"

"Yeah, and I get minimum wage, why?" Taryn was confused as to why her job and her money was any of his concern.

"I was just wondering why somebody as pretty as you would be wasting your time there, when you could be making more money somewhere else." This caught her attention. She could tell he was trying to choose his words carefully

"You ever thought about dancing?" Taryn scrunched her face up in confusion.

"You mean stripping?"

"Yeah if that's what you want to call it." She shook her head in disbelief.

"You should. My little sister does it on the weekends to help pay for school. She be racked up! It's nothing for her to make six bands in two days." Taryn was shocked. She knew strippers made money, but she didn't think it was that much. Taryn listened to Jeremiah go on for a little while longer before he was pulling into Kia's driveway. What he was saying sounded good, but the part she didn't get was why he was telling her. He had just asked her to be his girlfriend, now he wanted her to strip for other men? Something wasn't right about that. She thanked him for lunch as she closed his truck door. She was halfway to her car when he yelled through the window at her.

"Think about what I said." Taryn knew he was talking about her stripping. She waved at him dismissively and got into her car. She wished Kia was home from work so she could tell her about Jeremiah's interesting proposition, but she didn't get off for another hour.

Jeremiah sped down the interstate heading home. He hoped Taryn thought about what he was saying and decided to do it. He liked Taryn, but he loved money. He and the owner of the Luxx lounge were business partners and every girl he brought to the club, he'd get paid for it. He hadn't wanted to turn Taryn out like that, but she seemed like she could handle it. Besides, she wasn't trying to give him any play. In the beginning he thought she was too sheltered to expose herself to the nightlife, but as he got to know her, he realized she was just as ready as any other female. Being in a relationship with Taryn seemed to have its perks, but he wasn't feeling that with her anymore. She was still playing the good girl role while he had other women busting it open on call. Taryn was cool, but that was it.

*****

Taryn had just gotten back to the shelter when her phone vibrated with a text. It was Janay checking to see if she was in her room, because she was about to come by. Not even five minutes later, she heard a knock on her door. They talked about everything, eventually landing on her apartment search. Talking about her new apartment with Janay had her extremely excited. It was only when she thought about not having enough money for it that her mood changed. She'd been saving all of her checks from work, but it still wasn't enough. Her account held enough for a deposit and rent, but definitely not enough for a house full of furniture. She explained her situation to Janay.

"Just keep saving, we'll find something in your budget," Janay smiled as she prepared to leave. "Taryn, do you have a boyfriend?"

"Janay, where did that come from?" she smiled. "I was just asking because I've wanted to introduce you to my brother n law for a little while now, but I wasn't sure if you were single."

"I don't know about that Janay. I kind of have feelings for somebody else already." Janay looked a little upset. "Dang! Y'all would make a cute couple, but I understand. If you and your friend don't work out, let me know!" With that, she left. Taryn thought about it for a second, and she didn't know why she'd said that. She wasn't in a relationship with Jeremiah and although he was sweet, she didn't have any serious feelings for him. The one person she really did care about, she couldn't have. There was something about Demoto Youngblood that she just couldn't shake.

After talking to Janay, her mind was doing numbers. It was time for her to get her own place. She hadn't had anything to call her own her entire life. She visualized how she would decorate everything using ideas from Pinterest. The thought of having her own little home made her happy. She would never need anyone for anything else; anything she needed, she could handle on her own. Only thing holding her back was money. She had some saved on top of the money Mr. Buck had put up

for her, but that was for school. She wouldn't use that
unless she had no other choice, and right now she did.
How hard could dancing really be? She was beyond
confident in her body, unless Demoto was around. He
unnerved her completely. He looked at her with need and
desire, almost like he wanted to eat her. When he touched
her, her whole body shivered. When they'd had sex he
was so patient, not to mention skilled. Just then, the all
too familiar tingly feeling in her stomach came. For the
last couple of days whenever she would think about them
having sex, she got it. It would run through her stomach,
making her panties wet. She squeezed her legs together to
suppress the urge to feel Demoto inside her, but it didn't
work. Taryn noticed that by doing this, it only intensified
the feeling. *Damn, if this how dick make you feel, I
should have been getting it!* Taryn leaned over the bed
and grabbed her phone to text him.

> **Taryn:** *Dang it's like that?*

> **Demoto:** *like what?*

> **Taryn:** *You get my goods and I don't hear from
you no more*

> **Demoto:** *Nah that's my fault babygirl, I wanted to
text you*

> **Taryn:** *Why didn't you? I miss you friend...*

> **Demoto:** *...friend?...nah we more than that! I'm
out of town, I miss you too*

> **Taryn:** *oh I didn't know that, for how long?*

> **Demoto:** *Two months, you gon' wait on me?*

She was unable to respond back for a second due to smiling so hard. Her smile was so big she felt it on the inside.

Taryn: *you know I am*

Demoto: *Alright, I gotta go. I'll call you later*

Taryn: *I'll be waiting*

Hearing from Demoto put her right back into her feelings. She had to get a grip on her feelings for him until she figured out what they were. It was obvious by his messages that they were more than friends, but they sure as hell weren't lovers. *Or are we?* Taryn racked her brain for a few minutes longer before preparing herself for bed.

*****

The heat in the room mixed with the foul smell of urine had Demoto's stomach turning. He had been trying to hold his breath, but he had started getting light headed. This was the last month of his training, and they were learning a quiet death tactic. He had two more weeks to go before he could go home, and he couldn't wait. He had learned a number of different methods to torture and kill a person. He'd been trained to end a life no matter the time or place. From guns and knives to poison and his bare hands, he was a certified assassin. His instructor was extremely proud of him because he caught onto everything so quickly. The remaining two weeks were strictly passing tests. He would be placed in a series of situations to test his decision making and skill sets. In order to do your best, you had to be the best. His teacher told him every day there was more to being a killer than just ending a person's life, and he was right. Anybody could end an existence, but it took a professional to know how and when. Killing was an art. You had to know pain limits, correct doses, time frames, everything it would take to execute with no mishaps.

"Mmmm, mmmm," the man on the floor squirmed. He'd had the plastic bag on his head for almost a minute now, and he was about to pass out.

He had pissed on himself the moment Demoto attacked him and placed the bag on him. Demoto watched him twist and turn with his hands behind his back, just before passing out. The instructor clapped for Demoto before having someone wake the man up. He had done all he was required to do for this session.

"Excellent job, Youngblood. You're dismissed" Demoto exited the room and pulled the band from his dreads letting them fall around his shoulders. Grabbing his backpack and Gatorade, he headed up to his room. Cayman had flown him and two other people to Australia to complete this course. He wanted to be sure they weren't distracted by their familiar surroundings. He wanted them to be experts before giving them real contracts. In order to help the time pass faster, he worked out at the gym and read books. He hadn't talked on the phone much because he wanted to keep his head in the appropriate place. He knew if he talked on the phone to Alicia or Taryn, he'd lose focus. All Alicia ever wanted to do was argue, and Taryn made his mind go completely left. He could handle Alicia's little tantrums about him not calling or texting, but Taryn was a problem. After speaking with her, she stood firm in every thought that came across his mind. He had been going back in forth in his mind for a while about whether or not to take it to the next level with her, and still hadn't come to a conclusion.

His phone vibrated across the crisp white sheets of the hotel bed. Looking at the screen, he saw that it was Jacko but decided he'd call him back later. He was starving right now and needed to take a shower; he'd call him after that. An hour later, he'd finished eating and was in the shower thinking. The shower was big with a dark gray tiled pattern. Demoto was sitting on the small bench that was in the corner letting the water cascade over him. The hot steamy water massaged his aching body. He was sore from all of the workouts and training exercises. As he leaned his head back against the wall, he heard his phone ringing again. He wasn't going to answer it until he heard Lil' Johns *Ms. Chocolate* playing. He smiled and grabbed it off the counter.

"What's up Taryn-Lee," he answered as he pushed the shower curtain back closed.

"Nothing friend, what you up to? How's your trip?"

"What I tell you about that friend shit?"

"Oops I forgot! What you doing, it sound like you in the shower or something." Stretching his long legs out in front of him, he chuckled a little bit.

"I am, and my dick is hard as shit right now!" First he heard a gasp, then a loud laugh from her end. He joined her laughter before speaking again. "I ain't had no pussy in almost two months! A nigga going through it right now"

"Well you might need to do something about that, you nasty mouth boy."

"I wish you was here with that wet wet, so you could do something about it," he said in a husky voice. Between the water and the visions of her moaning beneath him, his dick was standing at full length. Talking to her on the phone brought back the memories of the time they'd had sex.

"I wish I was too!"

"Taryn you were so fucking tight and wet! Shit! Just thinking about how you felt on my dick got me about to bust," Demoto stroked himself at the thought of her.

"Damn Demoto, don't do this to me! You know how far away you are." Demoto could hear the need in her voice. She was obviously feening for him the way he was for her.

"I know T, you just don't understand how good your pussy is though. I ain't ever sharing that shit with nobody else." Demoto laughed at himself. He was talking to Taryn like he was her man. The night after she left his house, he couldn't stop thinking of her and her body. He'd already grown to love her personality but after being inside of her, he would never be able to resist her.

"You'll never have to Moto. It only wants you!"

"It better! Don't make me fuck you up over my shit."

"You won't. When you coming back? I miss seeing you." Demoto thought back to the last couple of days of training he had and ran his hand over his face. After telling her his schedule, they talked a little while longer before hanging up. *A couple more days of this shit.*

*****

Demoto sat in the chair at the salon getting his dreads retwisted. He had just gotten back from training and his head looked terrible. He'd called and his regular stylist was able to squeeze him in. He wanted to make sure he looked presentable for two reasons. He wanted to see Taryn, and because Cayman had something planned for all the top list of Double O tonight. He wasn't big on partying, but he would indulge just because he needed a release. He had been in serious mood for the past couple of months and he was tired. He would make his way to see Taryn and Alicia tomorrow. He hadn't even bothered to tell either of them he had made it back to the mainland yet. He looked at himself in the mirror as she styled his locs. He hated to look rough. When his hair needed to be done, he didn't even feel like putting on clothes. He felt incomplete. He had hats that he liked to wear, but it wasn't the same. Occasionally he just wanted to chill.

He had a few more hours before he had to meet with his company. Until then he would eat, relax, maybe even have a couple of drinks. The few hours he had left gave him time to think. Taryn had been on his mind heavily and he couldn't wait to see her. He was feeling her. There was nothing in this world he wouldn't do to protect her. Right now, all he wanted to do was hold her, feel her warmth in his arms.

*****

"Alright fellas it's about that time! Get ready to pull out them bands. We got a real money maker coming to the stage!" Taryn heard the DJ yelling over the microphone. At least once a month, every dancer had to do an individual set, and tonight it was her turn. She'd been working at Diamonds of Atlanta for almost two weeks and still wasn't used to it.

Jeremiah had talked her into doing amateur night one week, and she'd made close to three thousand dollars. She hadn't intended on making this a regular thing, but the money was good. He tried on many occasions to get her to dance at the Luxx in Columbus, but she wasn't having it. She didn't want it getting back to Mr. Buck or Demoto what she was doing. She decided to dance in Atlanta three days out of the week, and on the weekends.

So far it was going pretty good; nobody but Kia and Jeremiah knew what was going on. She decided to continue up until she started college in the fall. Her plan was to get the money for her apartment so she could hurry up and leave the shelter. Nobody besides Kia knew her current living arrangements, and that's how she wanted it to stay. Once the stage went completely black, Taryn pulled her mask down over her eyes, downed the shot in her hand, and walked onto the stage.

Unlike most dancers, she didn't go right out dancing. Instead, she walked past the pole and stopped at the edge in front of the VIP sections. Taryn stood still with her hands on her hips, until the lights came back on.

Taryn had the meanest stance the men had ever seen. She had a very commanding presence, which caused most of everybody to stop what they were doing. Tonight she had decided to dress up in a cute little Indian outfit. It was a brown spandex one piece, with red glitter on both nipples and down the middle of her back. There were blue and white feathers sewn on it to match the feather headband she wore around her head.

Taryn stood six inches taller than normal in her glittery red peep toe stilettos that tied around her calves and up to her thighs. Her big wavy hair fell down around her shoulders and back, making her look like a real Indian. Her smooth dark skin glistened beneath the flashing pink and white lights. Confidence radiated from her effortlessly. To the average woman, her existence was intimidating. Taryn looked around the club eyeing everybody through the glittery red and white mask on her face.

"Many of you may already know her, but for the ones who don't, my girl, chocolate Pocahontas!"

The beat to August Alsina's *Let me hit that* dropped, and Taryn started to move. The song was slow so she took her time dancing and twirling around the stage. She dropped and moved like a professional; no one would ever know this was only her second week. At one point, she leaned backwards grabbing the pole, and twirled only the bottom half of her body in a circle.

This move always got the crowd going, because it gave the perfect view. Men began running to the stage throwing money. Her entire show went well; she'd racked up enough and decided to go home early. She changed into a pair of pink Adidas jogging tights, a white v-neck, and a pair of running Nikes. She left her hair down, grabbed her bag, and headed out the door. Once she got back out to the main floor, the building had gotten super packed. There was an entourage of men in Double O shirts headed towards the VIP section. The men looked like money. Taryn was far from a gold digger, but they looked like they were about to spend some cash; turning around, she went back to the dressing room to change.

"Man I'm about to be drunk as fuck my nigga!" Jacko yelled at Demoto as they walked into the strip club.

He had just gotten back into town, and Cayman wanted them all to go out and unwind. Demoto didn't know everybody in Cayman's, crew so he'd asked Jacko to meet him in Atlanta. Jacko was his best friend, and they always had a good time when they went out together.

"Go ahead bruh, Double O paying for all this shit."

The group had taken up the entire VIP section. The girls must have had some type of money radar, because they all swarmed around. Demoto wasn't the strip club type. He enjoyed chilling and drinking with his friends. Jacko, on the other hand, looked like he was in heaven with the two girls shaking in front of him. Demoto smiled and waved off all the girls trying to dance for him. Word must have gotten out, because after a while they stopped coming his way, which was fine with him. After a few more drinks, he excused himself to the restroom.   Taryn stuck her head out of the curtains, checking to see what was going on with the men that had just come in. The floor around them was covered in money. There were about six girls over there, but Taryn knew just by looking at them she was getting ready to take all of their money. She'd switched into a pair of red thong panties and striped dark blue and white bra, with her same red shoes. She wore a small Braves jersey over it that she left open. She liked the idea of concealing her face when dancing, so she wore a dark blue mask that covered one side of her face. Taryn was easily the baddest female in the club. As she strutted across the room, men grabbed at her left and right but she had an agenda.

Before she could get to where the men were sitting, an older gentleman grabbed her arm. He told her he'd pay her three thousand dollars if she could get one of his young workers out of his shell. Taryn quickly agreed. She followed the man past the section they were sitting in to a table in the back. When she looked up and saw the boy sitting there with his shades on and a drink in his hand, she almost fainted.

"How about I get one of my friends to do it? I'm new and I'm really not that good," Taryn stalled.

"No I want you. This young man is very particular, and you're the best-looking thing I've seen all night. As a matter of fact, make that all my life." Taryn smiled at the compliment. All hell was about to break loose if he recognized her. Cayman pulled her towards the table

"I got something for you son."

Demoto looked up and waved his hand dismissively

"Nah sir, I'm fine. I just want to chill."

Taryn took this as her cue and turned to leave, but Cayman stopped her.   "Make him have some fun sweetheart." Cayman slid her a wad of bills wrapped in rubber bands. Her eye's almost popped out of the sockets. She nodded her head and smiled. The DJ was playing Rico Love's song *They don't know*. Taryn stood to the side and looked at Demoto out the corner of her eye; he was way past tipsy. *Thank God! Maybe he won't recognize me.* Taryn stood watching him a little bit longer before walking over to him seductively. She quickly turned around so her back was to his chest and started grinding on his lap. With both of her hands on his knees, she rubbed her backside all over his lap. Not long afterwards, he started to harden beneath her. She got mad for a split second because if she hadn't been there tonight, it would've been another girl all over him like this.

"We be in the same room, we don't ever say shit," Demoto started to sing. *Oh shit!* Taryn decided to put a little distance between them. She stood in front of him and danced with the beat of the music.

Demoto laid his head back and watched Taryn dance. He wanted so bad to cuss her out for being up in the club half-naked, but he couldn't. His plan had been to drag her out of there the moment he saw her, but she stopped him. The way her body looked in her little panties had him ready to fuck. He chuckled to himself lightly, because she probably had no idea he knew who she was. He had watched how nervous she'd gotten when Cayman brought her over to him.

He'd asked Cayman to bring her over once she came from the back. He, Jacko, and the Double O crew had caught the tail end of her Indian girl show, and he couldn't wait to get her alone. He had asked Jacko to sit on the other side of the club in the corner so he wouldn't see Taryn's body. Of course he hadn't told him that was the reason; Jacko thought once Taryn recognized him she'd leave.

As much as he hated what she was doing, she was good at it. Taryn was dancing her ass off and making his dick hard in the process. When Jacko had first told him Jeremiah had her stripping, he wanted to break both of their necks but he had to chill. Taryn was grown and Jeremiah couldn't make her do anything she didn't want to. Demoto figured it was time to turn up the heat, so he grabbed her by the wrist and pulled her onto his lap.

Taryn was now straddling Demoto's lap, and she was nervous as hell. Their faces were only inches apart; he was sure to recognize her now. She held her head down so her hair was covering most of her face. Demoto wrapped one arm around her waist and pulled at the little brave's shirt she had on so his mouth was close to hers.

"They don't know you belong to me."

Taryn smiled to herself as he sang along to the song. For a second, she thought he might have known who she was because of the lyrics he'd chosen to sing along with, but how could he? Taryn wanted so bad to say something back to him, but she already knew her voice would be a dead giveaway. For him to have acted like he didn't like strippers, he sure was enjoying the show she was putting on.

His hands roamed all over her body and stopped between her thighs. Taryn just knew she would melt when he began stroking her through her thong. She thought about stopping him, but she missed his touch. She began grinding roughly onto his fingers, causing her to get wetter. Demoto could tell Taryn was enjoying the way he was handling her. He was trying to see how far she was going to let him take it before she stopped him.

Sliding her thong to the side, he slid two fingers into her warm body. Her juices were dripping all over his fingers as he massaged her clit with his thumb. She moaned laying her forehead on his shoulder. He had her right where he wanted her so he took one of her nipples between his teeth, biting it softly through the thin material she had on. He loved the way Taryn's body responded to his touch. *Damn! I should have left her alone*, he thought to himself, because now he was hard and ready to sex her in the middle of the club.

Her thong and the top of Demoto's jeans were now soaking wet from her juices. He was working his fingers in and out of her so fast that she wanted to scream. He had worked her into such a frenzy; she was now clawing at his belt trying to get it a loose. She was surprised when he didn't stop her; instead, he helped her. She could feel the veins pulsating as she held his large manhood in her hands. It was so thick and heavy.

She couldn't take her eyes off it. She stroked him until she heard him let out a low groan. She lifted up a little and placed it at her opening. She made eye contact with him through her mask and tried to read the look on his face. The pretty green eyes shined with pure lust.

"Put it in Moto." She was tired of playing games; he had to have known by now it was her. Lifting her up a little more with one arm, he slid balls deep into her warmth. Taryn shivered at his touch

"I missed you baby."

"I missed your ass too girl." He was pushing hard and deep into her, causing her to bounce up a little.

"Ow Moto, I can feel it in my stomach." She scratched at his back through his shirt. "It's hurting me so good." She knew that didn't make sense, but that was the only way to describe the wonderful pain he was making her feel.

"Throw this shit on me T, show ya man what you got."

Taryn began bouncing her ass on him like she was dancing. She watched his eyes roll back as she rode him in a circular motion.

"I guess you did miss me," he mumbled.

Taryn was riding him like she'd been fucking forever. The way she was putting it on him had him in love. *Who knew lil scary ass Taryn could ride a dick this good.* Palming her butt in both hands, he pushed inside her as far as he could.

"I'm about to bust baby girl, lift up."

Taryn was obviously in a zone of her own, because she kept going.

"T, stop so I can pull out ma!"

"No, cum inside me Moto, it feels too good to stop." Taryn leaned down and sucked on his bottom lip once she'd felt the first jerk of his body. She bounced up and down on his dick faster. They climaxed together.

"Unnghh Shit Taryn!" He yelled quietly into her neck. He was breathing just as hard as she was. They sat there in the same position until he told her to go change and meet him out front.

Chapter 9

They rode down the dark road back to Columbus in silence. Taryn knew he was mad because the vein in his neck was jumping. She didn't know what to say, so she chose not to say anything. Demoto wasn't her man, but she didn't like him being angry with her. They were both lost in their thoughts as R. Kelly sang quietly in the background.

Demoto was pissed with Taryn. He didn't care what her reason was for stripping; she could have told him about it. What made him the angriest was that she was trying to sneak and do it. He couldn't protect her if he didn't know what she was doing. From the moment Jacko had told him about her new job, he'd put one of Double O's young soldiers on the task of watching her. He would wait for her to get to the club every night, and follow her to make sure she got home safely. Demoto knew that was invading her privacy in a way, but if it kept her safe he didn't care. He looked over at her out of the corner of his eye. She looked so pretty with her hair in a ball at the top of her head. The fitted V-neck shirt she had on hugged her breasts and flat stomach perfectly. The thin pink jogging pants she had on magnified the thickness of her thighs. Demoto returned his eyes back to the road. If he continued to look at her, he wouldn't be able to stay mad.

The entire ride home was quiet, but he obviously wasn't too mad because he'd brought her to his house. He hadn't even bothered to see if she wanted to go home. She had just gotten out of the shower and gotten dressed when he knocked on the door. Before she could say come in, he was already coming through the door. He flipped on the shower and stripped, like she wasn't even there. She tried not to look at his perfect body, but she couldn't help it. She watched him through the mirror until he got into the shower. Grabbing her things, she left the restroom and went into his room. She had no clothes over there, so all she wore was a pair of his boxer briefs and a tank top. She braided her hair down into two French braids and kneeled on the floor to say her prayers. As she got up, she noticed him standing at the door watching her.

"What?"

"I haven't prayed in so long, I think I forgot how." Taryn stood there, stunned for a minute.

"You want me to help you?"

"Nah, I'm good." Brushing past her, he turned off the lamp light and got into bed. Taryn slid in and snuggled up close to him. After laying her head on his back, she wrapped her arms around his waist and said goodnight.

"I love you," Demoto's eyes popped open because he knew Taryn hadn't just said what he thought she did. "I love you Demoto," she said again, this time a little louder. He turned over so they were facing each other. He didn't say anything; he just stared at her for a while with his hand caressing the side of her face.

"I love you too."

Taryn wanted to cry so badly, but she held it in. Her eyes were glossy, but no tears fell. She had known she loved him, but had no clue he felt the same. She had been going back and forth in her mind trying to decide whether or not to tell him, but she was tired of being on the side; they belonged together. She took a chance putting her feelings on the line and it paid off. Jeremiah and Alicia would just have to understand. If they didn't, then oh well. She couldn't care less about Alicia; she didn't like her anyways. Jeremiah was a different story. She never wanted to hurt him, but seeing Demoto love Alicia the way he should have been loving her hurt. If Jeremiah had to hurt in order for her not to, then so be it.

"Taryn, I'm so fucking mad at you right now. Why the fuck you out here stripping and shit?"

"I need the money," Taryn spoke so low that he could barely hear her.

"Right now ain't the time to get shy. Speak the fuck up! You weren't acting shy when you were in that club shaking your ass!" Demoto was practically yelling now. Visuals of her dancing on the stage flashed across his mind. He didn't want to be mad, but he couldn't help it. Taryn was supposed to be his; she was better than the stuff she was doing. He hated that she was out in the streets degrading herself for money. Money he would have easily given her. Demoto wasn't the richest man, but he was far from broke. Ever since he'd been working for Cayman, his riches had increased tremendously. He was something like a millionaire now. He'd done a few important jobs before leaving Australia that blew his account up. He would have given Taryn anything she thought she needed to dance naked for. Taryn knew Demoto wasn't trying to embarrass her, but listening to him rant made her feel like a piece of dirt. The water that glossed her eyes earlier was now cascading down her cheeks rapidly.

"I'm sorry Moto, but you don't understand."

"Understand what? Tell me what the problem is so I can fix it! I'm here for you T! How many times do I have to tell you that before you believe me?" Demoto sat up in the bed with his back to her. The sheet fell around his waist, exposing his broad shoulders and tattoo filled arms. Taryn knew she had messed up. Although she didn't want to, she knew the only way to ease this was to tell the truth.

"I'm homeless."

"You're what?"

"I'm homeless," she repeated again in a low whisper.

"Yo T, you ain't making no sense right now. What do you mean you're homeless?" Demoto didn't understand what she was talking about. She had told him months ago that she'd moved in with Kia and her father. How was she homeless? He knew Kia would never put her out, so he knew that wasn't the issue.

"IM FUCKING HOMELESS DEMOTO! What aren't you understanding? I don't have anything to call my own. I live at a fucking shelter with other homeless people." Taryn was now full out crying. The tears that were burning her eyes continued to fall. She couldn't stop them no matter what she tried. Hopping off the bed, she ran into the bathroom and slammed the door. Demoto sat there for a second trying to process what had been said. How could he not have known? Sliding off the bed, he slid on his basketball shorts and went to find her. He could hear her crying inside the bathroom, so he knocked on the door.

"T, come out baby. I'm sorry. I didn't know. You should have told me, you know I would have helped you. You could have moved in with me and you know that. You didn't have to stay at no damn shelter. Come out here and talk to me!" Demoto yelled through the door. Taryn sat on the other side of the door trying to calm her breathing. She was so embarrassed now that Demoto knew everything. Many nights she thought things might be easier with the truth out, but she was so wrong. She felt worthless and incompetent. Demoto was a young hustler that was getting it. He was only a few years older than she was and had more than people twice their age. Here she was, the homeless orphan sitting in his bathroom crying over shit she couldn't change. Thinking about her harsh reality, she started crying more.

"Taryn-Lee, I'll take care of you. I promise baby. Anything you need, I'll get it. Just come out and talk to me." Demoto was now kneeling on the floor with his forehead leaning against the door. He could tell by her cries that she was sitting behind the door. He had gotten onto his knees so she could hear him. He wanted to be as close as she would allow him right now. Just as he was pushing one of his dreads from his face, he heard his brother's bedroom door open. It was Adisa's girlfriend. She must have been spending the night.

"You alright Demoto?" she asked.

Instead of talking, he shook his head no. He was about to call Taryn's name again, but instead he knocked on the door. She didn't answer, but he could still hear her crying.

"Man Nay, I don't know what to do. My girl in the bathroom and she won't come out. I was mad and I think I went a little bit over board with her." Demoto was stressed out. He was afraid Taryn was about to shut down, and he didn't want that to happen. He knew she wasn't trying to hear anything he was saying, so when Adisa's girlfriend offered to talk to her, he moved to the side.

"Hey you in there, are you alright?" she asked through the door. There were a few sounds of movement before the door unlocked and swung open. Taryn rushed out and wrapped her arms around her, nearly making them both fall.

"Janay what are you doing here?" Taryn asked. When she first heard her voice, she thought she might have been hearing things until she heard it again. Demoto looked on in confusion. *How the hell they know each other?*

"I should be asking you the same thing?" Janay smiled as she broke their hug. Taryn smiled slightly before explaining to her that she and Demoto were friends. He looked out for her occasionally. Janay looked confused for a second.

"But didn't he just call you his girl?"

"Yeah she's my fucking girl. She's just so damn difficult all the time," Demoto answered for her. After Janay and Taryn explained their reasons for them both being there, they went into the living room to talk. Taryn vented for almost two hours before returning back to Demoto's room. A few times during their conversation,

Demoto popped in and out, pretending to be getting something from the kitchen. First it was chips, then water, now some skittles. Taryn knew he was only trying to be nosey, so she told Janay she would talk to her in the morning. Once she opened the door to Demoto's room, she found him sprawled across his bed with his Beats on. His eyes were closed and he was rapping along with some Drake song. Taryn stood and watched him for a few moments before his eyes opened and their gazes connected. Immediately, he removed his headphones and placed his iPod on the dresser. After turning back around, he reached one hand out for her to grab. He pulled her down onto the bed and kissed the tip of her nose.

"You still mad at me?"

"I was never mad at you Demoto. I was just ashamed of my situation. I didn't want you to know. I've never lived with Kia. I've been living at the women's shelter ever since the night after I stayed here with you our senior year. I wanted to tell you so bad, but I didn't know how. I'm making money at Foot Locker, but not nearly as much as I make at the club. I was against it initially, but when Jeremiah took me there and I made over three thousand dollars in one night, I couldn't stop. I'm too close to being where I want to be financially to stop. This isn't something I'm trying to make a career out of, I just want to stack enough bread so I can be comfortable."

"You don't think I meant it when I told you I would take care of you?"

"I know you did, I just didn't want to ask you for anything." Demoto didn't even bother to respond to her. Instead, he leaned over and pulled a Jordan shoebox from under the bed and opened it. Inside there were stacks of money sealed with rubber bands, along with two guns and some clear tubes filled with different color liquids. He moved everything to the side and grabbed the three bands of money, and gave them her. Taryn tried to protest, but he made sure she knew he wasn't having it. He returned the box to its rightful place before telling her to place the money in her bag.

"Thank you," she said as she snuggled against his chest. They were lying in bed wrapped in each other's arms. Taryn knew Demoto would take care of her, but she still didn't know how she felt about it all, whereas Demoto knew nothing would ever be the same with them again. His mind was in overdrive. First he had to pay Jeremiah a visit, then take Taryn to get all her shit from the shelter. She had come into his life unexpectedly and found a place in his heart. His world would never be the same again, Taryn was his forever. Tomorrow was a new day, and a fresh start. He was going to make every move count.

Chapter 10

"Can I have blue cheese instead of Zax sauce please?" Kia asked the Zaxby's employee that was taking her order.

"Excuse me sweetheart, can you add a Wings and Things with a large sweet tea and two chocolate chip cookies to that too please?" Jacko spoke from behind her. Kia turned around and smiled as he handed the lady two twenty dollar bills to pay for their food.

"What you doing here Jacko?"

"I was about to pick up my niece from school when I saw you walk in." Izzy's mom had called and asked him to pick her up from school because she was working late. Of course, he had no problem with that. Sitting at the stoplight, he saw Kia walking inside the restaurant. He checked the clock in his car and noticed he had thirty minutes to spare, so he turned and parked.

"Let me find out you stalking me."

"Nah shawty I'm not stalking you, I just figured we could have lunch together," he smiled. *Lord help me.* Kia squeezed her thighs together and turned around. She had been crushing on Jacko since the first day she'd saw him. She remembered it like it was yesterday

"Aye bitch don't get your ass beat!" Kia yelled at Taryn.

"Man fuck Alicia, I'll run through that hoe and you know it," Taryn said as her and Kia burst into laughter.

"That's what your mouth say—until she going upside that head." Kia and Taryn had been sitting on the porch all day laughing and playing. She'd spent the night over there after leaving the club last night, and had no plans of leaving any time soon. Kia had just stopped laughing when her daddy came out the front door holding Taryn's phone. It was Jacko and he was about to come over. As Taryn ran down the address, Kia drank some more of her mango Arizona.

"Girl which one of your men you inviting over here now?"

"Jacko ain't my man girl, that's my brother! He coming through to drop off the money for his shoes that's coming out Saturday. You know since these niggas found out I work at Foot Locker I'm everybody plug now," Taryn laughed.

Just as Kia opened her mouth to speak, a dark gray Corvette pulled into her driveway. It came to a halt, and out hopped a sexy brown skin boy with shoulder length dreads. He had on a black tank top and basketball shorts. Tattoos flooded his arms and neck. He was so pigeon-toed that he looked like he was going to trip over his own feet. He had the cutest walk Kia had ever seen. As he approached the porch, he caught her staring and smiled.

"What y'all pretty ladies doing out here?"

"Waiting on you," Kia flirted.

"Is that right?"

"You know it," she smiled at him. He smiled back and she thought she would faint. He looked good and smelled better.

"Pretty Lee, you been holding out on your boy. Why you ain't never brought this beauty around before?" he asked as he handed her five hundred-dollar bills.

"My bad Jackie, this my bestie Kia. Kia, this my brother Jacko." Kia reached her hand out to shake Jacko's, and when she did he kissed it.

"Nice to meet you beautiful. You got a man?" Jacko liked Taryn's friend. She was pretty and just his type. He'd always had a thing for brown-skinned women. She was small but not too small, which was even better. Jacko wasn't a big man, so he needed his women to be small.

"I do now," she smiled.

"Word?" Jacko asked as he smiled at her. She was feisty as hell too, definitely his style. He passed her his phone so they could exchange numbers. From that day on, they would text and converse over the phone occasionally, but that was it. She really liked him, but he didn't seem as interested in her so she fell back some. She was there when he needed her and vice versa, and that was good with her for now. She knew her attraction wouldn't stay this calm for long, but she had no other choice. She wasn't the type of female to beg for attention. If it wasn't given freely, she didn't want it. Jacko knew how she felt, so she wouldn't say it again. His attitude was so off and on that she didn't know when he was going to do what. Some days he treated her like a friend, and other days he almost flirted her panties off.

"You want to sit by the window or right here in the middle?" Jacko asked, breaking her from her walk down memory lane.

"Umm, we can sit by the window," Kia said as she followed him to the back. Jacko watched Kia eat the blue cheese-soaked French fries and smiled.

"What the fuck you smiling for, Jack?" Kia asked as she smiled across the table at him. He shook his head and continued eating his food. He liked Kia a lot; she was smart, beautiful, and a thug like him, but he couldn't be with her. She was one of the only women he'd met that intrigued him, but she was his boss's daughter. He and Buck had been talking Double O business for the past couple of weeks, and he wasn't ready to mess up his money over a female.

He'd never told her, but that day after he left her house he ran into Buck at a business meeting. Buck wanted him to run some money scams for Cayman. They talked for a while before he walked Buck out to his car. In the midst of their conversation, he noticed a picture of Kia and Taryn sitting on his dashboard. He hadn't wanted to ask who they were, but he had to. The moment Buck told him they were his daughters, he knew he had to back off. He explained to Buck that he knew the girls from school, but left it at that. He'd thought Buck was going to blow his cover the day he picked them up from the house, but he hadn't. If he hadn't needed them to pick up some money from him, he would have pulled off the moment he and Buck locked eyes. Being that Buck was a cool old dude, he just winked and continued to talk to the girls.

Jacko knew then why everybody in the hood loved and respected him.

"I'ma make you mine one day Kia, just wait on it."

"I been waiting, but we'll see."

"I'm for real," Jacko said as he checked his watch. It was almost time to get Izzy from school, so he had to wrap up their lunch. Before dumping their trash, he asked what she had planned for the day. When she said nothing, he invited her over to his place for a movie that night and she accepted. He was ecstatic because he thought she was going to say no. As he masked his excitement, they walked to her car. They leaned against the trunk as he pulled her in for a hug. The moment their bodies connected and he smelled her perfume, he got hard. He pulled her closer to him, kissing the side of her neck. Kia moved around a little once she felt his growing manhood along her thigh.

"Boy you so nasty."

"I can't help it. You looking and smelling good! I can't wait to see you tonight," he said with his voice full of excitement. Kia laughed and pulled the bottom of his face to hers until their mouths met. She kissed him softly, trying to pry his lips open with her tongue. She could tell he was skeptical at first, but obliged. When he did finally kiss her, she wished he hadn't. He kissed her so deep that her knees got weak. She was glad he was already holding her up. She let him kiss her for a little while longer before breaking their embrace and walking to her driver side door.

"I'll see you later sexy," he winked and walked to his car. Kia sat in her driver seat and watched him in the rearview mirror. She didn't want him to catch her looking at him, so she cranked up and drove out of the parking lot. He went one way and she went the other. *Tonight can't come fast enough!*

*****

Taryn's chest heaved up and down so hard you would have thought she'd just run a marathon. She sat in the passenger seat of Demoto's car with her arms folded tightly across her chest. She was so angry she could hardly keep still. She and Demoto were riding across town to Jeremiah's house, and she was pissed. She had done everything but flip over backwards for Demoto not to do this. She didn't want any friction between he and Jeremiah on her behalf. She and Janay had spent majority of the morning trying to convince him to let her tell Jeremiah herself, but he wouldn't listen. Taryn wasn't sure if she was angrier at him or herself. Had she been more careful, he would have never found out about her dancing.

"I don't care about your little attitude. You might as well go ahead and lose that shit!" Taryn let out a hard breath and continued to ignore Demoto.

"I don't care about you breathing hard either." Demoto looked over at her as he continued to drive. She looked so sexy when she was mad. If he didn't have other stuff to do, he would have taken her back home to his bed. Her eyes had turned into small slits, and she wore the cutest scowl. Had he not felt it was his place to straighten Jeremiah out for this, he would have let her handle it. From the moment he saw her in the park, they connected–a connection so powerful he'd go to the end of the world and back just to protect her. All she had to do was understand where he was coming from.

"If it'll make you feel better, I'm going to be nice."

"Whatever Demoto," she said as she began biting her nails. He chuckled a little at her; she was livid.

After deciding that she was going to have an attitude no matter what, he turned his music back up. He bobbed his head along with the music and continued to his destination. Another twenty minutes had passed before they pulled into a long white driveway. The brick house was surrounded by trees and flowers with a Georgia flag hanging on the porch. The car came to a complete stop before Demoto got out and called for her to do the same. She pouted the entire way to the door. She hated this was about to happen, because she actually had feelings for Jeremiah. She didn't want Demoto to act out and cause an uproar between her and him, or their own friendship. Demoto knocked and rung the bell a few times before somebody finally came and opened the door. Jeremiah stood there in nothing but some socks and boxers. He was practically naked at three o clock in the afternoon, but he didn't look the least bit sleepy. That only led Taryn's mind to one conclusion. He had company.

"What's up y'all?" Jeremiah asked as he faked a yawn.

"I need to holla at you real quick," Demoto spoke. Jeremiah nodded his head before turning around to grab some shoes. Taryn was trying her hardest to keep calm, but she couldn't shake the thoughts of him being with someone else. He and her weren't official yet and she obviously loved Demoto, but she still had feelings for him as well. The way he looked behind him before stepping out of the house added fuel to her fire. With her arms crossed over her chest, she bit her bottom lip to keep from talking. She knew herself and she knew that if she talked now, only foul things would come out.

"What's going on baby girl?" Jeremiah smiled at Taryn as she rolled her eyes.

"I don't know, you tell me."

Jeremiah was about to ask why she had an attitude, but Demoto cut him off before he had the chance to.

"Miah why the fuck you got T out here stripping?"

"Bruh Taryn is a grown ass woman. She can do whatever she wants. I didn't make her do shit she ain't want to do. I presented the opportunity and she took it from there. If you tight about this shit, then you need to take it up with her."

"Nah nigga! You know we were supposed to be looking out for her, and you got her out her shaking her ass for change. You know better than that shit Miah!" Demoto was practically yelling. His African accent was so thick now you could barely understand him. Along with him being so country, it was almost impossible to understand anything he was saying.

"Demoto I told you I'm grown. I can…"

"Aye Taryn, be quiet! Right now is not the fucking time!" Demoto said, cutting her off.

"I'm just trying to tell you!"

"T you don't have to tell me shit! As a matter of fact, you don't even need to be talking right now. This is between me and Miah! Go get your ass in the car!" Jeremiah was in the middle of correcting Demoto for talking to her like that when the front door swung open. There stood Ace, the same girl Taryn was about to beat down for Jacko a while back. She wore nothing but a pair of panties and Jeremiah's **Carver Football** shirt. Taryn was so mad she swore she could feel smoke coming from her ears. Ace made matters worse when she threw a sly smirk in Taryn's direction.

"What's going on out here?"

"Bitch none of your fucking business," Taryn spat.

"If it concerns my man, then it concerns me," Ace said as she wrapped her arms around Jeremiah's waist. Taryn didn't even bother to give Ace the fight she wanted; instead, she walked directly in front of Jeremiah.

"I guess I was wrong when I thought we had something huh? It's cool though. No love lost; just do me a favor and teach your hoes some manors," she winked at him just as she reached around his shoulder and popped Ace on her forehead. Ace tried to lunge at her, but Jeremiah held her back.

"Ace, chill the fuck out. You didn't have any business coming out here in the first place." She tried arguing her point, but he opened the door and pushed her back inside. He never wanted Taryn to find out about him and Ace this way. The feelings he'd formed for Taryn outweighed the lust he had for Ace. She was just a reliable freak to kick it with on the low. She had made it clear on more than one occasion that she wanted to be in a relationship, but that was never happening. He looked at Taryn once he turned around, and she looked completely unbothered by the situation. She broke their eye contact when she reached for the keys in Demoto's hand.

"Moto, I'll wait for you in the car."

"You good bae?" he asked as he held onto the hand she grabbed for the keys with. He didn't care that Jeremiah was standing there. He had tried to hide the way he felt for Taryn whenever they were around, but that was dead now. After the way Miah had just played T by having Ace there, he didn't deserve the courtesy. He would now make it known that Taryn didn't need anybody as long as she had him. Fuck Jeremiah, and fuck his feelings. If he couldn't accept that, then their friendship was over.

Taryn looked up at Demoto, shock evident all over her face. She didn't know what had gotten into him, because he'd just called her *bae* in front of Miah. Although she no longer cared whether he knew or not, it still caught her off guard. Not to mention, the total switch in Demoto's demeanor. He was just yelling at her like he was her daddy, and now he was being sweet. Maybe he was sorry she'd just had to

166

witness all of this foolishness on his account. Now that she thought about it, maybe she owed Demoto a thank you. Had he never insisted they come over here, she never would have known Jeremiah was sleeping around on her. She nodded her head and gave him a weak smile before heading for the car.

After Taryn had gotten in, Demoto turned around and stared at Jeremiah, daring him to speak on he and Taryn. In defeat, Jeremiah nodded his head in understanding and said nothing. It wasn't that he was afraid of Demoto, he just knew Taryn deserved better than what he was giving her. If he knew nothing else, he knew Demoto was loyal. He would give Taryn the world and ask for nothing in return. If they had something going on, which they obviously did, he'd make things right.

"Look Moto, you know me bruh. We been friends since our freshman year, you know I get money. I'm sorry I misused Taryn in the process, but in all honesty it was about money," Jeremiah said solemnly.

"I'm not about to stand here and act like this shit is cool with me, because it's not. But what I will say is I understand. You right, I do know you and you been about your cash since I met you. I just thought you were feeling T, that's all. You know what she got going on at home and we vowed to look out for her, and you neglected to do that. So from now on, you and her don't have shit to say to each other. Anything you need to discuss with her, you can tell it to me."

"Normally I would have some hot shit to say, but this time you're right. Just let her know I ain't mean for her to see this shit with Ace. On the real, it was never my intention to hurt her," Jeremiah explained. He tried

looking over Demoto's shoulder to see her, but she was
looking down. He shook his head and conversed with
Demoto a little while longer before they parted ways.
Demoto knew once he got in the car, she was going to be
feeling some type of way so he wanted to make sure he
handled it correctly. He took a couple of deep breaths
before he got in.

Taryn was sitting with her back facing him,
reading on her phone. He'd noticed that whenever she
had idle time, she would be reading. Before he said
anything, he reached over and took her phone. She
looked up immediately. Instead of seeing anger like he
thought he would, have, he saw hurt. Just as quickly as
she looked up, she looked away. He was sure she didn't
want to talk, so he cranked up and drove away. He'd
stopped by a local wing place and bought them some
food before heading back to his house. Taryn was quiet
most of the way. She sang along with a few songs on his
iPod, but that was it. Once they finally made it back to his
house and got comfortable, he gave her the phone back.
He put in his favorite movie *Baby Boy* while they ate.
Every so often, he would sneak a glance at her as she
watched the movie with a straight face; then out of
nowhere, she started talking.

"Demoto I'm not angry with you if that's what
you're thinking. I actually think I love you even more.
You are one of the only people in my life that's remained
constant. The way you take on my problems as your own
is unbelievable. You make it your business to take care of
me, and I appreciate that. You fight for me when no one
else does, and because of that I'll fight for you. Anything
you need, no matter what it is, I got you. Don't ever think

I don't notice the things you do because I do, and you'll always have my loyalty." Taryn finished talking and looked over at him. He was leaning back on the sofa with no shirt on, and his hair was loose and had fallen around his shoulders. He stared at her with such an intensity that if he had been anyone else, she probably would have been nervous. He didn't speak at first; he sat up instead.

"Taryn when I told you I love you last night, it was the truth. Never did I ever imagine that you would hold such a major part of my heart, but you do. The things I do for you, I do out of love. I'll always fight for and protect you because I'm supposed to. I'm your man. Any problem you have is mine now too. You're not in this alone anymore, so don't you forget that." Demoto leaned over and stuck his tongue in her mouth. They kissed for another five minutes before going into his bedroom.

"Je suis désolé (I'm sorry)…Je suis tellement désolé (I'm so sorry)," Demoto whispered over and over in her ear as he made love to her. He knew she had been through a lot; now it was his job to make it all better.

Chapter 11

Jacko had been running around for the past hour, trying to make sure everything was clean before Kia got there. His place wasn't the nastiest, but he wanted to make a good impression. He was already going against everything his mind was telling him by inviting her to his house, but it was too late now. How much harm could it do anyways? Kia was grown and so was he; they both knew how to control themselves. He had just walked out of his bedroom when he heard a knock at the door. As soon as he opened it, Kia smiled and walked towards him. She hugged him tightly before going in the living room. She wasn't familiar with the floor plan, but she could pretty much see everything from the front door. Jacko made small talk as he went to the kitchen for some drinks. When he returned, Kia had taken off her small jacket along with her boots. She was dressed comfortable in a CSU hoodie and some jeans.

"Come sit over here by me," Jacko said as he patted the seat cushion next to him. She had gotten up and was looking at his wall full of movies. She continued her search, like she hadn't heard him. Jacko knew she was trying to be funny, so he got up and walked behind her. He pressed her into his entertainment center with his body. They were pretty much the same height, so his manhood was right on her backside. He wrapped his arms around her waist and nuzzled his nose into her neck.

"Make this the last time you disobey me. When I tell you to do something, you do it!"

"Jacko, you are not my daddy."

"I know I'm not, but I'm your boyfriend; when I say do something, that's what I mean." Kia smiled inwardly because he was turning her on big time. She didn't take orders from anyone, not even Buck, but she would definitely take them from Jacko. The way he spoke to her with authority had her heart racing.

"Since when did you become my boyfriend? Last time I checked, you was still running around playing little kid games."

"Games? What games?" Kia ignored him and sat down on the couch. Jacko knew exactly what she was talking about, so she wasn't about to go there with him. It was obvious that he knew she wasn't because he left that conversation alone and kneeled in front of her. He used a little force and pulled her to the edge of the seat. After he wrapped both of her legs around his neck, he began biting at the warmth coming through her jeans.

"Jacko stoooop, what are you doing?" she whined.

"Just chill baby," he continued to bite and pull at her pants with his teeth. He knew Kia was hot because she was looking at him with lust-filled eyes. She was leaning back on her elbows watching his every movement. Jacko reached up and unbuttoned her jeans, and pulled them off. His dick jumped at the sight of her in her boy shorts. Once she was back comfortable, he pushed her panties to the side and began licking and sucking on her. Kia released some of the most beautiful moans he'd ever heard. When he could no longer take it, he stood up and removed his jeans. He retrieved the magnum from his pocket before picking her up, sitting down with her on his lap. He was surprised she hadn't stopped him yet.

"Look at you being a bad girl," he spoke as he helped her out of her panties. Kia was too shy to speak, so she didn't say anything; she just smiled. Jacko placed the tip of his penis at her opening before sliding her down onto him completely. Kia moaned so loud and sexy; Jacko thought he would bust right then.

"Oh damn Kia."

"What?" she asked confused.

"I'm about to fuck the shit out of you." Jacko switched positions so now he was on top, and began digging her back out. Being gentle was out of the question; he was hitting her with deep rough strokes, making her wetter. Kia was shy but she was no stranger to sex; she was throwing it right back at him. They were so in sync with one another you would have thought they'd done this before. Jacko was amazed at how Kia was working it. He figured she wasn't a virgin, but he didn't know it would be this good.

"You ready to cum for me?" Jacko asked. Kia nodded her head feverishly but still didn't say anything.

"Well cum on my dick Kia."

"I can't."

"What you mean you can't? Yes the fuck you can! Wet me up ma, let that shit go!" That was all Kia needed to hear before juices were squirting out all over Jacko. She had shocked herself with that one, because she'd never had an orgasm like that, let alone squirted. She moaned his name trying to catch her breath. Jacko looked at her and smiled as he continued stroking her. He was nearing his own climax when Kia squeezed her muscles, pulling him in tighter.

"Oh shit! That's my bad girl," he grunted before exploding inside of her. He lay on top of her for a few minutes before moving. Kia didn't mind either; yes he was heavy, but she still wrapped her arms around him. It took him a few minutes to get himself together before pulling out of her and removing the condom. Kia was a little embarrassed, so she grabbed her clothes and hurried to the restroom. She didn't know what it was about Jacko that made her feel like a little girl. He made her feel like she'd never had sex in her life. She had just turned the water on when he knocked on the door.

"Aye let me in Kia, I need to wash up."

"Okay I'll be out in a minute."

"Man Kia, open this fucking door." This time she opened it. He was standing there in nothing but his jeans—no boxers, or no shirt. He walked past her and flipped his shower on. He was in the middle of removing his pants when he stopped and pulled them back up. Once he got in front of her, he pulled her shirt over her head with a little protest.

"What you doing?"

"You're about to take a shower with me. And before you say something that's going to get you fucked up, I told you in the living room that was the last time you disobeyed me."

Jacko gave her a lazy grin and continued to remove her pants. Once they were completely undressed, they got in the shower. Jacko took his time lathering her up before doing himself. He could tell she was still a little shy, so he tried to be as gentle as possible. Kia was a grown ass woman; she was going to have to get out of that shy shit. He liked his women vocal; playing that quiet game wasn't going to cut it.

They washed off and returned to the front room. He wore nothing but a pair of basketball shorts, and she wore one of his oversized t-shirts and panties. She was so happy that she always brought an extra pair of panties with her. Taryn always laughed, but she refused to be caught in a situation like the one at hand and be unprepared. When she first pulled them out, Jacko had laughed too but, she didn't care. This was smart!

"So what do we do now?"

"We watch TV," Jacko said in a nonchalant tone.

"Don't be funny, you know what I mean."

"I'm not being funny. We're grown, we had sex. There's no need to start stamping labels, or acting crazy. You know you my girl, with your little bad ass," he said as he tickled her. Kia didn't necessarily like his response, but there was nothing she could do about that. For the rest of their night, they laughed, talked, and watched movies. When it was time for Kia to leave, she nor Jacko wanted her to go.

"Spend the night with me."

"I can't, my daddy ain't having that shit."

"Tell him you're at a friend's house or something. Please. I really want you to stay." Kia tried to think about a good lie to tell Buck before she called. Sure of herself, she called and surprisingly it worked. He was cool and said he'd see her tomorrow. She and Jacko were ecstatic. They chilled and had a good time the entire night. Jacko hit it one more time before they went to bed. Kia knew she was setting herself up for heartache dealing with Jacko, but she just couldn't shake it. The next morning, she woke up in bed alone. She ran her hand around the space where Jacko was supposed to be and felt nothing. She grabbed her phone from the nightstand and noticed she had two missed calls from Taryn and a text.

Taryn (bestie): *Call me girl!*

Kia laughed and texted her back, letting her know she had some juicy news to tell her and she'd call in a minute. She moaned to herself as she replayed in her mind the sex she'd had with Jacko last night.

"What am I going to do with this boy?" she mumbled to herself.

"You gon' get up and come sit on his face," Jacko said, startling her. Kia jumped up in search of his voice and found him sitting in the lounge chair he had in the corner. He was smoking a blunt and smiling at her. Kia immediately got nervous. Jacko was so nasty, and he didn't mind showing it.

"What you doing over there? Why aren't you in bed with me?"

"I wanted to smoke and I didn't want this loud to wake you up," he laughed.

"Boy please! I grew up around that shit. You could have stayed right here. Come back," she pleaded with her arms stretched out to him. Jacko put his blunt out and walked to her. He leaned forward and tongued her down before standing back up.

"Ima make you pay for that shit later. But right now we got to go. Moto need me to come by there."

"Okay, well I'll just go home. You can call me later when you're free." Jacko looked at her like she had grown two heads. She didn't know what she'd said wrong, so she asked.

"Why you looking like that?"

"Because I don't know who told you that you're about to go home. I run this shit Kia, not you. You're going with me," he smiled as he walked past and slapped her on the butt. Kia shook her head and tried to suppress the butterflies in her stomach. Jacko was so sexy, with his little pigeon-toed ass. After she grabbed her clothes, she got redressed and went into the bathroom to brush her teeth and do her hair. Once she was finished, she met Jacko in the living room where he was sitting on the couch with her phone.

"Why you all in my shit Jacko?"

"I want to see what little boys you got calling you."

"Okay well let me know when you find them." Kia went into the kitchen to get something to drink. She didn't care about Jacko looking in her phone, because for one he wasn't her man, and two he wouldn't find anything. She had long ago cut off all of her jump offs in hopes that he and her would get together. Jacko, on the other hand, had never been the jealous type. He wasn't really going through her phone; he was playing Candy Crush. He just wanted to see what type of female she was. If she was sneaky or had something to hide, she would have flipped out about her phone like most people did. That was a good sign in his book, so he got up and went to her. When he was in arms distance, she reached out and pulled him to her by his jacket and kissed his lips.

"Find anything?" she asked, still sucking on his bottom lip.

"My future wife," he said as he picked her up and placed her against the wall. They kissed as she ran her hand through his locs. He smelled so good Kia thought she would melt.

"I'm feeling the fuck out of you," he moaned into her ear as he placed her back on the floor. If they continued on the path they were on, he'd never make it to Demoto's crib. Fixing their clothes, they headed for the door.

*****

ZZZZZ...ZZZZZ...ZZZZZ. Demoto's red cell phone vibrated across the kitchen counter. He was busy taking a shower while Taryn made breakfast. They had gone to the shelter yesterday and picked up all of her things and brought them back to his house. She would be living with him and Adisa for now. Adisa and Janay didn't mind, and Demoto seemed to love the idea. Taryn wasn't too sure at first, because Demoto still hadn't ended things with Alicia and she didn't even care. She was too uncertain of what her and Demoto had going on, so she didn't push the issue. As she pushed a loose curl from her face and wrapped it into the ball on the top of her head, she picked up the phone. It had rang at least three times since he'd been in the shower. The caller had called from a blocked number so, she placed it back down.

"Somebody calling?" Demoto asked, coming around the corner in a pair of sweatpants and no shirt. His dreads were pulled back into two fishtail braids that Taryn had done last night before bed. Her nipples immediately poked through the thin tank top she had on. Demoto turned her on every time she looked at him. The white leggings she wore with no panties were sure to be wet by now.

"Yeah they've called like three times. I would have answered, but I didn't know if you would want me to."

"Nah it's cool," he said as he picked up the phone and made a call. Taryn eavesdropped on his conversation as best as she could without being too obvious. Once he hung up, he had a few stress lines across his forehead.

"You okay?"

"Yeah. I just have some work to do later on."

"Where you work at?" She placed his food in front of him waiting for an answer. He thought about not telling her, but he knew she could be trusted. He thought about the easiest way to say it and there wasn't one, besides the truth.

"I'm an assassin."

"Like a hit man?"

"Something like that but better. I work for a very important man and I handle very important assassinations. I don't do petty street bullshit; I handle inside jobs. Government officials, military missions, board of directors type shit." Taryn stood stunned for a couple of seconds before bursting out into a huge smile. Her reaction caught Demoto off guard.

"What you smiling at?"

"I know I thought you were sexy before with your tall African ass, but now that I know you're fine and a killer, I can hardly keep my panties on," she said as she fanned herself. Demoto burst out laughing. Taryn was so silly at times. He genuinely enjoyed being around her. Spending time with her wasn't a chore like it was with Alicia. Taryn was mad cool. She was low key and didn't pressure him. It was like chilling with Jeremiah and Jacko.

"Man T you a fool man."

"Boy I'm serious! How you expect me to act normal around you now? I know I probably shouldn't find this attractive, but I can't help it. That shit is hot Moto! Damn!" Taryn walked past him and headed for the restroom to take her shower. Demoto took a bite of his food and almost choked. It was disgusting! *Damn this shit nasty.* He thought maybe Taryn could cook, but it was obvious she couldn't. She had made eggs and grits and it was terrible! He looked over his shoulder before jumping up and putting it down the garbage disposal. He retrieved a banana nut muffin from the cabinet and gobbled it down before she came back. He didn't want to hurt her feelings, so he would just pretend that he ate it.

KNOCK KNOCK...BEEP BEEP.

His cell phone went off at the same time someone knocked on his front door. He snatched his red phone off the counter and headed for the door. He was so busy reading his text he didn't notice Kia was with Jacko.

Blocked: 7659 Blackmon Road. Tonight. 60 grand

Blocked: He should be alone. Finish clean!

"Damn bruh you cooked a nigga breakfast?" Jacko joked as he walked into the kitchen. Demoto finally looked up and noticed Kia sitting on the couch. She wore a nervous smirk, she knew they were busted.

"Boy hell nah. I didn't cook that shit, Taryn did," Demoto said before he knew it. He hadn't meant to let them know Taryn was there, but knowing her and Kia, she probably had already told her.

"Who cooked?" Kia asked. *Oops I guess she didn't know.*

"He said I did bitch, you heard him," Taryn said as she walked in and smiled at her friend. She had on some fitted jeans and a black shirt that crossed around her neck. She must had just washed her hair, because it was all down and still looked wet. The four friends stood and looked around the room at each other. Taryn spoke first.

"So I guess this the juicy news you had to tell me?" she said, pointing her finger between Kia and Jacko. Kia nodded her head slowly up and down as she hid her face with the pillow. Taryn and Demoto turned their attention to Jacko, waiting on his response. He looked at Kia and smiled slightly before busting out into a full grin at Demoto and Taryn.

"Fall back Pretty Lee, Kia my girl. She know that." What he was saying must have been true, because Kia was smiling like a little girl.

"Well alright then!" Taryn smiled.

"Nah, wait a fucking minute. What the hell you doing over here taking showers and cooking breakfast and shit, Taryn?" Jacko asked, and she answered with no hesitation.

"Demoto and I are friends. He looks out for me sometimes. Everybody in here know how fucked up my home life is, so it's no secret that I stay over here from time to time."

"Oh so we friends T?"

"Uhhh yeah…and have been for a while now." She was oblivious to how bad she'd just messed up. Demoto had begun to think of them as more than friends, but she was apparently still on her bullshit.

"Say no more." With that said, he walked into his room to get the things he needed to do his job later.

Kia and Jacko both looked at Taryn. Demoto was pissed, and they all knew it. The only thing that Jacko had up on the girls was that he knew how angry Demoto could get. Taryn had no idea what she had just done. He shook his head in sympathy for her and joined Demoto in his room. Taryn and Kia sat in the living room for a while, waiting on the guys and exchanging their secrets.

Chapter 12

The clouds of smoke danced in circles around his head. The weed that he was smoking was some of the best he'd ever had. He'd only taken three, maybe four pulls and he was already high. It wasn't very often that he indulged in his own product, but today had been one of those days. He had been stressing for the past couple of weeks trying to figure out how he was going to get out of the game. He had thought of every legit escape imaginable, but nothing seemed perfect enough. He'd given his job some of the best years of his life. It was time to call it quits. A couple of years back he would have done whatever it took, no matter the cost but that was no longer the case. He had two daughters now that he couldn't imagine living life without. Everything he'd done recently was for them. He just hoped when the time came, they would remain safe and free of the deadly street life. The streets was no place for his babies, but if he didn't play his cards right that's where they would be.

"Buck! We got a new contract. I already put #2 on his head, but I just wanted to let you know," his young worker Dee said as he burst into his office.

"Give me the rundown."

"It's the mayor's daughter. She addicted to drugs and she's ruining the campaign for her father. Someone on his opponent's team found out about her, and is threatening to bring it to the public. He's offered to pay 80 grand to get rid of her." Buck shook his head in disgust. He would never put a hit out on Kia or Taryn, especially for a job. If anything, he'd quit the campaign

182

all together and help them gain the help that they needed. That took him back to his earlier thoughts. He had to put things in motion. He wanted his daughters to always be protected, and he knew just the way to do it.

*****

His thoughts were clouded with long hair, thick thighs, and smooth dark skin. The way she stood full of confidence and authority. All of his thoughts were being consumed of her, and the fact that she wasn't even around made him angry. Here he was ready to break things off with Alicia and commit to her fully, and she was playing games. He had even gone as far as to call Alicia over earlier so he could tell her, but he changed his mind. When Taryn told Jacko and Kia he and her were just friends, he was pissed. He knew she was trying to protect her feelings or some girly shit like that, but she didn't have to string him along in the process.

Tonight was the Double O mansion party; everybody that was somebody was going to be there. He'd found out from Jacko earlier that Cayman's right hand man, Buck, was Kia's dad. More than likely, her and Taryn would be there. Demoto was hoping she decided to show up. He hadn't wanted to do her dirty, but he was tired of her changing her mind about them almost every day. He didn't need the extra stress. His job was stressful enough. As he sat in his truck, he watched the lights go off in the mayor's dining room, causing the entire house to be pitch black. He pulled his mask down over his face and grabbed his gun. He made sure the silencer was on it before exiting the vehicle. He'd been watching the house for almost two hours, and it was time to get this over with. Cayman had chosen tonight to do everything because everyone in his company would have an alibi. The city knew that whenever there was a Double O function, everyone was in attendance. Demoto made his way inside the house and up the stairs discreetly. Following the floor plan that was given by her father, he found the room effortlessly. He pushed the bedroom door open, and his target was kneeling on the side of the bed saying her prayers. *She'd never see it coming.* He put two pullets into her head and left as quietly as he'd come in.

*****

The windows in the mansion were shaking from the loud music. People were everywhere dancing and drinking. The rooms were already filled to capacity with different things going on behind each door. Taryn and her friend Nema had just gotten there and were looking for the room they were supposed to meet Kia in. Taryn and Nema had been specifically requested for this party. At first she had declined the offer, but changed her mind when she'd came from Kia's house earlier and Alicia was in Demoto's room. She tried to act like she didn't care, but when he got up and closed the door to his room that was it. She packed her an overnight bag and drove to Kia's house. After talking about it to Kia, her mind went back to why she needed her own spot. The only other way she could reach her goals quickly would be to go back to dancing. She'd called Nema to see was the offer still open about the party, and when she said yes Taryn agreed. She hadn't known until they got inside that it was a Double O party. Taryn wasn't completely familiar with the organization as a whole, but she knew these were the same guys Demoto was with the night he caught her at the strip club. She was hoping he wasn't coming, because he had to work tonight but she wasn't sure.

"Girl which room your friend said she was in?" Nema asked as they walked down the crowded hallway.

"She said the last one on the right."

"Okay well I think this is it right here." Nema turned the knob and went in. Kia was sitting on the bed kissing Jacko. When the door opened, they both jumped.

"I caught y'all ass!" Taryn laughed.

"What's up Pretty Lee? Kia didn't tell me you were coming," Jacko smiled as he made his way over to hug her.

"That's because I wasn't sure yet. Y'all better be glad I wasn't Buck busting up in here."

"I know right! That nigga would have killed us both; it's a good thing he doesn't do parties," Kia laughed. Jacko leaned in and kissed her again before excusing himself. Taryn threw her bag on the bed and sat down.

"Nema this is my best friend Kia, Kia this is Nema, we work together." Kia and Nema exchanged smiles and hellos before Nema took a seat on the bed next to them.

"Taryn, what if Demoto is here tonight? He's going to kick your ass. Didn't he already tell you one time about this stripping shit?"

"Girl I didn't know this was no damn Double O party. I should slap your ass for not telling me."

"Hell I didn't know either until I got here with Jacko. You know Buck sure didn't tell me. He probably don't even know I'm here. He hates for us to be around this Double O stuff. But what I can tell you is that Jacko said the stripper part is only for the Bosses. Even if Demoto is here, he shouldn't be in there."

"Man I ain't worried about Demoto. He got Alicia. What I do ain't none of his business."

"Who is Demoto?"

"That's her *boyfriend*. He and she are trying to act like everybody stupid. Like they ain't got shit going on but we all know. They may as well stop hiding it. He already got onto her for stripping one time, and here she is again. So Nema if you see a fine ass nigga with dreads and green eyes, you better run. He's about seven feet tall with brown skin and blonde hair. You'll know him because his looks are rare as hell! Get as far away from Taryn as you can, because he gon' beat her ass," Kia was laughing so hard tears were coming from her eyes. Nema and Taryn joined in because it really was funny.

"Man whatever Kia! We got time before we're supposed to start dancing, so I'm finna go out here and find me another man. Both of my boos kicked me to the curb. First Jeremiah, now Demoto–I must not be as fine as I thought." Kia and Nema burst out laughing again. The three girls stayed in the room for another thirty minutes getting their hair and stuff together before joining the party. Jacko had given Kia the key to that room. It was just for her; no one else from the party was allowed in there.

"It's so packed in here!" Kia said as they passed through the bottom half of the house. She was talking to both girls, but Nema was the only one to respond. When she looked over to see why Taryn hadn't said anything, she noticed her attention was on something. Kia followed her gaze and landed on Jeremiah in the corner with Ace. Jeremiah was leaned against the wall while Ace danced on him. He was so busy kissing the side of her neck he didn't even feel their gazes on him. The sight before them pissed Kia off, so she knew it had to have gotten to Taryn. Just like she figured when she looked over, Taryn's eyes were glossy.

"Don't you dare Taryn-Lee. You better not let one tear fall and I'm not playing!" Taryn blinked a couple of times before looking at Kia.

"I'm straight sis, let's keep walking."

"You want me to go slap that girl?" Nema asked. Taryn had to laugh at her. Nema was so sweet and quiet on most occasions. She stuck to herself when they were at the club, and that was what drew Taryn to her. Nema was average height, light skin, and had a body that could kill. She wasn't the prettiest girl in the world, but her personality made up for it. She and Taryn had been friends since her first night. She had just gotten dressed and was a ball of nerves, until Nema brought her a drink. Nema drank and made jokes with Taryn until she was comfortable enough to go out. Even then, she made sure to dance next to her the entire night. Next to Kia and Demoto, Nema was her girl. Taryn didn't trust easy, but Nema had proved to be a good person.

"Nema I knew I liked you! I was thinking the same thing!" Kia said, giving her a high five.

"I don't know how I got caught up with y'all two crazy asses," Taryn laughed as she looped her arms through theirs. After stopping to get a few drinks, they headed into the main room to dance. Taryn checked her watch and let Nema know they had another hour and a half before their show.

*****

"Bruh are you coming or not?" Jacko yelled into the phone.

"Yeah nigga I had to get dressed," Demoto answered. He had just left his house and was on his way to the mansion. He'd gotten two texts and three missed calls from Alicia, begging for him to call her back, but he had yet to respond. He wasn't really in the mood to deal with her drama at the moment. He kept seeing visuals of the girl's brain matter splattered across the light pink comforter. No matter how many jobs he'd already completed, it never got easier. He hated to kill women and children, but that came with the territory. It wasn't often that he accepted those types of jobs because of this reason.

"Alright, well hit me when you get here." Jacko hung up the phone and walked back into the house. He wasn't even in the door good when he noticed Kia, Taryn, and her friend on the floor dancing. Taryn's friend was dancing with one of the double O security guards, while Taryn and Kia danced alone. Dudes all over the floor were trying to get next to them, but they continuously dismissed them. Jacko laughed to himself because they obviously knew he and Demoto would fuck them up. His laugh must have caught Kia's ear, because the moment she looked up their eyes connected. The way she looked at him and bit her lip made him hard. *Her lil ass knows what she doing.* He nodded his head in the direction of the room before walking away. Kia's face held a knowing smile as she told Taryn she'd be right back. On her way up the stairs, she was stopped by loud yelling. The voices were coming from the room to her left. Whoever the two people were obviously didn't mind others hearing their conversation, because the door was cracked. Kia, being the nosey person she was, wedged her head inside just enough to hear without being noticed. She had to cover her mouth once her eyes focused. It was Demoto's girlfriend Alicia, and she was kissing some old guy. *What in the world? This lil hoe!* Kia was just about to turn around and walk away when they stopped. Now the guy's face was more visible. Before his tongue was so far down Alicia's throat that Kia couldn't see anything. He was way older than them, with the ugliest scar across his forehead. Why on earth would Alicia cheat on Demoto for him? Whatever the reason was, it was none of her concern so she continued on her way.

"It took you long enough," Jacko said as soon as she entered the room.

"I know. I just saw Alicia kissing some old man."

"Demoto's Alicia?"

"Yep! They was going at it! At first they were arguing, and by the time I was able to look at them, they were kissing. She nasty because that nigga look old as dirt, he must be paid!"

Jacko just shook his head at Kia. She loved drama. She was like a walking soap opera. As he snatched off his hoodie, he made a mental note to tell Demoto about his girl when he got there. Right now it was time for some loving. He picked Kia up and walked her into the bathroom. After he sat her on the counter, he kissed her neck. He'd figured out just recently that was her spot. The light grey joggers she had on were definitely working out in his favor. He was able to slide his hand in her panties with no problem. He played in her wetness, drawing loud moans from her lips. Jacko ran his hand up Kia's body and stopped at her neck. He choked her lightly while he massaged her clit.

"You ready for me Kia?"

"Umm, yes Jack! Yes!"

"Come on Kia baby, let me have it," he spoke in her ear. She was grinding on his fingers feverishly. Jacko knew how to make her whole body shiver with just his touch.

"Right now Kia! Come for me." Jacko's demands pushed Kia over the edge; she came all over his hand.

"Yeah, that's my baby," he moaned as he wrapped his arm around her body and pulled her off the sink. He had lowered his jeans enough to release his dick without getting fully undressed. With the other hand and Kia's help, he pulled her sweats around her ankles. Kia was ready for the D, but his mouth looked so good that she had to kiss it. Before she turned around, she slithered her tongue in his mouth. He moaned as he ran his hands all over her body. Kia bit his bottom lip softly as he pulled away and turned her around. She was leaning over the counter when she moaned to him.

"Go slow Jack." Jacko nodded his head yes, but he already knew that was a lie. He rolled his magnum on and slammed into her.

"Ahhhh!" she yelled. He knew he'd caught her off guard, but it didn't take long for her to get with the flow. She was matching his stokes with expertise. Kia looked at him over her shoulder; she thought she would bust in that second. He looked so good to her. He was holding the bottom of his shirt with his teeth, exposing his tattoo-filled abs. The tight grip he had on her waist mirrored the intense look on his face. He was filling her insides up with his deep manhood.

"You so fucking sexy Jacko! Shit!" She was almost breathless.

"Yea you too baby," he said as he leaned over and kissed the middle of her back. Jacko's hand was up in midair when he heard voices outside the door. Somebody had just come in their room.

"I thought you locked the door," he whispered.

"I thought I did."

Jacko didn't plan on stopping until Kia came. He wasn't about to stop pleasing his baby because they had an audience. Besides that, she had to pay for not locking that door. Whoever it was would just have to hear her. He slapped her ass hard.

"What I tell you about disobeying me? Didn't I tell you to lock that door?" he was slamming into her so hard her juices were splashing against his thighs. Kia always got wet when he was rough with her. He could tell she was enjoying herself, because whatever it was she was saying, he couldn't make it out. She was trying to say something, but it was mixed with her moans so he didn't understand a word of it. He smacked her ass again as he continued to thrust into her. Kia's legs began shaking as she squirted all over him.

"AHHHH JACKO!!!"

"Shit" he grunted as came right behind her. He stayed inside her for a moment before he pulled out and flushed his condom down the toilet. He fixed his clothes and wet the washcloth that was hanging on the towel rod. Kia's body was so weak she could barely move. Jacko turned her around and washed lightly between her legs, cleaning her up. He stared into her eyes the entire time, which only made her wet all over again.

"Give me this damn rag, before we be in here fucking again," she smiled as she snatched the rag from his hand. She made sure to wash everything over again before Jacko pulled her panties and joggers up around her waist. He leaned against her and stuck his tongue in her mouth for a few minutes before pushing her behind him. He wanted to see whoever was in the room before she came out. He was a man; he didn't care if people knew he was fucking in a bathroom at a party, but he didn't want them to think that about her. He really liked Kia; he wasn't about to embarrass her like that.

192

"Um huh, bring y'all nasty asses on out here," Taryn smiled once she noticed Jacko at the door. Her and her friend were sitting on the bed smiling. Jacko laughed and opened the door all the way. Kia came out, but pressed her face against his back.

"Nah freak nasty, don't try to hide now; you wasn't being shy when your ass was in the yelling for the whole house to hear." Taryn had gotten up and pulled a laughing Kia from behind Jacko.

"Man Pretty Lee, chill out," Jacko smiled. Taryn, Kia, and Nema were so busy laughing they couldn't even respond. Jacko knew it was time for him to leave the girls to themselves, so he kissed Kia on the lips again before leaving.

"Y'all two so fucking lame! I know y'all was sitting out here listening."

"You damn right we were, with your disobedient ass," Taryn laughed as she hit Kia on her butt.

"That lil thug ass nigga look just like he can put it down too," Nema said.

"Nema girl, put it down ain't even the word! That dick be so good I don't be able to process one coherent thought," Kia said as she high-fived her. The girls laughed a little while longer before it was time for Taryn and Nema to get dressed for their show.

Chapter 13

"Okay fellas I have a special treat for y'all tonight. It's my way of showing appreciation for a job well done."

Taryn could hear the bullshit Cayman was speaking from the other room. Her and Nema had just gotten dressed and been taking a few shots while they waited. She hadn't danced since the night Demoto had caught her, and her nerves were all over the place. She still hadn't gotten completely comfortable with the lifestyle yet. She paced around the floor in her six-inch glittery gold heels. The gold and white sequined slingshot she wore was banging! Nema had gotten them matching pieces for the first show. Tonight the men had paid for an entire round, meaning they would do four shows. The first one they would do together. The next two would be individual with Nema going first, and lastly would be a bonus. They would only do that one if the men were tipping generously. The bonus round was always their customers' favorite because they got completely naked. Taryn was hoping it wouldn't come to that one tonight. Nema on the other was ready. She had been stripping for years, so this type of thing was nothing to her. She actually favored private parties over the club, because you get paid more. In the club you had to split a lot of the money, but at private parties you split it with one or two other girls and that was it.

"You gon' be alright Pretty Lee," Nema said as she put gold glitter over Taryn's eyelids.

"Ima tell my brother you stole his nickname."

194

"I couldn't help it! It's so cute and fits you perfectly! You're really pretty Taryn. I don't know why you're nervous. But for real–if you want, we can do it how we did your first night at the club. I'll dance by you the whole time until you get comfortable."

"Thanks Nema girl, but we can't do that tonight. It's only us two. If we want our money we have to show out!"

Nema thought about it and Taryn was right. She wanted her money by all means, but Taryn was her friend. She would do what made her feel comfortable. The way the show went depended on Taryn anyway. Nema was a person that fed off other people; she'd tried not to be like that, but she couldn't help it. If Taryn was live, then she would be too. After she finished their makeup, she checked to make sure their music was in the player and ready to go. By the time she got back, Taryn had put her one sided mask on and let her hair down. Nema had never told her, but she loved the whole mask thing Taryn did. She was the only dancer she knew that wore a mask every set. She knew it was to make her feel more comfortable, but it definitely added spice to the show. Nema looked at Taryn and the way her hair fell around her shoulders to the middle of her back. She was flawless. Nema knew she wasn't the prettiest girl in the world, but she was confident. If she hadn't been, there was no way she would have ever been able to do a private show with Taryn. After spraying on perfume, Taryn walked up and grabbed Nema's hand; she said a quick prayer and then smiled. Together they walked to the door to get a closer look. She could see through the peephole that there about thirty to forty men either sitting or standing. She wanted to make sure Buck hadn't decided to show up; he would kill her. The only familiar face she saw was Cayman. He was the same man that paid her three thousand just to dance with Demoto at the club the last time. Most of the men there were old, with the exception of maybe ten young ones. She had turned to give herself the once over again when the door opened. In walked a man looking to be in his mid-thirties with a baldhead and a double O shirt on.

"They're ready for you ladies," he smiled.

"Once we get to the door, press play and we'll come out," Nema instructed. He left the room and they could hear him fumbling with the big entertainment system in the closet. Surprisingly, Taryn took the lead with Nema standing behind her. As soon as Taryn heard the beat to Cashout's "*She Twerkin*" blare through the room, she walked out. The room erupted in noise from the men. She smiled a knowing smirk and began to dance. She had picked this song to go first because it always got her hype. The music mixed with the liquor she'd consumed had her ready. She was so busy dancing she hadn't even noticed Nema had the men put a pole in the middle of the floor. This was right up Taryn's ally. She was acrobat on the pole. The men had already been throwing money, but once she climbed the pole and started doing tricks, it really started flying. The floor was covered in green bills.

"Turn up then baby!" Nema screamed at Taryn as she twirled down the pole and landed into a split on the floor. Nema reached over Taryn's head and began climbing the pole for her show. Taryn was good, but Nema was better. She got off the floor as Lil Ronny's

Circle came on. Taryn stood and looked around the room at the men. They looked like thirsty little puppies to her. There was one sitting in the front row with a wad of cash in his hand. He looked to be about her age, so she sashayed over to him.

"Oh shit young buck, she finna get you!" some old man yelled. The young handsome boy in the chair smiled and winked at Taryn in response. He motioned for her to sit on his lap, but instead she stood in front of him and bent over. Her hands were on the floor as she made her butt shake. This was a move courtesy of Kia. She'd taught her different stuff once Taryn had disclosed her part time job. There were a host of "oohs" and "ahhs" sounding off in the room. She was sure she'd even hear a couple of "Oh shit's" to go with it. She had already known they would like it. Money was flying all over her head, and onto the floor around her. By the time 2 Chains *Extremely Blessed* went off, Taryn had sat down on the boy's lap and was grinding. He had wrapped one arm around her waist and held her hair in the other. The entire time she danced, he had been kissing her shoulders and feeling on her body. She normally didn't allow this type of thing, but he was cute and had thrown at least a couple thousand dollars off this one song. The stack of money he held was filled with twenties and fifty dollar bills. The grip he had on her felt so good; every time she tried to stand, he would pull her back down. He was obviously favored, because the older men just laughed and continued to hand him money.

"You can't handle all that woman Jarrett!" one of them yelled.

"Shit! I can if she let me!" he said loud enough for Taryn to hear. She smiled and kept dancing. That's one thing that wasn't happening–no matter how much money he threw. She didn't mix her personal life with men she met at work. When the last song for their first show went off, Taryn and Nema grabbed the bags of money and left the room. Cayman had one of the bartenders pick up their money and place it in two clear trash bags for them.

"Man Pretty Lee we just racked up girl!" she squealed, wrapping her arm around Tayrn's neck.

"Didn't we though! We don't even have to do anymore sets after all that damn money!"

"You crazy! There's more where that came from. You better go out there and get that damn money!" Nema joked as she stripped out of her slingshot.

Taryn stripped from hers as well as she walked into the bathroom. She hopped in the shower to rid herself of sweat before her next show. She had ten minutes to hit the hot spots, get dressed, and be back out there. Once she'd gotten out and dried her hair, she wrapped it in a bun on the top of her head. Her next ensemble was one she'd gotten custom-made. It wasn't made for tonight, but the way things are going, she'd probably never end up wearing it. It was a black leather one piece with red words written on the back. The sides were cut out with a plunging neckline. She wore big red earrings and her red heels that had small pom poms on the front. She topped it off with a full mask. This one was half-red and half-black, with gold designs on it. The gold letters were the same as the red ones on the back of her outfit. Overall, it was simple, but Taryn was killing it.

By now her drinks had worn off, and she was ready to get it all over with. She was so glad she only had to dance to two songs this time. Fully dressed, she waited for the man to come and let her know it was time again. He'd been paid to get the girls whatever they needed that night. Taryn checked her phone for any missed calls, but she had none. She had one text from Kia letting her know she would be waiting on her downstairs once they were finished, but that was it.

*****

Demoto had just gotten to the party and was immediately glad he'd come. There were wall-to-wall women, drinks, and food! It was just what he needed to get his mind off his previous tasks. He texted Jacko to let him know he was there as he made his way through people. He'd just gotten into the kitchen when he got a text from Jacko. After grabbing a beer and a bottle of water from the cooler, he walked down the hall in search of him. After passing a few doors, he got to the last one on the left and walked in. Kia and Jacko were sitting on the bed playing cards.

"It's a whole party going on, and y'all in here coupled off, playing cards."

"Bruh you know I don't do much partying; besides, I didn't want to leave Kia alone."

"Why you come by yourself Kia? Where your best friend at?" Demoto asked, trying to be funny, but he really did want to know where Taryn was.

"She had to leave for a minute with her friend, she said they'd be right back." Kia was hoping Jacko and Demoto didn't see through her lies. It had been easy to lie to Jacko because he didn't care either way, but Demoto was different. He was paying attention because he actually cared. He looked at her for a long minute before nodding his head. Kia breathed a sigh of relief as he sat down in the corner. He texted on his phone for a few minutes before saying anything else.

"So you don't know where they went?"

"They said to the store. Her friend needed some Tylenol or something," Kia continued to lie as she pulled out her phone to text Taryn.

"Aye Jack, where that nigga Jarrett at? Cayman said I'm supposed to be picking my money up from him."

"He upstairs. They having a private meeting," Jacko said, oblivious to the fact Taryn was one of the strippers. He hadn't officially started anything with Double O yet, so he hadn't been invited. Demoto grabbed his keys and headed for the door. Kia wanted to do something to make him stay, but she didn't want to give herself away. She just hoped like hell Taryn was getting her text messages. After speaking with a few employees, Demoto found out where everybody was and headed there. He didn't know what kind of meeting they would be holding in the middle of a party, but he was glad they hadn't called him. He'd had enough of Double O for one night. He needed a few hours to recuperate. Half way up the stairs, he heard loud music playing. As he got closer, the music got louder. *The meeting must be over*, he thought as he opened the door. When he went in, he saw a short light-skinned stripper. He wasn't really into strippers, but she was moving. He watched for a few seconds before heading over to Cayman. He was sitting at the bar drinking, so Demoto took a seat next to him.

"Everything Good?" he asked.

"Yes sir."

"Good. Your money is in your account."

"I thought you wanted me to get it from Jarrett."

"Change of plans," Cayman smiled as downed the rest of his drink. Demoto shook his hand and got up to leave when he heard Usher's *Superstar* come on. He would have continued out the door if his thoughts hadn't hit him like a ton of bricks. *Taryn better not have her ass up here*, he thought. He thought about hiding amongst the other men, but quickly changed his mind. If she was in here, he was about to show his ass. The lights were off right now, so when they cut them on, she'd see him. He stood against the wall to the side of where she would be dancing. He had one foot on the wall with his hands in his pockets. His heart dropped when he saw her silhouette in the door. He could already tell it was her.

*****

"Last show," she mumbled to herself as she stood at the door. She was waiting for the right part to come on before she walked out. She stood there a few more minutes looking at her feet until she heard it. Once the beat dropped, she walked out. She had instructed Nema to keep the lights off the first minute to build suspense. The darkness also helped her keep a cool head; she had gotten back nervous. She was twirling and grinding all over the floor as the men showered her in money. She had just climbed the pole when the lights came on. She kept her eyes closed as she circled around it a few times. As she slid to the floor, she bent over with her butt in the air again and wound it in a slow circle. She was making sure to give whoever was behind her a good show. When she stood up, a familiar scent hit her nostrils. *It can't be, Jesus please no!* She turned her head to the side, and sure enough there he was. Demoto looked so angry that his skin had a red tint to it. His green eyes shined with hate and hurt mixed together. She looked away as quick as she could. She couldn't bear the look that was in his eyes.

As Demoto stood watching her, he realized he was more hurt than angry. He had asked her not to do this, and she disobeyed him. He hated to see her degrading herself like this, but she wouldn't listen to him. He wanted to be angry, but by the look that was on her face the entire dance, he could tell she didn't want to be there. The men in the room probably had no idea, but Demoto knew her inside and out; she was in serious discomfort. He tried to soften the look in his eyes, but she had turned her head. When she walked away, he noticed the words on her clothing. It read **Forever Yours** across her back and **Youngblood** written across the top of her butt. The words were made to look as if blood were dripping from them. For a long moment, he had mixed feelings because she was here dancing for other men, in something that was obviously made for him. Taryn had his mind all over the place. He didn't know what to think. By the time he'd stopped daydreaming, her show was over and she was gone.

*****

"Taryn, was that your boyfriend you was looking at like that?" Nema asked once they got back into the room.

"Yes! Girl I'm so scared. I don't know what he's going to do." Taryn paced around nervously. She was so busy trying to figure out whether Demoto was mad or not she hadn't even changed yet. She tried calming her nerves a few more minutes before grabbing her bag to change. Nema had already put on a short form-fitting dress, some boots, and a jacket. She was sitting on the bed waiting for Taryn so they could go. She had packed their money in the duffle bags they'd brought along and was playing Candy Crush on her phone. Taryn snatched off her clothing, showered again, and pulled her hair into a smooth ponytail. She put lotion on her body and sprayed it with perfume. She dressed herself in a pair of maroon jeans and a gold, navy blue, and maroon crop top that stopped at the top of her pants. She put on her necklace, bracelets, and earrings before walking out. She slid her feet into her dark blue converse, and grabbed her backpack and duffle bag. Once they'd gotten into the room, the men had begun to disperse. Taryn was grateful for this because she didn't want any of them trying to hit on her. There was only one face she wanted to see, but it was nowhere to be found. She looked around the whole room, turning down men along the way. When she couldn't find him, she looked for Nema so they could go. Just when she'd found her, she felt a strong arm wrap around her neck from behind. Her back rested against his front with his arm resting around her neck. He wrapped his other arm around her waist, holding her tightly against his body. At that moment, Taryn thought all of the breath would leave her body. She felt so calm in his arms. His cologne mesmerized her as he spoke in her ear.

"What I told you about this shit?"

"I'm sorry."

"I know. Let's go," he said, finally releasing her. When she turned around, his face was void of anger; in its place was love. She was so happy that she could hardly contain it. Tears began to leak from her eyes.

"You're such a crybaby," he laughed as he pulled her in for another hug. He had already known she was sorry, but her tears reassured him. Demoto grabbed the duffle bag from her and threw it over his shoulder. They locked hands and headed for the door.

"Wait, I have to get Nema." Taryn turned around and walked towards her. She was standing in the corner talking to one of the men. When Taryn got her attention, the man handed her his card and they left. They were almost down the stairs when the young boy from the party yelled to get Taryn's attention. He raced to where she was standing. He gave Demoto a pound before speaking.

"I was wondering could we exchange numbers." Taryn looked at Demoto before answering. She hated he'd done this right now.

"I already have a boyfriend, I'm sorry."

"Well he sure is a lucky man," he smiled before retreating up the stairs. Demoto looked at her and walked away.

*****

Demoto didn't mean to get angry all over again, but that was one of the reasons he hated for her to strip. He knew men probably approached her all the time, but he was sure Jarrett had done it strictly based on her show. He practically gulped his bottle of water as he sat in the kitchen with Jacko. Kia had stayed behind to catch up with Taryn. Jacko had spent the last twenty minutes trying to explain to him how he was wrong, and he still didn't see it. Yeah he had a girlfriend and still wanted Taryn to himself, but so what! She'd made it very clear she loved him, so why should she be with anyone else? He had gotten angry with her for dancing, but it wasn't like he gave her money on the regular. The more he thought about it, the more he understood what Jacko was saying. He was going to have to fix this, especially since he'd just found out Alicia was fucking with somebody else. That relationship was a wrap!

*****

The cool air from the ceiling fan felt good to her aching body. The heels she'd worn tonight had her ankles on fire. That was one of the cons to dancing; your body ached like crazy afterwards. She lay in the spacious bed in nothing but her t-shirt and panties on. Her hair was still in the ponytail from earlier with her scarf wrapped around it. The soft sounds of Jeremih played in the background. She had been home in bed for about two hours and still hadn't fallen asleep yet. There was so much on her mind she couldn't keep her eyes closed longer than five seconds.

Tomorrow she was going apartment hunting and she couldn't wait. Demoto and Adisa were past welcoming, but she was ready for her own space. She'd been living off people her entire life, and she was tired of it. The seventeen thousand dollars she'd made tonight on top of what she already had in the bank was enough cushion for now. After Demoto walked away from her at the party, he hadn't said another word all night, but it was fine. She loved him, but she was tired of the games. She'd decided tonight was her last night dancing; she would stick to Foot Locker for now. With the money Mr. Buck had stored away from her, and her checks and savings, she was sure she could maintain.

Taryn lay there trying to figure out what would become of her and Demoto once she moved out. They had been feeling each other all of this time and nothing had come of it. They'd had sex, expressed their feelings, and once again nothing happened. Taryn was sick of trying to figure it out. Maybe some space between them would be just what they needed. She let out a loud breath as she sat up in the bed. She reached to get some water from the bottle on the nightstand, but it was all gone. She hated to get up but the Patrón she'd drank earlier had her mouth dry. She unlocked the door to her room and walked into the kitchen.

Being that this was an apartment, she could see the living from where she was standing. Demoto was lying down on the sofa wrapped in a blanket. She knew it was him because his hair was hanging off the side. When he heard the fridge open, he looked up and made eye contact with her. Instead of either of them saying anything, they turned their heads. Taryn was tired of his little tantrum, so she got her water and went back to her room. She closed the door and got back into bed. She'd grown tired of listening to music, so she cut the TV on. As she flipped through the channels, she noticed her favorite movie Pretty Woman was on. Taryn was bent over looking under the bed when she heard someone fidgeting with the knob on her door. She knew without them saying anything it was Demoto. She slid on the floor and sat there for a moment debating, whether or not to let him in. She really didn't feel like being bothered with him not one bit, but this was his house. She didn't necessarily have the right to lock him out of anything in his house. That's why she needed her own place. Pulling herself from the floor, she went against her better judgment and opened the door. To her surprise, he wasn't there. Taryn rolled her eyes and continued down the hallway to his room. He was lying in the bed watching TV.

"You need something?"

"Nah."

"If you don't need anything why did you come to my door?"

"I didn't."

Demoto could tell she was irritated. She looked at him a little while longer before slamming his door shut and going back to her room. She hadn't been in bed no longer than five minutes before he was at her door again. This time she hadn't bothered to lock it, because she knew he was coming. He came in and got into bed with her without saying a word. Truth of the matter was, he couldn't sleep knowing she was in the house with him and he couldn't touch her.

Demoto had formed an attachment to her that he couldn't deny. Her scent alone was intoxicating. Her hair, her eyes, her nose–everything about her drew him in. When it came to her, he was hopeless. He laid next to her in bed watching her movement. Every time she laughed her breasts would move, and it was turning him on big time. He didn't care if he was being a pervert; Taryn's body belonged to him. He lay there a little longer before reaching over to cut her television off. At first she looked like she wanted to protest, but changed her mind. She had just scooted down in the bed when he pulled at one of the butterfly nipple rings she had in.

"What are you doing?"

"I love you Taryn."

"Whatever Demoto."

"What you mean whatever?

"Exactly what I said! I'm tired of playing games with you. You know I love you. You go around here like you some kind of King or something. Alicia may let you string her along and do whatever you please, but that's not happening with me. I'm grown. If you want to act like a child, then be my guest. Just believe me when I tell you, it won't happen with me. I've had enough of your bipolar ass. If you want me then say so; if you do, but you don't want to be with me, that's fine too. Just please make up your mind; all this back and forth is giving me whiplash."

Taryn had shut him up that fast. He couldn't think of anything to say, because she was right. Once he'd gotten out of the bed and made it back to his room, his mind was made up. He walked into his closet and pulled a pair of sweatpants and a jacket out. He grabbed the Jordans next to the bed and went back into Taryn's room. Upon entry, the look on her face told him she was confused.

"Put on some clothes real quick, take a ride with me."

Taryn watched him leave the room with no further explanation. She snatched her scarf off and brushed her hair back into a neat ponytail. Dressed in her Adidas track suit and sneakers, she grabbed her phone and went to the bathroom to brush her teeth and wash her face.

Chapter 14

The blue lights flashed so brightly that Taryn had to squint her eyes to see. Cop cars lined the block for miles. There were news vans on three different areas of the street. People had gathered behind the police's yellow caution tape. Some onlookers were crying while others were watching, exchanging stories amongst themselves. The further down they drove, the more she could see. They were closing in on the scene when the car in front of them was stopped by a young officer. Whatever he'd said had the car turning around. He made his way to Demoto's car next.

"I'm sorry young man, this street is blocked off. You can turn around in this driveway right here," he tipped his hat and walked away. It wasn't until Demoto pulled into the neighbor's driveway that Taryn saw the coroner's car parked in the driveway of the house that was taped off.

"Oh my gosh! Somebody died Demoto!" Taryn couldn't believe her eyes. She'd never been that close to a crime scene in her life. She looked over at Demoto and he showed no signs of concern, so she looked back out of the window. As they drove back past the news cameras, Taryn noticed the Mayor talking to one of the reporters. *What's he doing out here?* She was quiet the rest of the ride. Unaware of what Demoto had planned, she chose not to ask any questions. There weren't very many places they could be going at four thirty in the morning, so she figured she'd find out soon enough. They eventually came to a stop outside of the Waffle House on the north side of town. Demoto came around, opening the door for her. He didn't speak until they were inside and seated at a table in the corner.

"You okay?"

"Yeah, are you?"

"Not really," he slumped down in his seat a little more. After running his hand through his locs, he looked back at her. He didn't say anything, and she didn't want to pry so she waited for him to disclose more.

"That was the Mayor's house we just went to. His daughter was killed tonight." He could tell by the way Taryn's eyes bulged that she hadn't expected to hear something like that.

"How do you know?"

"I took you there because if we're going to be together, we need trust. I don't want any secrets. In a relationship, trust and loyalty is everything. If I can't be real with anyone else, I need to be able to be real with you. Taryn, you are the one person who needs to have my back at all times. No matter what the situation may be, always trust me. If there ever comes a time you're not sure what to believe, believe me. Believe in the love I have for you, the love we have for each other. I'm a man of my word, T; if it comes down to you and anybody else, it's going to always be you. It has been since the first day we met. The things I'm involved in are tough. I need you." Demoto looked at Taryn for some type of response, but she gave nothing. His nerves were starting to get the best of him.

"T, say something. Tell me how you feel about me or something. Anything!"

"What exactly are you involved in?"

"I've told you already once before." Taryn bit her nails trying to figure out what he could have possibly told her. "Why did you take me to that house? What did that have to do with anything?"

Demoto looked at Taryn like she grown two heads. She couldn't possibly be this naive. He had obviously given her more credit than she deserved. He was sure the look on his face mirrored the thoughts in his head. They were in a public place; it wasn't like he could say it out loud.

"You remember the conversation we had in the kitchen that day when you asked where I work?" Her face frowned as realization set in. Her eyes got big as saucers, then returned to their normal size.

"That was you tonight?" she asked in disbelief. She had thought Demoto was joking when he'd told her that. That wasn't a job people had in real life. It couldn't be. She knew it was indeed true when she looked at him and he was nodding his head up and down.

"How? You were with me at the party," her words trailed off as she realized it had taken him a while to get there. *Wow!* Taryn mumbled her thoughts to herself. She probably looked like a fool to him right now, although talking to herself had been something she'd done since childhood.

"Moto I don't understand, you're always so gentle with me. You've never given any inkling of being a...well...you know...a...ummm, well you know what I mean," she said, unable to say the word.

"That's because I love you, T. You and my contracts are two different things. It's not something I chose to do; it was offered and the pay is good. As cruel as it may sound, it's not that personal." Taryn got up and sat on the same side of the table as him. With her arm looped through his, she laid her head on his shoulder. Demoto rested his hand between the thickness of her thighs and relaxed. With her body next to his, Demoto felt the best he'd felt all night.

"I'm here forever Moto." She meant those words with every fiber of her being. Many people would probably judge her for loving a man that killed others, but so! Fuck them and their opinions; anybody got out of line, she'd just have Demoto handle it. She knew she should have been running for the hills by now, but she wouldn't dare. Who was she to judge? Her livelihood wasn't that great either.

"Now T, this is between us. Nobody besides Jacko and Adisa knows." Taryn nodded her head in understanding. She had so many questions, but chose to leave them unanswered. The less she knew the better. An hour had passed, and they'd finished and were headed to the car when Taryn's cell phone rang. It was Jeremiah. She pressed the ignore button and put in her pocket. In her seatbelt and ready to pull off, it began to ring again. This time Demoto pulled it out of her pocket to see who was calling. Taryn held her breath waiting for his outburst, but it never came. Instead, he was chillingly calm.

"Why Miah keep calling?"

"I don't know. He was just at the party with Ace all hugged up and kissing. I don't know why he calling me now."

It bothered Demoto to hear the hurt in her voice. He didn't want her hurting behind another man. If she was feeling sour about Ace, that meant she still cared about Jeremiah. Demoto clinched his jaw tight while running his hand over his dreads. He hated that she loved another man. He wanted to be the only recipient of her love.

"You sound like you care." His response came out a little harsher than he wanted it to. She picked up on it right away and looked at him. With her hand resting on his leg, she leaned over the console and kissed the muscle jumping in his jaw. She rubbed the side of his face for a minute before moving his hand to her chest. She placed it over her heart so he could feel it beating.

"My heart belongs to you and only you, Demoto. I don't care who Jeremiah is with, it just pissed me off that he's so sloppy."

"It better," he smiled as they headed back towards his house.

*****

The smell of lavender and vanilla filler her nostrils as she lay on the floor of her living room. She had been shopping all day and she was dog tired now.

Against his will, Demoto had let her get her own apartment. Mr. Buck had co-signed her lease and she'd gotten her keys that morning. Taryn chuckled to herself as she thought about the fit Demoto had when she'd told him she was moving out. He didn't understand why she couldn't just live with him. He only gave in once she agreed to live in the same apartment complex as he did. All of her belongings were in the right places; all she had to do now was hang pictures. She had been in her apartment for almost two weeks now and she had yet to do so.

Between Demoto and Mr. Buck, her entire place was furnished. The two insisted on paying for all of her things. Taryn was even more excited now that Kia was about to move in with her. She hadn't wanted to leave her dad at first, but he insisted. Taryn had moved into a two-bedroom in hopes that she would, and she'd finally agreed.

"Why you laying on the floor?" Kia asked, walking into the house. She had an arm full of clothes as she headed towards the back. When she came back, she was empty handed and exhausted. After kicking her shoes off, she lay on the floor next to Taryn. They were in deep conversation when there was a knock at the door.

"That's probably Demoto. He's been trying to get over here all day," Taryn laughed as she got up to get the door. As soon as she opened it, greedy hands were on her. They roamed freely over her body, pulling her against his hard chest. His full lips devoured her smaller ones until they were breathless. He looked down at her, happy to finally be in her presence.

"I missed you today," he said as Taryn freed his hair from the band around it before kissing his mouth again.

"I can tell."

"You busy? I need to talk to you about something." He looked around and noticed Kia getting off the floor. She waved as she bypassed them and headed for her room. Once the door was closed, Demoto pulled Taryn to the couch so they could sit down. He observed her appearance, taking in her beauty. Her face was serious, awaiting his words.

"I got a contract today. It pays two hundred thousand up front, and another two once I'm finished." Her eyes got big at the amount of money he mentioned. "The only thing about it is, it's going to take some time. One month minimum." Taryn's face dropped with sadness. She hated when he had to leave. She barely made it through nights without him; how was she going to spend an entire month, maybe longer, alone?

"Where is it? Is it in driving distance from here?"

"No babe, I have to fly. It's in New York." He watched her fall backwards onto the sofa. Her arms were crossed around her waist as she poked her lip out. Although he expected this type of reaction, he didn't know it would make him feel this bad. He stroked her hair as he fought with himself about what to say next. He thought long and hard, trying to make a decision.

"How about you go with me?" She perked up at hearing this, but quickly deflated when she realized she had to work.

"How long will you be gone? I have to work."

"No you don't. You might as well quit that little Foot Locker gig, I can handle things from here on out."

"Handle things? Have you forgotten who you're talking to? I am not about to sit around and let you take care of me. If we're in this relationship, we're in it together! Don't ever in your life insult my hustle like that again. Whatever we do from now on, we will do as a team! Know that!" Demoto was at a loss for words. Taryn had never spoken to him like that. She was always so meek and mild-mannered, but not today. He hadn't meant to insult her; he was simply being the man she deserved. "Don't sit there looking crazy, just give me a kiss and I'll forgive you," Taryn smiled at him as he leaned in to kiss her mouth. After pulling away from her soft lips, Demoto stood up to stretch.

"Go pack your things; we're leaving in the morning."

"What? Didn't I just tell you I have to work?"

"Didn't you just tell me we're a team?" He watched her eyebrows relax across her face "Yeah, that's what I thought! Now go pack your bags, we're leaving tomorrow. It's a little colder in New York, so pack accordingly T." He kissed her once more before heading out the door. Taryn sat there for a minute engrossed in her thoughts until Kia came back.

"So where y'all going?" she asked as she plopped down on the sofa. Taryn stared off into space for a moment. Demoto had told her not to tell anyone, but Kia was her best friend. She could trust her with her deepest secrets, but what about Demoto's? Concluding it wasn't her business to tell, she kept it to herself.

"Demoto has a business trip to New York tomorrow, and he wants me to go."

"Girl you better go! I wish Jacko would take me to New York," she blushed. Kia and Jacko had gotten pretty close lately, and had recently made it official. Taryn was so happy they were a couple; they looked so cute together.

"I'm going. I just hate to miss work! Plus I don't have much cold weather attire."

"Girl you act like you work a corporate job or something; you do nothing but ring up shoes all day! As far as clothes go, the mall doesn't close until nine baby girl!" Kia smiled. Taryn laughed at her as they headed to their rooms to change. There were no explanations needed when it was time to shop.

*****

The atmosphere was cold and stale as he waited in the sitting room. He had a meeting with Cayman in twenty minutes, and was ready to get it over with. He was already tired of waiting; it was freezing! There was absolutely no reason for it to be that cold. He ran his hands up and down his goose bump-covered arms trying to keep warm. That only worked for a few minutes before he was right back cold. After looking down at his watch, he noticed he had ten minutes left until his meeting started, so he was going to walk to the Starbucks across the street. Just as he stood to leave, the door opened and out walked Cayman's second in charge, Buck. Demoto immediately went to shake his hand. Buck was the definition of a real OG. He didn't talk much, but when he did nothing but wisdom percolated out. He had all of Demoto's respect. He hadn't had the opportunity to work with him yet, but he hoped to in the future.

Buck grasped Demoto's hand in a firm grip. He had been meaning to talk with Demoto for a while; he just never had the time to before now. Gathering him and Jacko up for a talk had been his plan, but the girls and business continued to interfere. He didn't know whether or not Jacko had told Demoto about him being Kia and Taryn's father or not yet, so he would do that now.

"Handling business, Youngblood?"

"Yes sir. Getting my assignment right now."

"Good. I've been seeing nothing but great things coming from you and I expect it to continue. You're a hard worker, and passionate about your craft. You're a very respectable and trustworthy young man, which brings me to my next point. You and my daughter have gotten very close, I assume?" The bewilderment displayed on Demoto's face gave him his answer. Jacko hadn't told him anything. "You are the Demoto Youngblood that my Tee-Tee speaks so highly of, correct?"

"Mr. Buck I am Demoto Youngblood, probably the only one around, but I don't know a Tee-Tee." A hearty laugh escaped Buck's lips as Demoto stood convoluted.

"Taryn, Taryn-Lee is my daughter. Tee-Tee is a nickname I gave her. She's told me about you on more than one occasion, and from what I gathered you two are pretty serious. I expect that you will treat her accordingly and keep her out of harm's way. She's been through enough. I don't want her going through anything else that's going to cause her pain."

This was news to Demoto. Not one time had Taryn mentioned Mr. Buck's name. She'd told him Kia's dad had taken her as his own, but all he knew him by was daddy, because that's how she referred to him. *No wonder Kia tough as nails.* It all made sense to him now. Kia was street smart in too many ways to count. Now he saw why; she had been groomed by the best. He had to make sure to tell Jacko.

"Yes sir we are. I love her. I will protect her with my life, as she will for me. I'll fight the world for Taryn-Lee and she knows that. My loyalty to her surpasses that of a normal relationship, Mr. Buck. I promise you have nothing to worry about; when she's with me, she's safe."

"This I already knew, Youngblood. I've had my eyes on you and your little friend Jack for some time now. I hope you didn't think Kia and Taryn were out without my knowing. Never. I have eyes on them at all times, along with you two. I'm not here to threaten you, just to give my blessing. You two young men are some of the best I've seen in a long time. Real is rare around here these days. As long as y'all continue to keep them safe and happy, you have your life. The moment something goes bad, you will see me," Buck said as he patted Demoto on the shoulder before walking away He was halfway down the hall when he stopped and turned back around.

"Leave this conversation between us. I don't want the girls finding out, they'll kill me," he smiled and got onto the elevator. Demoto was baffled by this news, but obviously he was doing good. Buck wasn't the man to make idle threats, so he had to stay on his A-game. It was funny though, because when he spoke of the girls killing him, he wore a smile only a father could. The love he had for Kia and Taryn was real, and Demoto respected it.

"Come on in Youngblood," Bradley Marks, Cayman's secretary, said and motioned him inside the office. Demoto followed closely behind and sat down. He looked around for Cayman, but there were no signs of him.

"I thought I was meeting Cayman?"

"That's what I called you here to talk about today. There have been some things going on lately that we aren't too sure about, and we need to make changes. Our leadership isn't what it's supposed to be, so let's just say it's time to clean house. There are people working this organization to the bone, and our security is something we can't play with. We have to be able to ensure the work we're doing is under the radar. In order to keep it that way, jobs will only be given and taken by the best we have. Demoto you are one of the most loyal people on our payroll, and without you our proceeds would decrease drastically. The job you've taken in New York will seal the deal for your promotion. If you can handle that, upon your return, there will be an extensive amount of gain." Marks held eye contact until Demoto nodded his head in understanding.

The two went on for another thirty minutes going over his job. Bradley informed Demoto that there was a family living in New York that had the background folders of everybody to ever come in contact with Double O. Each folder contained the person's entire life, on paper. From family to school and arrests, they had it. The father was the Senator of New York, and a longtime member of Double O. He had been the legit spokesman since the organization started. He married the bookkeeper of Double O and had two children. The oldest son was also a member of Double O, and a computer technician. Anything involving electronics and scamming, he was the go-to guy. Lastly was the daughter; she was the youngest of the family, but the most beneficial. She was the accountant. Every dollar Double O owned had gone through her hands. She was in charge of the budgets and payroll. She made sure all dirty money was accounted for before it was washed clean. If it wasn't for her, Double O would have never made it this far. Double O was a respectable and legal organization because she assured the money appeared legal.

Overall, the family was one of the most detrimental assets to this company, but they'd been slipping. They had begun to get sloppy and were bringing negative attention to the Double O Corporation. The reason this particular job was going to take so long was because trust had to be established. Being that this family was veterans in this game, they trusted no one. You are going to have to be around longer than a few days to get in their good graces. Demoto had been chosen for the job because not only was he knowledgeable and inventive, but he was ardent and dependable. If anybody could get the job done, it would be him. Demoto leaned forward onto the front of the Bradley's desk.

"Okay, so you want the whole family taken out?"

"Correct! Make it clean and undetectable. The father is a senator. You have to be sure this looks like a hit, and that it doesn't blow back on Double O," Bradley finished as he handed Demoto a backpack. "Everything you need is in here. Be sure to be safe and smart, Youngblood."

"No problem. Nevertheless, I have one question, why didn't you pick the number one for this? If this job is so important, wouldn't you want your best assassin on the job?" Bradley smirked at Demoto's question before answering.

"You are the best assassin. He's number one simply because he was here first. Like I said at the beginning of our meeting, changes are in order. Good day Demoto." They shook hands and Demoto left. He had to go home and get everything together for his trip.

Chapter 15

The plane ride to New York was nothing short of eventful. Trying to explain to Taryn the various aspects of this trip was exhausting. Her catching on wasn't the problem; convincing her she couldn't help was. She wanted to help him take this family down. Demoto was stressing because he knew how important this was, and couldn't afford any mistakes. Taryn was a smart girl, and could probably help as some point, but not now. These people were professionals; he couldn't have her ruining things before he even got it started. She was adamant about helping, and it was giving him a headache.

After the first two hours of telling her no, they viewed the contents of the backpack together. Inside were fake identification cards for him, a folder with private information on the family, and a set of keys for the house he would be living in. Inside the folders was everything he would need in order to move in on the family. He just had to figure out the right way to use it. After leaving Bradley's office yesterday, he had Double O's computer tech make Taryn fake IDs as well. He hadn't told her yet because he wasn't sure how she would fit into all of this. The main reason for him having them made in advance was so no one could trace their names while in New York.

After their two-hour flight, they'd just landed at LaGuardia and were headed to get their bags. The airport was packed with people. Everyone was moving along to their destinations without acknowledging the presence of the next person. That's how Demoto liked it. Whenever he was on a job, he maintained a low profile. He didn't want to converse with anybody that might remember him being there. When the time came, he wanted a clean break. As he stood quietly behind Taryn, he watched the people that continued to bypass them. He wanted to stay alert and aware of his surroundings. Taryn was standing next to the carousel waiting for their bags. She'd insisted on getting her own, so to avoid the argument he let her have her way. She'd caught an attitude right after the plane landed and hadn't spoken to him since. He thought her tantrum was funny. How she was going to get around and do anything without speaking to him was amusing. He was busy watching her wrap her long hair into a bun when his pocket started to vibrate. He retrieved his vibrating phone, noticing it was the red one. He pressed the answer key, but said nothing.

"I know you've made it. You have approximately one month to make this happen. Don't disappoint me," Bradley said before hanging up.

Demoto listened before hanging up and heading to get Taryn. He grabbed for her arm expecting for her to pull away, but she didn't. She placed her smaller suitcase onto the larger one and grabbed his hand with her free one. They walked hand and hand to the front of the airport to catch a cab. They were slapped with a rude awakening once they got outside. They were no longer in Georgia. The wind brutally assaulted their faces as they stood on the curb. Snuggling against Demoto was like second nature for Taryn. He placed his free arm around her body, pulling her closer. They were standing the closest to the street, so when the next cab came Taryn hopped in. Demoto put away their bags before he got in and they pulled away. Nearly twenty minutes later, the car came to a stop in front of a Starbucks. Demoto could tell by the look that was on Taryn's face that she was confused; he'd explain it to her later. After paying the cabbie and retrieving their bags, they walked inside. He ordered them both a caramel latte with java chips and sat down. Taryn had found them a table as soon as they walked in.

"So are you going to tell me why we're at Starbucks and not at our hotel?"

"Nope! But I'll tell you how pretty you look," Demoto smiled as her face grew serious. She was obviously not in the mood for games. "The cold weather sure is making you bitter," he laughed. Taryn was casually dressed in a purple Adidas tracksuit with all of her hair down. It was wild from the blowing wind, and she looked absolutely beautiful.

"Come on Moto, tell me please. I'm tired and cold, I just want to go take a hot shower and lay down." She watched him as he stood up and reached his hand out to her.

"Come on crybaby."

"Where we going?

"To take a hot shower," he smiled as they grabbed their bags and left the building. It was still extremely cold outside, so their walk down the street was torture. Demoto watched the faces of all the people that were passing and they didn't look the least bit fazed by the temperature. They carried conversations easily. It pained him to open his mouth, or breathe for that matter. Taryn-

Lee didn't look to be doing much better. She was keeping his pace, but she was shivering so hard her teeth were chattering. A few buildings up they stopped in front of a high rise and went inside. They both breathed a sigh of relief as they made their way to the elevators. Neither spoke a word, just observed in silence. The elevator came to a stop on the sixteenth floor before Demoto grabbed the back of Taryn's arm and led her down the hall.

He pulled out the keys that Bradley had given him in the backpack and went inside. Once the door was closed, he and Taryn stood still in amazement. The flat was breathtaking. It had hardwood floors and massive windows that stretched from the floor to the ceiling. The entire apartment was white, from the walls, to the décor. The only color was the blood red curtains and pillows on the sofas. The pictures that hung from the walls were immaculate and unique. The kitchen was decorated in black and gray, as well as two of the bedrooms down the hall. The last bedroom was the master, and it was draped in teal and gold. The bed took up majority of the floor, minus the small sofa set in the corner. The cinnamon smell of the atmosphere was so relaxing; it made Taryn feel right at home.

"I never want to leave!" she gushed as she admired the master bathroom. Demoto followed closely behind. He too was in awe at the apartment, but not as much as Taryn. Whenever he did work for Double O, he was treated like a King. He was given nothing less than the best.

"It's a good thing you don't have to."

"Yes I do. When do we start?" Demoto left the room to get his bags. He was not about to have this argument with Taryn again. At least that's what he thought. She followed him back into the living room.

"Demoto, I don't understand why you won't let me help. I mean it's not like I'm asking to shoot them or anything. I just want to help! Let me make friends with one of them or something."

"Taryn I appreciate it, but no! You're too naive for something like this. You are the same person that was about to let a stranger know where you're laying your head. We're in unfamiliar territory, and you're ready to trust anybody! The moment we got into the cab, you started telling all of our business. That man didn't need you to tell him we're not from here; it's obvious as fuck! Secondly, suppose we'd let him drop us off here, then he'd come back later to rob us? Huh? I bet you never thought about that. But it's cool because it's not your job to, it's mine. Just like it's my job to keep you safe. You're not helping me, and that's final!"

"Well why did you even bother to bring me then?"

"Because, I miss your ass like crazy when I'm gone! That shit fucks with my head, and I need to do my best while I'm here. I knew if I could come home to you after dealing with bullshit all day, it would keep me ready for the next day. If you had stayed in GA, I would have been miserable every fucking day and fucked over this job."

"Don't try to say all that sweet stuff so I won't be mad," a smile crept across her face as she unzipped her jacket. She would let this go for now because he was right. She didn't know the first thing about what he did. She just wanted to help in any way she could.

"I ain't worried about your ass being mad. I knew you would be alright after I gave you this good D," he laughed as he motioned towards his hard length with his eyes. Taryn couldn't help but laugh at his silliness. After tossing her jacket over the back of the sofa, she went to retrieve the rest of her things. She wheeled them straight to the master bedroom without even asking. She wasn't the least bit surprised when Demoto came rolling his stuff in behind her. The look he gave dared her to object to them sharing rooms. She smiled at him and rolled her eyes.

"Demoto you are not my daddy!"

"Oh but I can be!"

"Your nasty ass! I should have known you would say something slick." She continued placing her clothing on the hangers in the closet. If she was going to be living there for a month minimum, she was not about to live out of a suitcase the entire time. Demoto left his things in the suitcase and put it in the closet. *Just like a man.* He wasn't even going to put his clothes up. He probably wouldn't mind one bit living out of his suitcase. Once she finished hers, she'd do his as well.

******

It had taken her thirty minutes to unpack their things, and they had retreated back to the extra large great room. Demoto was busy looking over the files of each folder while she made them dinner. She wasn't the best cook, but she tried. She had baked some steaks and made baked potatoes and salad. The kitchen had been fully stocked when they got there. Taryn was in love with the Double O treatment. Less than an hour later, she was done cooking and had called Demoto to taste it. To her surprise, he actually looked like he liked it. She made their plates and sat them on the table in the dining room. It took Demoto a few more minutes before he joined her. They said their prayers and dug in. It was quiet the first few minutes while they ate. Demoto looked like he had a lot on his mind, so she decided to break the silence.

"Find anything useful in the folders?"

"You have no idea! These people are loaded bae. They have stacks of money, and the dumb daughter is blowing it all. She has the worst gambling problem known to man. This girl is losing thousands of dollars at a time in casinos, and stock markets. Anything you can think of, she's betting on. She has money on cockfights, horses, racecars, even football games. I've never seen anything like it."

"Well it's not like they don't have the money."

"They're not going to have it too much longer. She's spending more than they're making back, and I don't even want to get started on the brother. This man is scamming some of the largest names in the world. The files from his computer alone can shut down the whole white house. He has taps on everything. The only thing is, that fool has a meth addiction." Taryn ate another piece of her steak while she waited for him to finish. "The father, he seems like a pretty stand up dude. There's nothing much on him besides the fact that he cheats like a fucking maniac. He's had four paternity suits this year alone. Which brings me to the last member of the family, the mother. She is suffering from depression and sees a psychiatrist twice a week. Between the four of them, they'll be broke within the next three months. The shit these people are in could kill Double O. None of them are stable enough to be in charge of a business this prominent. One mishap and the whole team could go down. They've been maintaining thus far, but they have to go before it's too late." Demoto shook his head as he thought about all of the information he'd just taken in. Each folder was thick with information on the family, from their friends to their favorite hangout spots. This was going to take a lot of work, but it could definitely be done.

"Dang! Who are these people?" Demoto got up and came back with a family portrait they'd taken last month and slid it to Taryn.

"Taryn-Lee, meet the Elmores."

*****

DING! DING! DING!

The siren from a winning slot machine sounded. People were moving all around the room. They were drinking, serving drinks, or changing tables and machines. Taryn had accompanied Demoto to the Resorts World Casino about an hour ago, and she was already ready to leave. He had come to watch Emily Elmore, the gambling nut daughter. The only reason he'd let her come was because she had begged. Now she wished she hadn't. There was nothing appealing about continuously and unnecessarily losing your money. She had tried to endure the pain like a trooper, but she was bored out of her mind. After a few more minutes of roaming around, she shot Demoto a quick text.

Taryn: I'm about to go shop! Call me when you're done

My Love Moto: No the hell you ain't! Keep your ass in this Casino!

Taryn: LOL Demoto please! I keep telling you, you are not my daddy

My Love Moto: I keep telling you I can be! Just be safe and don't talk to nobody

Taryn: Yes sir daddy ☺

My Love Moto: Call me daddy when you taking this dick

Taryn: Nasty ass!

My Love Moto: You love it! Don't talk to nobody!

Taryn put her phone back into her purse and headed out the door. She checked to make sure she had her fake IDs and walked into the brisk air. There were stores everywhere. She couldn't wait to get in Nordstrom and Burberry to find her a good coat. It was fucking freezing in New York! She missed home already; hopefully Demoto would get done sooner than later. On her way to Burberry, she was stopped by the Apple store. It was big and clear, she'd never seen anything like it. She rushed inside. By the time she'd left, it had been thirty minutes and an iPad later. She'd heard Demoto tell

Adisa he'd broken his last night before they left, so she got him a new one. She stopped and ate as she made her way down the street. She enjoyed the scenery as she basked in the happiness of her current situation.

"Welcome to Burberry," the sales woman greeted as she entered. She smiled and headed for the section she saw jackets in. There were so many styles; she couldn't choose. Thumbing through the racks, she could hardly contain her excitement. The various shades of browns caught her eyes instantly, until she saw red out the corner of her eye. As she turned around, the sight before her made her eyes bulge. It was the cutest red Burberry Reyna Trapeze coat. She'd saw one similar to it on fashion week when she was watching TV a while back. She had to have it! After having a salesman retrieve that coat along with two others, six pairs of boots, a scarf, and three hats, she was ready to check out. Her total was close to 32,000 . She had just reached in her purse to get her black card when the clerk grabbed her arm.

"There's no need for that ma'am, your things have already been purchased." Taryn looked at her like she had spoken in a foreign language.

"Excuse me, what? How? By who?" Taryn rambled off questions as they packed her things into bags. The clerk didn't say another word until she had finished bagging her items.

"The gentleman in the corner next to the window has given strict instructions for this spree to be on him." Taryn turned around and looked towards the window. She turned back around quickly, because she didn't know that man from a bum on the street.

"Are you sure you have the right person? I don't know him." The lady behind the counter gave Taryn a disapproving look. One day young girls would learn; when a man was spending money, let him. Not bothering to acknowledge Taryn's question, she walked around the counter to hand her the bags. Taryn could tell the lady felt some type of way, so she took her things and headed for the man. As she got closer, she still didn't recognize him. She made up in her mind that she would just pay him back and leave.

"Hello sir, I'm not sure if I have this right, but did you just pay for my things?" The man was an older white gentleman dressed in a sleek suit. His hair was groomed and he looked to be in his mid-fifty's. He smiled at Taryn as she waited for a response.

"That is correct. I like for beautiful women to have beautiful things. I think you're beautiful and the green trench coat you tried on compliments your skin very well. As well as everything else you tried on."

"Thank you, but you didn't have to do that," Taryn said as she reached to pull some cash from her purse. A large hand covered hers, stopping her movement.

"You're money is no good here, pretty girl. You're welcome" He smiled and left the store. Taryn thought about going after him to give him money, but decided against it. She grabbed her things and proceeded to finish shopping. Hopefully there were some more men looking to fund her trip. She hit at least five more stores, racking up on cold weather clothing for her and Demoto. Neither of them had packed the appropriate clothing for this trip. She had bought so many things she could hardly carry it all. She knew there was no way she was going back to the casino. Demoto had texted and called her a few times to check in, so she told him she'd wait for him at the apartment.

By the time she got inside the apartment, she was beat. She didn't think she'd ever been this tired in her life. She showered, washed her hair, and braided it down. It had gotten dark and she was lying on the sofa watching television when her phone rang. It was Kia. They talked for a while about nothing before Taryn fell asleep. She didn't know how long she'd been asleep when she heard the door slam shut. She looked up to find Demoto standing there with a smile on his face.

"Honey, I'm home," he sang playfully as he leaned down and kissed her. He took a shower before joining her on the sofa.

"So how did spying go?"

"T, that bitch is paid! The only sad part is, she's so fucking sloppy. It's going to be a cakewalk getting to her. How was shopping?" he asked. Taryn told him all about the clothes she'd gotten them, and the man that had treated her in Burberry. He wasn't too fond of that, as she figured he wouldn't be. They talked for a little while longer before he picked her up and carried her to the bedroom. He snuggled up close to her and lay his head on her breasts. With her arms wrapped around his head, and his around her waist, they drifted off to dream land.

Chapter 16

It had been one week since they'd gotten to New York, and things were going great for Demoto. Taryn, on the other hand, was bored and ready to go. She'd done all the shopping she could and had grown tired of the cold. She and Demoto were getting ready to head out to a club that the son, Bailey Elmore, frequently attended. Demoto had pretended to meet him two days ago at a local meth house. Bailey immediately took a liking to the African meth head, or so he thought. He and Demoto had talked for a while before he invited him to the club. He'd even gone as far as to put him on the VIP list. Being that women were free all night anyway, Taryn didn't need any special treatment. If need be, Demoto would just pay for her to skip the line. They'd agreed to separate once they got inside. He didn't want any extra heat on Taryn, so he kept her at a distance. Demoto explained his rules to her over and over to make sure she understood. Once they got into the club, they wouldn't be together but she was to stay in his line of vision. Looking her over in the mirror almost made him change his mind about the club all together. She was dressed in a white two-piece ensemble with pink pumps. The cropped top showed her flat stomach while the satin pants hugged her shape. Her hair was French-braided into one long braid in the center of her head. The large gold hoops and gold watch was her only jewelry. Taryn-Lee Alvarez was bad, in every way. She had to be the most beautiful woman walking the planet, and all his. He walked up behind her and kissed her neck.

"You making my dick hard girl."

"Well what you want me to do about that?" she asked as she turned to face him. She loosened the buckle to his belt a little and stuck her hand down the front of his slacks. As she ran her hand over the tip of his throbbing wood, it jumped in her hand.

"It's yours baby, get it," his voice was husky and filled with lust. His accent seemed to get thicker when he was ready for sex. Demoto turned her on something terrible. She had been watching him get dressed all night. She pushed him to the wall as she squatted in front of him. After freeing him from his pants, she licked her lips. Demoto's dick was the most beautiful thing she'd ever seen. It was long, thick, and heavy. The pulsating veins protruding out the sides led straight to the perfectly ripe head. It was begging to be kissed, so she did. Once she'd kissed the head, she continued to lick up and down his shaft before taking as much of him in her mouth that could fit. The moan that escaped his lips made her panties wet. Her head bobbed up and down as she sucked him harder and faster. She could tell he was getting close because he started speaking in broken French. Whenever he was about to cum, he would moan to her in French.

"What are you saying?" she asked as she paused and looked up at him. He was looking down at her with eyes blazed with lust.

"I said you look so beautiful with my dick in your mouth. I love the way your lips circles it while you look up at me. Shit Taryn-Lee, you make me fall deeper in love every time I look at you" His hand was now resting on the side of her face. He had reached to touch her hair a few times, but she kept moving his hand. It had taken her too long to get her braid right; she was not about to let him mess it up. She smiled up at him as she thought about how she must look with his hard dick still hanging out of her mouth. She pulled it out, kissed the head, and went back to sucking. It had been another five minutes before she felt the slight tremble in his legs as he pulled out of her mouth and bust in his hand. He had wanted to see if she would swallow, but he didn't want to push her too far just yet. She was still new in the sexual area of life. When he returned, she was putting on more lipstick. He smiled at her as he fixed his pants. Once they were put back together, they left the building and headed for the club.

*****

"I told you this shit was going to be live brother!" Bailey shouted over the music.

"I know, I'm glad I came!" Demoto yelled back. He, Bailey, and a couple of other dudes Bailey had invited were all sitting in the VIP booth above the dance floor. They had bottles of Jack Daniels circulating, along with small pipes of meth. Demoto indulged in neither. He told Bailey he liked to get high in private, so he would pass for tonight. Surprisingly Bailey didn't give him a hard time about it. He was cool. He poured him a glass of Jack instead. Demoto pretended to be drinking it, but in reality he was watching Taryn. She was in the next VIP booth over with a couple of other girls. To everyone around them, they looked to be a group of friends out having drinks. Taryn had met the girls in line and invited them in her booth so she wouldn't have to sit alone. Every so often, she would look his way and smile before returning back to her new friends. Demoto winked at her and turned his attention back to Bailey.

"You should go talk to her brother," Bailey said into his ear.

"What? Talk to who?" Demoto asked. He didn't know he was that obvious.

"The black girl in the white. She keeps looking over here giving you the eye; I think she wants your cock man," Bailey laughed at his own joke. Demoto joined in on the laughter to play it off. *She's getting the cock alright,* he smirked to himself.

"I don't know man; I don't really want to get turned down."

"Dude fuck that! I'll go tell her for you" Demoto reached to stop Bailey, but he was already on his way. He watched as the girls in the booth with Taryn swooned over him. They obviously knew who he was, and figured he had money. Demoto watched as he leaned in Taryn's ear and rubbed his hand down her exposed back. Shortly after, he pointed in Demoto's direction with Taryn's eyes following his finger. She smiled and gave a light wave before nodding her head no. Bailey talked to her for a few more moments before returning to their booth.

"She said you're not her type," Bailey said as he slapped Demoto's shoulder in sympathy.

"Not her type? Well let's see about that, I love a challenge," he rubbed his hands together as he watched Taryn get up and head to the dance floor.

"Jason, I'll bet you one thousand dollars and a bag of meth that you can't get her number," Bailey said, calling Demoto by the fake name he'd given him.

"Bet." Demoto rose from his feet and headed towards Taryn. When he walked up behind her, she tried walking away but he pulled her back to him.

"So I'm not your type?" he whispered as he bit her ear. She giggled and shook her head no. Both of them were aware that Bailey was watching; Demoto looked up and winked at him. Bailey raised his drink, acknowledging the bet. Demoto smiled before turning his attention back to Taryn.

"Tell me what's your type so I can be that for you." Taryn was getting weaker by the second. Demoto was pressed up against her so tight she could barely move. She pretended to pull away a few times to make it believable, but stopped when her favorite reggae song came on. She wound her bottom all over him. She could feel the massive hard on he had for her.

"You see what you're doing? Rubbing your ass all over me and shit."

"I need you inside of me Moto," she moaned with her eyes closed. Her head was lying back against his shoulder as they danced. He reached up and choked her lightly, startling her.

"You riding my dick all night tonight, you hear me?" She nodded her head.

"I'm making you cum all over my face when we get back. I can't stop fantasizing about all the shit I want to do to your pretty ass." She clenched her muscles tighter, trying to compress the feeling he was giving her, but it was no help. She couldn't think straight with him on her like that, so she pulled away. She turned to face him before holding her hand out for his phone. When he handed it to her, she programmed her fake name and number in there before handing it back. After that, she walked away.

Demoto was so proud of her. She did an excellent job at pretending. He readjusted his hardness in his pants before heading back to his booth. Bailey was waiting there with a smile on his face. In one hand he had a stack of bills; in the other he had a small baggie of meth. Demoto smiled and freed him of both items. For the rest of the night, they partied and talked. Demoto was past ready to go, and had been for a while. Every time he looked up, there was a different man in Taryn's face. It was like she was a man magnet tonight or something. After looking her over again, Demoto realized that's exactly what she was. Men gravitated to pretty women, and Taryn was that effortlessly.

*****

"Keep it moving!" the bodyguard yelled as everyone exited the club. It was a quarter past three, and the city still had life. Taryn, on the other hand, was barely making it. She'd danced and enjoyed herself for half the night, the other half spent feening for Demoto. He and her had been secretly *sexting* since their dance, and she wanted him something terrible. He and Bailey had just walked out behind her and were deep in conversation.

She could barely hear them because of the drunk partiers around her. She didn't want to seem too suspicious, so she texted Demoto that she'd meet him at the hotel, but that was a quick no. Well, more like a hell no! With her body wrapped in her arms, she aimlessly walked down the sidewalk. She was about to lean against the VIP pole when one of the bodyguards walked up to her. He wrapped his arms around her body and leaned his chin on her shoulder.

"Let me help you stay warm." Taryn was about to pull away, but he smelled so good, not to mention he really was warming her up.

"Oh, so this is your way of helping me stay warm?"

"It sure it! Where are you from? It has to be the south; I haven't heard an accent so sexy in all my life." He leaned back against the pole, pulling her with him. Taryn was about to tell him Georgia when she remembered what Demoto said about telling their business.

"Thank you, but I don't know if you should be hugging all over me like this. My man might not like it."

"Sweetheart I'm not trying to be disrespectful or anything, but if your man is here with you, why are you by yourself?"

"He's talking business with a friend, that's him over there," Taryn motioned towards Demoto. The man was friendly and keeping her company, but that was it. He needed to know he didn't have a chance.

"Bailey Elmore is your man? No offense darling, but you can do better. That meth head doesn't deserve you."

"You don't know him like I do."

"You're right, I probably know him better. I did security for his pedophile ass father a few times. I'm sure you already know that though. If you've been around him, it's obvious; you're just his type. Do me a favor sweetheart–run as far away as you can. That family is poison. Listen, you seem like a nice girl so I'm only trying to help you out. I know you guys aren't serious because he's over there kissing that brunette right now. He'll be dead before the month is out; there's people looking for him. He's owes money to a lot of people. Please don't get too caught up with him; you're too beautiful to take a hit because of him."

He kissed her cheek before letting her go. She turned around and his face caught her off guard. He was gorgeous. He was tall and had muscles everywhere. The blonde hair on his head was cut short and pushed up in the front. His piercing blue eyes were making her hot. She reached out and grabbed his hand, pulling him back to her. Once he was close enough, she wrapped her arms around his waist and lay her head on his chest.

"I thought you were keeping me warm."

"What if Elmore comes over?"

"After what you just told me, I wouldn't care. How about I give you my number and we hang out while I'm in town?" She smiled up at him, enjoying the feel of his strong arms around her. For a brief moment she thought about what Demoto must be thinking, but she'd handle that later. He smiled and handed her a business card from his pocket before kissing her cheek again and leaving.

*****

Demoto was busy talking to Bailey about meeting up tomorrow when he looked up and saw Taryn. It was like a flash of heat came over his body. She was all hugged up with some white dude, like he wasn't even there. He didn't know where this had come from, because one minute she was alone and the next she was holding on to him. He focused on his conversation with Bailey trying to calm his nerves, but it wasn't helping. The vein in his jaw jumped as he clenched and unclenched his fist. *Who the fuck does she think I am?* His heart was beating so fast he could hear it. He was just about to go over there and hem her ass up when he noticed the man had walked away.

"You okay brother?" Bailey asked as he looked in Taryn's direction. "Oooh, you want to say goodnight to the black beauty? I feel you my man, go ahead. I'll just call you tomorrow."

"Shit, you caught me man! I'm going to see if she wants to go home with me! I'll catch you tomorrow," Demoto said as he shook Bailey's hand and walked away. On his way over, he noticed Taryn reach out to the man again. He stopped in his tracks. He had to go calm down before he caused a scene and blew his cover. He paced for a few seconds before he looked back in her direction.

This time she was alone again, and standing on the curb. He made his way towards her.

"Why the fuck you was all over that nigga?" She turned around and looked at him like he was crazy. Before she spoke she held her hand up in face.

"Demoto chill. It's not what you think."

"It looked like you were all hugged up with that fucking security guard to me. That's not what I think?"

"Listen Demoto, I said calm your ass down." She turned and headed towards their building. The club they'd attended was right down the street from their hotel . He walked behind her furiously. *She acted like she got some room to have a fucking attitude.* He watched the way her hips swayed and hated that it was affecting him. Her ass in those white pants had his joint brick hard. As he stuck his hands in his pocket, he sped up so he could catch up with her. They walked side by side in the freezing cold until they reached their building. It was quiet and warm as they boarded the elevator. Taryn stood in the corner with her arms folded across her chest. She was pissed, and it was funny to him. He held out his hand to her, and she slapped it away. He chuckled lightly as the doors opened, and in walked three ladies. They looked to be in their late fifty's. *What they doing out this late?* Demoto wondered as he walked around them and stood in front of Taryn. Even with her heels on, he towered over her. After placing both hands on the wall behind her head, he kissed the tip of her nose.

"Ne pas être en colère contre moi BELLE. (Don't be mad at me beautiful)," he kissed her eyes before leaning down some more to kiss her lips. She stood still trying to hold on to her attitude. "Je suis désolé. (I'm sorry)."

"Move Jason," Taryn said. He smiled hearing his fake name. Instead of moving, he got closer. He pressed his body hard against hers and ran his hands down her back and onto her butt. When he kissed her, a small moan escaped her lips. He knew she wouldn't stay mad long. As much as he hated to, he pulled away and looked at her. She looked back at him with need. Demoto would never get tired of being in her presence. She was the best thing to ever happen to him, and he hadn't even known he was looking for her. The elevator dinged and the ladies got off. Well, two of them did; the last one touched Demoto's back so he would turn around.

"You two look lovely together."

"Thank you ma'am," he smiled as the door closed behind her. With Taryn's hand in his they waited until they got to their floor. Once in their apartment, Taryn began to undress for the shower. She wasn't in there a good five minutes before Demoto came in behind her.

"I don't like you talking to other men."

"Well baby, that's a fact of life; it was nothing. When I talk to anybody other than you, believe me it's friendly. Nobody makes me feel the way you do."

"I can't tell! He was all over your ass and shit, then when he let you go you went back to him." Demoto didn't like sounding jealous or possessive, but when it came to Taryn he couldn't help it. Taryn smiled as she pulled his naked body to hers. She licked the tribal tattoo that covered his upper body until she stopped at his neck, where she left a kiss. Demoto being jealous was the cutest thing ever to her. A man as fine as him wanted her. She felt so exhilarated. Demoto Youngblood was all hers.

"It was for you. He meant nothing. Don't be jealous baby, there's not a man on this planet that could take your place." Taryn placed his hand at her opening. He instantly took the lead and played in her wetness. The ragged breath escaping her mouth escalated the faster he moved his fingers. She looked into his green eyes as his free hand roamed her body. The water cascaded over them as he pulled away turned her around. She leaned against the wall as he entered her from behind. She screamed once it was all the way in. The shower bar was in the perfect place for her to keep her balance. He was sliding in and out of her when her head jerked back lightly. He had a hand full of her hair, and had pulled her head back. His mouth was inches away from her ear as he spoke sensual things in his deep voice.

"You still need me inside you?" he asked, referring to what she'd told him at the club earlier. She nodded her head the best she could with her hair still wrapped in his hand.

"You're fucking beautiful! Seeing you with other men fucks me up." He had sped up his pace now and was slamming into her. She was sure the people on both sides of them could hear her. She was moaning and screaming so loud. Demoto was so big and vigorous when it came to sex. The pain was a welcomed one.

"You're hurting me Moto."

"Good! Tomorrow it'll remind you how my dick felt inside you." When Taryn heard that, she got weak.

"Ah shit Moto! Hurt me more baby."

Demoto let out a small laugh laced with lust. He slapped her butt and pulled out of her. As soon as she turned around, he sat down and pulled her onto his lap. She slid down on him and his head fell backwards against the shower wall. He moaned and bit her shoulder lightly. She rode him so good he could barely talk. She stared into his green eyes. She'd never love another person the way she loved him. The pleasure was evident on his face as he bit his bottom lip.

"You love me baby girl?"

"Always."

She rode him faster until they both climaxed. She was so tired she fell forward and lay her head on his shoulder. Neither of them bothered to separate from the other. Demoto wrapped his arms around her body and held her. He'd never known a happiness so profound until he met Taryn. It was unexpected, and nothing he had been looking for. Now he couldn't imagine not having it. He had to be her one. He wanted to be the one person she had to see every day, the one she missed, the one she trusted–he wanted to always be the one person she needed. She made him whole; she made him feel things he'd never known were possible. Before he saw her in the park that night, he couldn't see himself being with just one woman. Just the thought seemed boring to him back then. Now he never wanted to see a day that didn't include Taryn. He looked down, and she had fallen asleep. He kissed her forehead before turning off the water and taking her to bed. He dried her off and was about to slide his shirt over her head when she woke up. She smiled and drifted right back to sleep. *The D got my baby gone.*

*****

As the shag rug beneath her feet warmed her toes, the fire lit in front of her warmed her hands. She'd just gotten to Bailey's house with Demoto and she was nervous as hell. She didn't want to slip up and say the wrong things, so she sat quietly. As far as Bailey knew, this was her and Demoto's first time seeing one another outside of the club. Demoto had made up some lie about his place being a mess, so Bailey offered his place for them to chill.

Demoto had been with Bailey nonstop for the last two weeks, and Taryn busied herself with school and shopping. Her fall classes had just started last week, and she was loving college already. She'd told Demoto everything the security guard had told her, so now he was in overdrive. He wanted to handle the family before someone else had the time to. It was even better, because now he would have someone else to take the fall for the murders. Hearing that other people were after them as well gave him the extra push he needed. He'd been strategizing his plan every free minute he had. Like today, the family was having a party and Bailey had invited Demoto and told him to bring Taryn. He said it was a small gathering for his father's birthday and there would be a lot of people they needed to meet. Bailey turned out not to be a hard person to crack. He was friendly and whenever he was high, he got loose lips. He'd just about told everything except the password to his computer. She was casually dressed in a pair of jeans and a sweater. Her hair was flat ironed straight today with a crème knit hat on her head. The high-heeled boots she'd worn matched perfectly with her Burberry coat. She was cute and would fit right in with the rich family. Today her name was Jessica, and she was in New York doing an internship. She was a student at USC in California, and was only in the city for a few weeks. Her and Demoto had gone over her story a thousand times before she left the apartment. He left first, and she would join an hour or two later. That was over three hours ago, and she was just getting there. Bailey's sister Emily had answered the door and from the looks of it, didn't care much for her. She had no idea why being that they had just met, but that was not her concern. After Emily pointed towards the living room without bothering to open her mouth, Taryn took a seat and waited for Demoto to come. She had been sitting there for five minutes or so before Bailey came in and greeted her.

"Hello pretty lady," he beamed.

"Hello, Bailey right?" He took her outstretched hand and kissed it.

"That would be me. Jason is in the great room with my mother, follow me and I'll take you to him." She followed Bailey down a large hallway and down some stairs until they reached an extravagant living room. It was decorated in pale gray and pink colors. The furniture was beautiful, and the woman Demoto was talking to looked even better. Mrs. Elmore was a pretty lady with long blonde hair. She smiled at Taryn, but she could still see the sadness behind her smile. She came around the counter and grabbed her into a hug.

"Hello dear, how are you? I hear you're a friend of Jason's?"

"Yes ma'am, I'm fine. You are absolutely stunning, Mrs. Elmore."

"Well thank you sweetie, you are a beautiful young lady as well. You compliment my Jason very well." Taryn smiled and looked at Demoto. He was smiling like he had won the lottery. The way he looked at her made her feel special. He wore a proud expression; like this was his real family she was meeting. She knew he had been spending a lot of time around them these last couple of weeks, but she had no idea they'd taken a liking to him so fast. Then again she could understand, there wasn't anything about Demoto for a person not to love.

"She's not that great," Emily said from the door. She had to have just walked in, because she wasn't there a minute ago. Taryn turned her head towards Emily and smiled.

"And you are?"

"Although it isn't any of your business, I'm Emily Elmore. Please don't bother telling me who you are, because in my eyes all you are is unwelcomed," she rolled her eyes and grabbed some water from the fridge. Taryn was shocked by her attitude, but dismissed it. She'd hate to mess up what Demoto had going on for beating the shit out of Emily. She looked at Demoto and caught the pleading look in his eyes before refocusing on Emily.

"It's a good thing I'm not here to see you then, isn't it?" Emily had opened her mouth, but was cut off by Bailey.

"Knock it off Em!" She walked past and slammed her bottle of water on the counter so hard it splashed on Taryn. Before Taryn could respond, she was gone. Mrs. Elmore tried to apologize on her daughter's behalf, but there was no need. Taryn didn't care; that would just make killing her easier when the time came. Bailey had just shown her to the restroom to dry her pants off when she heard the door open. The bathroom was big and favored Jeremiah's the way it was made. The part she was in with the toilet and sink was locked, so she wasn't worried about who it was. In the back of her mind, she figured it was Demoto anyway. When she came out, she got the surprise of her life.

"Nice to see you again darling."

"It is. How are you?"

"Better now. Can I have a hug?"

Taryn thought about it for a minute; what could it hurt? She walked into his open arms and melted in his tight embrace. His cologne was mesmerizing. He held her tight, but let her go faster than she'd hoped. He smiled at her with those sexy blue eyes.

"I guess you didn't take my advice."

"Actually I did. I'm here on business," she gave the half-truth. "I'm no longer seeing Bailey, but I had to attend this function for my internship."

"That's great news, beautiful. Just stay clear of him and you should be fine. I'll see you later," he kissed her cheek and left the bathroom. She stood there for a minute trying to regain her composure before joining the party. Once she finally got herself together, she opened the door and bumped into a hard chest, a chest she was familiar with, a chest that held her head perfectly; she looked up into Demoto's angry green eyes. He pushed her backwards and back into the bathroom before locking the door behind them. He didn't say anything; instead, he snatched at her belt until he was able to get her pants unbuttoned. He couldn't get them off because she still had her boots on, so he pulled them down as far as they would go before ripping her panties off. Taryn didn't know what he had going on, but she was scared to say anything. She just let him have his way with her. She grabbed the side of the counter to steady herself as he sat her on it. He pushed his own pants down in a rush and out popped his already hard pole. It was thick and throbbing. He pulled her to the edge of the counter roughly and entered her. He sucked on her neck to muffle his moans. Her warmth was surrounding him, pulling him deeper with each stroke. She had her arms wrapped tightly around his neck, with her hands running through his dread locs. She tried to pull his head back to look in his eyes, but he wouldn't let her. Every time she would do it, he would turn his head or move her hand. It wasn't until he spoke that she knew why he wouldn't look at her.

"I saw him in here with you T," his voice was a low whisper. Taryn almost hadn't heard him.

"Nothing happened."

"You're mine. Why was he here?" Demoto's voice broke as he tried to finish his sentence. Taryn squeezed him tighter in her arms before trying once more to look at his face. This time he let her. His eyes were red and wet with tears. The scowl on his face displayed the anger in his heart. His breathing was rough and hard as he continued to slide in and out of her. Taryn didn't know he was that jealous. She had no idea Demoto had even saw the security guard leave. She hated that she'd caused him to feel this way. He looked at her; his eyes were no longer angry, they looked scared almost.

"I'll kill him," he said as his eyes turned from a light green to a darker one. His face zoned out for a minute until Taryn kissed his mouth. She had to kiss him a few times before he refocused on her. She hugged and kissed him as he began to slam roughly into her. He sucked on her neck, but she could hear the moans leaving his lips. They came more frequent when she started grinding back against him. Before long, she felt moisture on her neck. He was crying. It was getting harder to distinguish between his sniffles and his moans. She knew Demoto loved her, but she didn't know it was like this. Hearing him cry brought out her own tears. A few slid down her face as he exploded inside of her. He didn't move right away; he just stood there with his head on her shoulder. A few seconds later, he pulled away and fixed his clothes before grabbing a washcloth from the cabinet and washing her off. He then helped her fix her clothing and leaned on the wall. They watched each other, neither saying anything.

"I was drying my clothes off and he came in here. Nothing happened, he just warned me to stay away from this family. I promise. I know how it must look, but nothing happened." Demoto still said nothing; he just looked. She walked to him and grabbed his hands in hers. His breathing was still ragged from crying as he tried to get himself together. His eyes looked withdrawn and weary.

"I fucking love you T! Damn I love you so much! When I saw him walk out of here, I almost went crazy. I'm sorry." His eyes were watering again. He didn't know what had come over him but when he saw the man leave the same restroom he knew Taryn was in, his mind went blank. He kept envisioning her moaning beneath another man, and it made him livid. He saw her eyes closed tight from pleasure given by someone else, and he wanted to punch the wall. As he looked at her now, he knew she would never do that to him. Her eyes told him so. He'd heard it out of her mouth a million times before, but she showed him on a daily basis. He had to get a grip when it came to her; she could easily be the death of him.

"T just know you could end me. You could break my heart forever, okay?" She nodded as water dripped nonstop from her eyes. After a few minutes, her head took a different direction and started shaking from side to side. She opened her mouth to speak, but his lips on hers silenced her. He knew she was trying to tell him she would never do that, but he already knew. He had gotten caught up in the moment and let his feelings overtake his logical thinking. They stayed in the restroom for another ten minutes before rejoining the party. The living room was packed with people now. They found their way to the back room looking for Bailey. When they did, he had a pretty blonde girl sitting on his lap; she looked high. Demoto sat down next to them while Taryn excused herself to get a bottle of water.

She gotten stopped a

number of times to talk to the people there. When she finally reached the kitchen, Mrs. Elmore was in there; she looked sad. She smiled when she saw Taryn before excusing herself. Taryn felt bad for the woman; she wanted to sit and talk to her. That was a bad idea though, because it would only make it harder when the time came to end their lives. She grabbed her water and wandered around the house, taking in its beauty. Once she reached the great room, there was a man speaking and everyone was listening. When she saw him, she felt like she was having déjà vu. It was the same man from the Burberry store. They caught eyes and he winked. She left the room so fast she didn't even realize she was practically running. Once she slowed down enough, she went to sit in the room she'd been sitting in when she first got there. She wasn't there a good five minutes before she felt someone's presence. When she turned, it was the man from the Burberry store.

"Don't run, beautiful girl."

"I'm not. I just needed a minute to myself" *What the fuck is going on?* she wondered. *This must be sneak up on Taryn day or something.* This was the second time in one day she'd gotten cornered by a man.

"I didn't know you were a friend of my son."

"Yes sir, I met him at a club a little while ago."

"Pity. I wanted you for myself," he smiled before touching the side of her face. She leaned away from his touch, but his hand followed. He leaned forward and smelled her hair as he rubbed her face. She was about to move his hand, but she didn't have to. There was the

256

sound of someone clearing their throat by the door. There stood Emily. Mr. Elmore saw Emily, but acted as if it was nothing. He smiled at Taryn again before kissing her hand and leaving. He didn't even acknowledge Emily's presence as he exited. She stood in the doorway shooting daggers at Taryn with her eyes.

"Have some class, you black bitch. My mother is here; you could at least have enough respect to not do it where she could catch you!"

"Emily listen to me, and listen to me good sweetheart. You don't know me. I advise you to stay the fuck out my face before I beat that little ass."

"Whatever you whore. You are just his type! I've never known what he sees in pussy the same age as his fucking daughter. He loves your kind; the least he could do is cheat with someone worth his time. You black girls never want anything but money." Taryn closed the distance between them

"I wouldn't want your daddy on his best day. The only thing his old ass could do was give me his money, because I wouldn't do shit with that old ass dick except pump it with fucking Viagra. I have my own money baby, I don't need his! What I do need is for you to stay the fuck out my way before I give you what the fuck you're asking for." Emily stood stunned.

"I thought you were here for my father."

"No! I'm here with Bailey's friend Jason. You would have known that if you would have taken a minute to ask." The look on Emily's face was priceless. She apologized profusely before Taryn forgave her.

"It's cool, this black girl has money," they laughed together before walking away. The rest of the party went pretty smooth. They hung out and drank until it grew late. Bailey and his friends were sitting around getting high while Taryn and Emily sat in her room talking. It was sad, because Emily obviously had no friends. She opened up and told Taryn everything about herself, even that she worked for Double O. Taryn soaked in as much as she could to relay to Demoto. The more she listened, the worse she felt. This family was in shambles in one hundred different ways. Demoto would be doing them all a favor by ending their lives.

Chapter 17

It had been one month, and Taryn and Demoto were finally where they needed to be with the family. They could end it now, or they could get a little closer. Demoto could tell Taryn was ready to go home, but was being a good trooper for him. After she'd told him about the father and his infatuation with young black girls, he knew he tried to keep her away from the house. Of course, she refused and continued to hang out with Emily. He didn't stop her from doing that because Emily was harmless; Taryn could snap her into two if need be. The only thing that was causing him friction was finding the right time. He'd gotten a copy of everything on Bailey's computer and forwarded to Bradley, along with his backup hard drives. Emily had shown Taryn the way she made everything work with Double O's money.

258

Demoto shook his head at how naïve Emily was. She hadn't know Taryn long, but when she heard Taryn's lie about being a student and interning there in New York, she wanted to show off. Taryn picked up on everything instantly; it was so easy. Demoto was beyond proud of her and the way she was handling things. Today Mrs. Elmore had an appointment with her therapist, and Demoto was staked out across the street watching her. He had been sitting in his rental car for the last hour and a half when he spotted her coming out of the building. She looked like she'd been crying as she headed to her car. He followed her to the house and waited a little while before getting out. Once she was in the house, he waited another thirty minutes before knocking on the door. He already knew she would be alone; that's why he'd waited until today. She opened the door and forced a smile.

"Hello Jason, how are you sweetheart? Come on in." He followed her into the kitchen. She had various vegetables on the counter, obviously preparing dinner. He took a seat on the stool when she told him Bailey wasn't home and invited him to wait for him. They talked about nothing for a little while before she asked him about his meth habit. Demoto fabricated everything he could think of while she listened intently. Before long, she pulled out her wine bottle and had just about drank the whole thing. *These people have problems.* Demoto spent another hour there with her before he left. He'd had enough for the day. He was tired of the Elmores; all he wanted to do was spend time with Taryn. He'd called her and she was on her way back from the mall with Emily. She was going to meet him at their apartment. When he got there, she was already there and putting away the clothes she'd just bought.

"Boy you know you fine!" she said as soon as he entered the room. He blushed, causing his brown skin to turn red. "Come give me a kiss. I missed you today."

Demoto kissed her intimately. His hands were all over her body while hers were in his hair. She broke their kiss with a smile before going back to folding her new clothes.

"Your ass been spending money like crazy," he smiled.

"I know, I can't help it. You said I could, don't be getting amnesia now." He lay across the bed and watched her.

"I'm not. You deserve it; buy whatever you want. Let's go out on a date tonight. I'm so tired of spending all my time with these people. I just want to be with you today." This made Taryn happy. She enjoyed Emily and Mrs. Elmore, but she too missed it just being them two. She stopped folding clothes and climbed on top of him. She sat on his lap and looked down at his beautiful face. Never in a million years would she have thought she would love so deeply. Her whole life was spent trying not to grow too attached, and the moment she met him, that went out of the window. His tattoo-filled chest and neck was so sexy. His blonde dreads lay around his brown face as his green eyes sparkled up at her. Taryn was so in love with this man.

*****

That night they decided to go out to eat and see a movie. Taryn had washed and re-twisted his hair earlier, then styled it in two French braids. Her hair was still straight, so she added a few curls to the end and did her makeup. She'd only been on a real date twice, both times with Jeremiah. They walked down the windy streets of New York hand in hand. They looked around at all the different buildings and cars that were different from the things they were used to back home. When they finally reached the restaurant, they had a ten minute wait. Taryn sat as close as she could to Demoto without sitting on his lap. When she looked at him, his eyes were circulating around the building. Anytime they went anywhere, he always scoped the place out first. She assumed it was something he was taught while working for Double O.

"I sure wish my date was paying attention to me." He looked down at her and smiled.

"I am paying attention to you. I just got to make sure everything is good first. You enjoying our trip?"

"Yes and no. Yes because I'm here with you, but no because the reason we're here is getting harder."

"This is exactly why I didn't want you to help. I knew you'd get too attached." He looked at her and could tell she felt bad about they Elmore's family fate, but oh well. This was his job; he never got in too deep to handle his business.

"I just feel so sorry for them, Moto. Emily and Mrs. Elmore are really nice. I like them." Demoto shook his head; bringing her had been a bad idea. The best thing he could do was not have her around when the time came.

They waited in the front for another twenty minutes before being taken to their seats.

"Moto, tell me about Cameroon."

"Tell you what?"

"Your home, your family, anything. I just want to know about you. You never told me why you aren't there anymore. You've also never told me about your parents," His attitude was dry and his entire demeanor began to change. He looked away and watched the cars driving up the street. The faraway look in his eyes told her that this was a sensitive subject.

"It's okay; we don't have to talk about it. How much longer do you think we'll be here? I miss my daddy and Kia."

"It's fine baby girl, we can talk about it. I was just trying to find a place to start. Cameroon is such a long story, so I'll give you the short version. My parents are very wealthy people. I lived there up until I was eighteen before my father sent Adisa and I here. We didn't want to come at first, but he said it was for our safety. He'd arranged English tutors, school, work, and a place to live. His long time buddy offered his assistance, and that's how I became the person I am today." Taryn could tell there was more to the story, so she waited for more. He looked like he was done talking until he looked in at her face. She wasn't settling for just that. He let out a long sigh before continuing.

"My family is royal, Taryn. We're wealthy and well known around Africa. Life was good until my father died." That made Taryn hate she'd asked. "I'm a prince, Taryn." Her eyes looked lost for a moment.

"That's so cool! Why would you leave?"

"I'm not a good prince. My family is in charge of the XX-16. It's an army of killers. They are used to keep the people of Cameroon in order. One of the generals was Rasheed Cayman. The man I work for now. He and my father were best friends before shit went left. For a while, the city was under attack and people were dying left and right. My father wanted us gone immediately, so he set it all up. Adisa and I were both trained and fierce; he knew we'd be okay here. Neither of us wanted to leave him, but he insisted. Growing up, he'd taught us everything. He was always so patient with us; no matter what it was, he made sure we knew about it. The day after we arrived here, we got word from Cayman that he'd been killed. It almost tore me apart. I didn't want to do anything but go back to Cameroon and make any and everybody bleed, but I couldn't. He'd left strict orders with Cayman that we were not to return. He wanted us to have a life outside of murder, and that still didn't happen." Demoto drank some of his water as he ran his hand over his head. He hadn't talked about Cameroon to anyone. Taryn was the first person to ever know his past. Talking about it made him too emotional. It put him in a difficult state of mind, one he didn't know how to handle. He'd been a part of things you could only read about in books or watch on TV. It terrorized him to think about the person he used to be.

"Did you ever find out who killed your father?" He looked at Taryn for a long while. He watched as she waivered beneath his icy gaze. He could tell she was rethinking being so nosey, so he tried to redirect his energy. After taking another sip of water, he finally nodded his head yes.

"My mother."

"Your what? Are you serious?"

"Yes. She knew he was fighting to end the murderous reign she had, and she had him killed. They cut his head off and burned his body in the middle of the street. She treated him like he wasn't shit, even in death. If I ever get my hands on her again, she's dead." Demoto thought maybe he should have spared her the last detail but hey, she asked. He observed her face looking for a reaction, but it was blank. She didn't have one ounce of emotion on her face. It was straight and void of any feeling. Finally, after a good five minutes she made eye contact. Her eyes were glossy, but no water fell. He immediately got up and sat on the other side of the booth with her. He grabbed her hand and held it as he pulled her face towards him. She kissed him the moment they locked eyes. Her kiss was filled with emotion. She was kissing him so hard her upper body was practically sprawled across his. Obviously remembering where they were, she leaned back and crossed her hands nervously in her lap.

"You okay T?"

"Yeah, I just feel bad. Here I am laying all my problems on you, and you have your own." Demoto pulled her into him so that her head was lying on his shoulder.

"Don't feel bad bae, that's my job. I'm your man; I'm supposed to take on your problems. What do you think I'm here for? Everything that's stressing you, give that shit to me! I'm here to make life easy for you girl. In my arms is where you should find peace. Don't worry about me and the shit I have going on, I can handle that. Trust me to be your man."

Taryn squeezed Demoto's hand tighter as she let tears stream down her face. She didn't understand how she'd gotten lucky enough to find him. Demoto Youngblood was the epitome of fortitude and love. There was no one in the world like him. Taryn hadn't known this side of him at first; he was so playful and happy that she would have never guessed. She was consumed by her thoughts when she felt his hand wiping her face.

"I wish your crybaby ass would stop all this crying, you're embarrassing me."

"Shut up!'" Taryn laughed as she wiped her face. The rest of their dinner went great. They didn't talk anymore about each other's past. Not that there was much to hers. When they were done, they left hand in hand headed for the movies. They were sitting in the theater watching The Equalizer when she felt Demoto's phone vibrating. He checked his message and noticed he had to go. Taryn wanted to finish the movie, but she didn't put up a fight. Once they were back at their apartment, Demoto changed clothes and grabbed his backpack. He was dressed in all black, including his jacket. He instructed Taryn to do the same. Once they were dressed, they headed to the office of Mr. Elmore. The text had told him that it was time to wrap everything up. He knew from past experiences that if he got a text like this, then the time was running short. His opportunities would be gone soon. The last time he'd gotten a text like that on a job, his target was about to be captured by another family he owed. He didn't know what it was Mr. Elmore had up his sleeve, but he was about to find out.

*****

"I'm tired of your bitching Helen!" Mr. Elmore shouted. He was standing next to the window in his office while his wife sat in a chair in the corner. Her head was down and you could hear her sniffling.

"I just don't understand why you treat me like this. I'm depressed because of you! If you would just respect our marriage and leave these young girls alone, things would be fine," she continued to cry as he looked on in disdain.

"Helen, I do it because you bore me! We never do anything; you're always at the fucking shrink!"

"So you running away to The Dominican Republic with this little girl is your way of escaping?"

So that's why it's time to wrap it up? Demoto thought to himself. He and Taryn had been hiding in his secretary's office for the past twenty minutes. Taryn was sitting beneath her desk in the corner while he hid behind the wall. He wanted to be close enough to not only peek into the room, but to hear as well. His plan was to sneak in and kill them both while Taryn waited. He knew that was risky because she might see or hear something she didn't want to, but she hadn't wanted him to come alone.

266

He listened a little while longer as he watched Mr. Elmore pack up his things.

"So what do you plan on doing about Double O?" Mrs. Elmore whispered.

"Fuck Double O! I have enough money saved, I'll be fine and you and our indolent children will be fine as well." This drew more sobs from her. Demoto had grown tired of watching him verbally abuse the lady. She had been sweet to him from day one. After checking to make sure he had the large syringe, he motioned for Taryn to stay put before pushing the door open. The look on their faces was one of shock, then horror. Mr. Elmore tried to make a dash for his desk, but was stopped by Demoto's voice.

"Don't even bother, it's not there." Demoto had disarmed the entire family a couple of days ago. He knew his time was winding down and had to make a move soon. He wanted to be prepared when it came. The gun the man was reaching for was long gone.

"Who sent you?" Mr. Elmore scoffed.

"A friend." Mrs. Elmore looked at Demoto with calm eyes, not a hint of fear in them.

"Kill me first please. I've grown very tired of this life, I'm ready," she began walking towards Demoto, but he stepped back and ordered her to sit back down. She was going to die, but he wasn't the one that was going to kill her. He looked over at her husband and nodded his head in her direction. He was going to make him do it. Not only had he caused her all the pain, but Demoto needed this to look like a set up.

"If you want us dead, you'll have to do it yourself! I knew it was something about you when I first saw you. I've never seen a meth addict look as healthy as you! Who do you work for?" Mr. Elmore asked again.

"Sir, get your ass over here and stick this needle into your wife's neck."

"I will not!" he yelled. Demoto shook his head because he'd hoped this would have gone smoother. He was tired and not in the mood for disobedience, so he'd just do it himself. He walked to where she sat on the couch and sat down. She willingly laid back on the small sofa and turned her head to the side. Demoto hated to do this; he really liked her. He stared for a moment before injecting her with the poison. His heart was began beating faster as he watched her eyes start to close. He found comfort in knowing this was what she wanted. Her death would be slow with minimal pain. He'd decided to use this lethal injection drugs for her because she didn't deserve anything harsh. Her husband, on the other handv was about to get it. Demoto rose to his feet and walked towards the coward hovered down in the corner. He had lost his nerve quickly and was now shivering like a bitch. Demoto smiled as he made him stand up.

"Give me everything you've got connecting you with Double O. And don't bullshit me!" His eyes lit up like saucers. Realizing Double O was behind his death was unarming. He'd done nothing but good by them, for this in return. Sure he'd grown tired of his association with them over the years, but he'd still held his end of the bargain. He sat at his computer and unlocked the safe beneath it. Inside were folders and a small crown royal bag filled with thumb drives.

"This is everything."

Demoto surveyed the things quickly before pulling his hunting knife out. He slit his neck in one swift motion and he fell face forward on the desk. Once he'd gathered everything he needed and placed it in the backpack, he checked both of their pulses. They were both dead, and his work was halfway done. Looking over the office, he made sure everything was in place before leaving.

*****

Demoto zipped through traffic as he drove down the street. He was headed to finish the rest of the family, but he had one more stop to make. He looked over at Taryn and could tell she was scared, but she said nothing. When he finally stopped, they were back in front of their apartment. Taryn turned to look at him.

"What are we doing here? I thought tonight was the night?"

"It is, but you're not going. I want you to stay here."

"What? No! I want to go with you Moto!"

"No T, stay here. I need you to stay. Once everything is complete, we can't stay any longer. This is a well-known family and the police are going to be coming. You have to stay here and pack all of our things. Once everything is packed, book our tickets and wait for me to get back. Find the first flight back to Atlanta."

Taryn stared at Demoto before agreeing. She wanted to put up a fight, but what he said made sense. It took her a moment to say yes because she wanted to be with him. If something went wrong, he would need someone there to help.

"What if you need my help?" He chuckled lightly before kissing her lips.

"Thank you baby, but I got it. I'll be back. Just go do what I told you, I need you to handle this for me bae." With that, Taryn nodded and hopped out of the car. She was so scared because all night, things hadn't seemed right. Everything just felt wrong, a wrong she couldn't explain. When she got to the room, she began packing their things. She tossed their clothes in whatever suitcase was open. They'd fix it once they got home. She was so nervous she could barely hold it together. She knew this night would come and she thought she was ready, but obviously wasn't. To get her nerves in check, she kneeled on the side of the bed and began to pray. She prayed for what seemed like hours until she heard her phone ringing. It was Demoto. When she answered, she expected to hear his voice but she didn't; she heard Bailey's.

"Just thought you should know, your little sweetheart is dead bitch," he laughed the most hideous laugh she'd ever heard before the line went clicked. She dialed his number back and Bailey answered again.

"He's fucking dead! I'm feeding his ass to my fucking dogs. You two thought we were stupid? Hell no! We used his ass to get rid of our fucking parents. I've known who you both were all along. We didn't make it this far being that naïve." Taryn shrieked at the news. She began crying and screaming at him to let her speak to Demoto, but all he did was laugh and hang up. She was about to throw her phone against the wall when it beeped with a text. She had picture mail from Demoto. She was scared to open it, but she had to know the truth. Her heart wasn't prepared for what she saw. It was a picture of Demoto's head. It had a hole the size of a gold ball in the side. The blonde dreads she'd grown to love was painted red with blood and brain matter. His eyes were open and fixed in a daze. It looked like he was looking at her through the picture. In that instant, her world was over. She threw the phone at the wall and let out one of the most gut wrenching screams known to man. The pain in her chest was excruciating. It was like she could feel her heart shattering into pieces. She yelled and screamed so loud she was sure the people down the street could hear her. Falling backwards onto the floor, she kicked and screamed like a child. The feeling she had was indescribable. She was so distraught she didn't know what to do with herself. She began to pull at her hair, snatching it until her head hurt. She carried on like this for another hour or two before her phone started to ring again. She was scared to look at it thinking it may be Bailey again, but she noticed it was Jacko's ringtone. She was so weak she didn't even bother to say hello after answering it.

"Yo T, where's Moto?" he asked in a breathless plea.

"Dead." Hearing the words from her mouth started her tantrum back up. She began crying all over again. She could hear Jacko yelling obscenities in the background.

"I just got a picture of him from his phone. Who did this shit?" Jacko asked, but Taryn was unable to talk. "Taryn, listen baby girl, give me the address where you're staying. I'm going to send someone over there to get you." Taryn pulled herself together enough to give Jacko the address before falling into a heap on the floor. She lay there and cried herself to sleep until she heard the front door slam. She figured it was probably Bailey coming for her, but she didn't move. Hopefully he'd blow her head off, and she could be with Demoto again. To her dismay, it wasn't him. It was the security guard from the club. This confused her.

"What are you doing here?" she asked.

"Listen Taryn-Lee, I work for Double O. Jacko had Bradley Marks send me over. I've been working on this family for the last few months. I was here to help just in case you guys needed it. I was on strict orders not to let you two know who I was because I do a lot of undercover work. I came as soon as they told me what happened with your friend. I have to get you out of here and on a plane back home. Things are about to get bad up here."

He kneeled down to pick her up, and she deflated into his arms. He carried her into the bathroom and turned the shower on. After undressing her, he bathed her and washed her hair the best he could. She stood limp in his arms the entire time. When he'd finished, he helped her get dressed before loading all of their things in the back of his truck. With everything packed, he carried her down the stairs and sat her in the front seat. He had to lock her seatbelt for her because she wouldn't move. He drove two hours outside of the city and pulled up to a private airstrip. There was a private plane waiting there. She was slumped down in the seat when her door came open, and Kia rushed to her. Taryn looked utterly distraught. Kia hugged her friend tight as she could. Her and Jacko had flown up the moment they got the news. Double O had charted them a private flight there and back to pick up Taryn and Demoto. Nobody told Taryn, but they were bringing Demoto back as well. The moment Cayman got the picture of Demoto's head, he sent another team in to finish the job. They'd killed both Emily and Bailey. After retrieving Demoto's body, they packed it for the plane ride and brought it to the airstrip. Taryn was the last to arrive.

"Taryn come on sis, we have to go," Kia pulled the hair wrap from Taryn's head and put her hair into a better ponytail. When she realized Taryn wasn't moving, she called for the security guard. He lifted Taryn with no problem and placed her in her seat on the plane. It took another ten minutes to get everything ready for the flight before it took off.

Chapter 18

It had been a week, and Taryn felt like dying. The void in her life was indescribable. It was ten o' clock in the morning, and Taryn's whole world felt dark. The sun was shining, but all she saw was grey. The light in her life was permanently dimmed. She'd never see another happy day as long as she lived. The brightness of her life was put out the day Demoto died. She'd been in her room sulking since she'd gotten home. She hadn't eaten or bathed all week. Sleep was a thing of the past. Every time she closed her eyes, she would see the picture of him with that hole in his head. She hated Bailey for ruining her life. She hated him for putting that image in her head. She hated him for taking her one true love. She just hated him! Every time she took a breath, she was reminded of him. Since he'd killed Demoto, breathing had become a task. It actually took effort to take a breath. She was busy wiping more tears when she heard Kia come in her room. She flipped the lights on and snatched the covers away.

"Taryn, it's time to get up sis. The funeral is in another hour and you need to be there. I know you want to lie here, but you can't! You have to be there for him."

"I can't Kia. My chest feels empty. There's like this gaping hole where my heart belongs. I can't do it, I just can't!"

"You have to, T. Moto would want you there. I know it hurts sis, I know it does, but this too shall pass. It'll get better soon; you just have to take the first step, which is saying goodbye."

"I don't need any steps, Kia! I don't want to live in a world that he's not in! If there's no Demoto, then there will be no Taryn! He was my heart, and now he's gone and I feel dead." Kia cried as she observed the pain her best friend was in. She sat next to her on the bed and hugged her as they cried. They cried until they felt better. Before long, Taryn had gotten up and was heading to wash her face. When Kia watched her plug her iPod in, she knew she was going to make it.

"I guess we should get dressed before we're late," she smiled lightly.

"Okay well I'm in my room, call my name if you need me," Kia exited quietly. Taryn sat on her bed and looked around her room. She looked at his cologne on her dresser, his clothes in her closet, and got weak all over again. She took a few deep breaths and willed herself not to cry. Just as she got herself together, she heard Ace Hood and Trey Songz *Ride* start to play. She instantly thought of Demoto. He and her use to listen to that song all the time. Tears fell uncontrollably as she thought about the life they'd never have. She thought of the wedding, the kids, and the life that had been ripped from her.

Even though I'm in the streets, you know exactly what I do, when I chase this paper you ain't gotta wait for me to bring back home to you, cuz I ride or die girl we gon be good, and if you ride or die, we gon make it out this hood."

The song blasted through her speakers as she walked back into her closet. Taryn-Lee sang along to the song as tears ran down her face. How could she have gotten to this point? Where had she gone wrong? She had been alone basically her entire life, and the one time she found true love it was taken away. She had given all the love she could, been loyal from day one, and where did it get her? Nowhere! Only place it had gotten her was in her apartment with a broken heart, and a closet full of his clothes to pack. She knew exactly how Ace Hood felt; they were supposed to always be good. She was his ride or die. Taryn was so out of her mind, she tripped over a shoe in the middle of her floor. As she fell into her closet, she hit her head on the doorknob. While lying flat on the floor, she lifted her head a few inches and came face to face with the black safe beneath her shoeboxes. At that moment, she figured there was no way her life could get any worse. Either hitting her head on the door magnified her pain, or the amount of self-pity she was feeling had consumed her. She reached for the case and opened it. The small pink Cobra .22 felt heavy in her hand. As she leaned back against the wall, she stared at the gun for a long moment; she had nothing else to lose, and nothing to look forward to. The only person she had was in a big church with a suit on, waiting to be eulogized. Shaking back her tears, she raised the gun to her mouth and stuck it inside. *Lord please forgive me*, she prayed in her mind before pulling the trigger.

*****

"Taryn! Taryn!" Taryn stirred a few times before opening her eyes. When she did, she smiled. *Finally we're back together*. She looked at his face and remembered placing her gun into her mouth. *We're in heaven!* She reached out and touched the side of his mouth. She ran her hand over his hair, and eyes. She

276

touched the side of his head where the hole was in the picture and smiled, it wasn't there!

"T, get up baby girl we have to go."

"Go? Go where? I want to stay here with you. I don't want to leave! Demoto please don't leave me again! I want to stay in heaven with you. Demoto please, please Demoto please don't make me go!" she begged as she grabbed onto him.

"Yo T, you good bae? Did you take anything?" he asked, shaking her lightly. He looked into her eyes, but she looked fine. "T talk to me, did you take something?" he asked again. Taryn shook her head no and rubbed her eyes. Looking around, she noticed she was still in New York, in the apartment they'd been staying in. *What in the world?* She looked at her packed suitcases and tried to figure out what was going on. Demoto was standing there fully dressed, still wearing his black jacket and jeans he'd worn when they left to see the Elmores.

"What's going on?" she asked. Demoto noticed the confused look on her face.

"T, you must have fallen asleep. When I walked in you were on your knees beside the bed, sleeping." Everything came flooding back to her. She was packing so they could go before she began saying her prayers. She had fallen asleep talking to God. After her memory returned to her, she jumped on Demoto. She wrapped her legs around his waist as she clung to his neck. She was squeezing him as tight as she could. He wrapped his arms around her and squeezed back. He didn't know what was wrong with her, but he was just as happy to be back in her presence. He walked to the bed and sat down with her still on his lap. They held each other for another five minutes before he pulled away.

"What happened?"

"I thought you were dead. Bailey called me and said he'd killed you, he sent the picture and everything." That set off a thought in her mind. She hopped up and ran to grab her phone. She scrolled through her and Demoto's messages, and there was no picture. She held her phone close to her chest and breathed a sigh of relief. "It was a dream." She put her head down and started crying. "Demoto, I never want to live without you. That was the worst time of my life. I tried to kill myself before your funeral." Demoto looked at her with sympathetic eyes. She looked so distraught. He'd thought something was wrong with her when he came in and heard her crying. Upon entering their bedroom, he saw her kneeling on the bed asleep. The cover beneath her face was soaked from her tears.

"I'd never survive without you," she cried. It took her a few minutes to stop crying before she began packing their things again. When she finished, she began to clean. She needed to do something to calm her nerves. She still felt the pain of thinking Demoto was dead. By the time she'd finished cleaning everything, he had taken a shower and gotten dressed. He told her he'd load everything in the car and book their tickets while she got ready. Taryn took a shower, washed her hair, and got dressed. By the time they got into the car and on the way to the airport, it was almost five in the morning. Their flight was set to take off at six thirty. Taryn wanted to know what happened with Bailey and Emily, but judging by their immediate departure he'd taken care of it. She didn't even care to think about it anymore, she was just happy it was them and not him. She laid her head back against the seat and relaxed.

*****

As always, the Double O building was cold as hell as Demoto and Jacko walked to meet Cayman. He'd called and wanted to meet with them earlier that morning. Demoto was a bit shocked that he'd asked him to bring Jacko along. When they got there, they waited in the sitting area until it was their appointment time. Jacko was looking though his phone when it dinged with a text message.

Pretty Lee: *Y'all good?*

Jacko laughed before texting her back.

"Bruh, can you tell your girl to stop texting me?"

"Man I told her ass to stop all that crazy shit," Demoto joined Jacko in laughter

"It's cool, how's my sis doing anyway?"

"She's good now. It took her a minute to wrap her head around me still being alive. That dream had my baby girl shook. I can't go nowhere by myself no more. She was about to come here until I told her you was with me."

"My sister n law wilding ain't she?"

"You have no idea, her little crybaby ass." Demoto went on to tell Jacko about the dream. They were in deep conversation when Cayman's door opened. Bradley walked out and motioned for them to come in. Once they got inside, they noticed Cayman was nowhere in sight. Instead, Mr. Buck sat behind his desk.

"Take your seats gentlemen." Once everybody was all settled in, he began to speak. "Demoto, job well done son. I expected nothing less. However, you did do one thing I didn't approve of–why did you take Taryn-Lee with you?" Demoto looked at Mr. Buck unsure of what to say. He thought about lying, but decided against it.

"I love her. I knew if I'd left her here, she would have clouded my thoughts. It was easier to work knowing she was with me."

"Suppose she'd gotten hurt, then what?"

"I would never let that happen." Buck was heated when he'd found out Taryn had gone along with Demoto to New York. He was about to send Jacko to get her, but Kia begged him not to. Of course, she hadn't known Jacko was who he was going to send; she just didn't want him bothering Taryn. He had planned to chew Demoto upon sight but the humble and confident young man sitting in front of him didn't need that. He believed Demoto when he said he'd never let that happen.

"For your sake, that better be true. As for you Jackson, how would you like to take over the jobs of the two Elmore children? They were in charge of our money system, so to speak." He watched Jacko's eyes look to the ceiling for a few seconds before coming back down.

"Thank you sir, I'd be honored."

"I've been watching you; you're a dependable young man. You're serious about your money, and I respect that. I won't bother asking can you handle this, because I know you can."

"I'll do my best sir."

Buck took a pull of the Cuban cigar he was smoking before he continued.

"Now aside from the business tip, I have other business to speak with you two about. Kee-Kee and Tee-Tee are my babies, and they've obviously taken a liking to you two fellas. I'll make this short. I approve as long as you're serious. Don't fuck them over. I'm not saying y'all have to stay with them forever because I'm a realist, but what I will say is end it respectably. Don't be out in the streets embarrassing my girls." He looked both boys in their eyes waiting for acknowledgement. Jacko wasn't a man of many words so he nodded, but Demoto spoke for them both.

"I'll admit in the beginning we didn't mean for it to go this far with the girls, but I'm glad it did. I can't speak for Jack, but I love T and I plan to keep her."

"And I Kia," Jacko said. Buck was thoroughly pleased with the men his daughter's had chosen. They were strong, business-minded, and not easily intimidated. If they committed to his girls the way they committed to their hustle, he knew there would be no problems out of them. After going over more issues involving the company, the boys left.

*****

Taryn lay in the bed with Kia watching *How to Get Away with Murder* and eating fish and shrimp. They had been at home all day doing nothing, and Taryn was glad. She was exhausted mentally and physically after her and Demoto's trip. She missed Kia and was happy to be back home with her. The episode had just gone off when Jacko stuck his head in the door.

"Pretty Lee, get your ass out of my bed!"

"Boy please! This is my bed. I had Kia long before you came along; I'm just sharing her with you."

"I ain't stun that shit you talking about girl, Kia know what it is. Don't you baby?" She smiled at Jacko so hard Taryn could feel it on her face. She laughed as she got off the bed.

"Damn bitch, your ass cheesing hard!"

"Taryn-Lee you know you my baby, but daddy's home. You got to go!" Kia and Jacko both laughed as he walked in and Taryn walked out. He laid in the spot Taryn had just been in and kicked his shoes off. He pulled his shirt over his head and lay his head on Kia's lap. He told her about the conversation he'd just had with her dad, including the job offer. Kia was shocked to hear her father had known she was with him all along. She thought she had been doing a good job keeping it a secret. She should have known better; Buck knew everything. The job offer made her happy. She knew as long as Jacko was involved with Double O, he would be paid. That meant he wouldn't have to spend so much time working. He could quit some of his side hustles and spend more time with her.

"I'm so happy for you Jack."

"I'm happy too baby. I'll be even happier if you marry me." He had been thinking about marriage for a long time now. Long before Kia came along. He'd always wanted a wife. When Kia came along, he knew she was the one. She held him down no matter what it was. Her feisty attitude matched his. They were like two peas in a pod. Marrying her would only strengthen the bond they shared. They'd only been dating a few months, but they were the realest months of his life. No woman had ever made him want to commit like Kia did. She was his baby. He'd asked Buck before he left, and he had given his blessing. All he needed now was for Kia to say yes. He looked up in her eyes because it was taking a long time to answer. Her smile was a mile wide.

"Stop all that damn cheesing and tell your man yes."

"Yes Jack I'll marry you!" she squealed as she leaned down and placed kisses all over his face. In the middle of their kiss, she hopped off the bed and ran out of her room. She moved so fast she forgot all about Jacko's head being in her lap.

"Taryn! Taryn! Where you at girl?" she yelled as she went into her room. Her and Demoto were sitting on the floor working out. Well, he was and she was sitting there watching him. Kia shook her head at her girl before gushing out her happiness. "Jacko and I are getting married!" Taryn jumped off the floor, practically stepping on Demoto's head, and hugged Kia. Taryn was so excited she made them bump into the door.

"Jacky Boy come here!" she yelled. He came down the hall a few seconds later. She punched him in the chest the moment he got close enough. "I told your ass to wait until I was there!"

"You knew?" Kia asked.

"Yep! I got your ring!" She opened her top drawer and pulled a small velvet box out. Jacko had told her a long time ago he wanted to marry Kia. She'd even gone as far as to pick her ring out for him. He'd sent her the money while she was in New York to pay for it. She was so happy! Kia and Jacko were perfect for one another. If there was anybody that matched more than she and Demoto did, it was Kia and Jacko. Demoto was sitting on the floor smiling at Kia's excitement.

"Congratulations sister in law," he said as he stood to hug her. He grabbed the ring from Taryn and handed it to Jacko. She had it in her hand like she was the one proposing to Kia. "Get this shit before Taryn put it on Kia finger for you." They all burst into laughter as Jacko got on one knee and asked again. Kia smiled and jumped up and down, like he hadn't already asked her one time. She bum rushed him, knocking them both to the floor as she said yes a thousand times. Taryn stood with Demoto's arm wrapped around her waist, wondering when her time would come.

*****

Looking at the water beneath him, Demoto smoked the last of his blunt. The sound of the water and his kush mixed together had his mind at ease. He had come out here about an hour ago to think. Normally he wouldn't stay so long, but tonight he had a lot on his mind. The river walk wasn't the safest place to be at night, but he would kill anybody that tried him. His mind was so overwhelmed with thoughts that he couldn't sleep. He had thought about going to Taryn's house, but he changed his mind. He needed to be alone for a little while. He was trying to wrap his mind around the facts that had been given to him earlier by Buck.

No matter what way he set it up in his mind, he couldn't believe Cayman was no longer in charge of Double O. He had been scamming everyone of their cash from the beginning. He'd been robbing all of his employees from day one. Although that was bad, that wasn't the part that bothered him the most. He couldn't believe Cayman had been in on having his father killed. Buck had gotten an anonymous letter from someone in Cameroon letting him know the details of his father's death. Demoto knew it was his mother. She was vindictive like that. She had been sending anonymous post cards and letters for years, but he and Adisa never responded. As bad as he wanted to just let it all go, he couldn't. His mother and now Cayman would pay. Cayman had thoroughly messed up crossing him. His death would come when he least expected it. Once he'd finished smoking his blunt, he went back to his car and headed home. When he got out of his car, he was attacked by a group of men. They punched and kicked him until he fell unconscious. When he woke up, he was lying on the floor of what looked to be Cayman's living room. He couldn't believe his life right now. He sat up on the floor, and across from him was the last person he expected to see. Taryn was sitting on the couch with a scared look in her eyes. Demoto got up and went to her, but she didn't say anything.

"Don't be scared baby girl, I'll protect you."

"She better be scared because I'm going to kill her ass." Demoto looked around, and there stood Alicia. She had her arms crossed, and she was leaning against the counter. She didn't appear to have any weapons, so he didn't know why Taryn looked so scared. He knew it had to be something, because his baby would have ate Alicia up whole a long time ago if it was that easy.

"Alicia, what's going on? Why are we at Cayman's house, and why do you have Taryn here?"

"I had you all brought here," Cayman said from the top of his long staircase. Fire burned in Demoto's eyes as he laid eyes on him. He wanted to get up and break Cayman's head off his shoulders, but that would have to wait. Right now he needed to figure out what was going on. When Cayman got downstairs he went to Alicia and kissed her. Demoto wasn't surprised; Jacko had told him a while ago Kia saw her kissing some old guy. *It was his old ass.* From the looks of it, Alicia wasn't feeling it the way he was. She moved her head slightly as his lips touched her cheek. Cayman noticed, but kept on walking until he stood in the center of the room. He rubbed the hideous scar on the side of his face as he walked over to Taryn and rubbed his hand through her scalp. Demoto jumped to move his hand, but Alicia pulled a gun and pointed it at Taryn. He wanted to kill her.

"I knew you loved her more than me. I hate her!"
she screamed. Cayman simply walked away and sat
down.

"Demoto, I called you here because I love Alicia.
I know you may think that has nothing to do with you,
but it does. See the thing is, she loves you." Demoto
looked completely unbothered by the situation; that had
nothing to do with him.

"Well I don't love her back, so that shouldn't
matter."

"It won't, by the end of this night. Tonight is
about her. You'll give her the passion she craves. The
affection you show Miss Alvarez will be directed towards
her. Many may judge me for this because they don't
understand. What man would want his woman to gain
things only he is supposed to give her, from someone
else? I'm different; I like my women happy by any means
necessary. So in order for her to be happy, I've promised
her one night of love from you." Demoto objected
immediately.

"Hell No! That shit is not happening."

"Oh but it is. If not, I'll give your sweet little
chocolate lover here some serious attention," he said with
a sinister stare. Demoto balled his fist and let out a loud
breath. He wanted so bad to kill Cayman and Alicia, but
now was not the time. If he wanted him and Taryn to
leave alive, he had to play by Cayman's rules. He looked
over to find her fear stricken eyes with water in them. As
quickly as he thought about cooperating, he changed his
mind.

"Fuck no! I'm not doing this shit while Taryn is here."

"You have no choice."

"Yes the fuck I do, come on T," he stood and pulled Taryn with him. He was prepared to head for the door when Cayman slapped him across the head with a gun.

"NO STOP! PLEASE STOP! It's okay Moto, just do it!" Taryn belted out. She couldn't stand to see him getting hurt on her behalf. She would have to take this L like a champ. She watched as his green eyes turned dark. Blood leaked from the gash on his head as he stared at Cayman. She rushed to him and grabbed the bottom of his face to make him look at her. It took a second for his eyes to meet hers, but when they did his expression softened. She looked at him and nodded.

"It's okay. Just do it." He let out a deep sigh and rested his face into her palm. The whole scene was too much for Alicia to take. She walked over and slapped Taryn across her face. Before anyone could stop her, Taryn punched the taste from her mouth. She was in a very unfair situation, but she wasn't about to let that bitch keep putting her hands on her.

"Listen lil bitch, don't fuck with me," she said as she made her way to the couch and sat back down. Cayman and Demoto both smiled for their own reasons.

"Alright, well let's move this party to the bedroom shall we?" Taryn looked at him, tooted her nose up, and declined the offer. Her tune changed quickly when Cayman told her otherwise. Once they were all in the room, Taryn and Cayman sat on the small sofa in the corner. His gun was pointed to her head. Cayman instructed them to get undressed. Taryn could tell Demoto was heated, but he didn't say anything.

When everything was in order, Demoto and Alicia got into the bed. The look on her face was priceless. You could tell she was happy. She so pathetic! Demoto looked back at Taryn one last time before he leaned in to kiss Alicia. His hand cupped her neck as he tongued her down. They were kissing for a few seconds before a moan escaped her lips. Taryn looked on in pure agony. It made her skin crawl to hear Alicia's moans. Demoto looked back at Taryn again before positioning himself on top of her. He had just finished putting his condom on before sliding into her. The scream that sounded in the room made tears fall from Taryn's eyes. She knew the feeling Alicia was having because she'd become familiar with it. Those same screams she was hearing now, she'd made a few herself. Demoto slid in and out of Alicia while kissing her lips. They way he was being so gentle with her was driving Taryn insane. He looked like he was enjoying it. Alicia's eyes were closed and her mouth was slightly opened. Pleasure was written all over it.

"They're in love sweetheart, they'll never be a place for us in their lives," Cayman said to Taryn as he looked in pain. He too hated this. He hated that he couldn't satisfy the woman he loved. This was his way of getting revenge on Demoto for making Alicia love him. He'd already made up in his mind to kill her once this was over. He'd tried everything he could to turn her and Demoto against each other. He'd made up lies, paraded he and Taryn's relationship in front of her, he'd even had him jumped in front of her, but nothing helped. He thought maybe seeing him get beat up would push her away from him, but it hadn't. Alicia wasn't the type for drama, but even the fight hadn't scared her away. He didn't want to lose Demoto as an employee back then; he just wanted her to himself.

Cayman's words weighed heavy in her mind as she watched Demoto bite Alicia's bottom lip. *No matter what the situation may be, always trust me. If there ever comes a time you're not sure what to believe, believe me. Believe in the love I have for you, the love we have for each other.* Demoto's words were the only thing that kept her sane. She sat up in the chair and took slow breaths. If she was going to get through this, she had to believe it was all a show. The closer attention she paid, she realized that's exactly what it was. What he was doing with Alicia was different than what he did with her. He was always so gentle with her. He talked and massaged her body the entire time. When they were together, he made her look into his eyes, not to mention the kissing. It was hurting like all hell to watch him give away her love, but if that's what kept them alive she would do it.

The final nail in the coffin was when he ejaculated. Demoto never came that quick when he was with her. It had only been about ten minutes before he stopped. He had just pulled out when he looked over at her. He made eye contact for only a few seconds before looking at the floor. He was notably embarrassed. Taryn wished she could comfort him, but their circumstances wouldn't permit that.

As Demoto and Alicia got dressed, Taryn followed Cayman out of the room. They went to his wet bar and he made them both drinks. Taryn was a little hesitant at first but after the night she'd just had, she drank the whole cup in one swallow. He was refilling her glass again when they were joined by the porn stars. Taryn looked at them both and turned back to face Cayman. He looked at her and winked. Although it was his idea, she was sure they were feeling the same way at the moment. The whole thing was forced, but she still felt a little angry. The room was quiet with an awkward silence for a good twenty minutes.

"Can we go now?" Demoto asked as his thick African accent boomed out. Taryn could always tell when he was the angriest, because his accent was next to impossible to understand.

"You may," Cayman said as he nodded his head for the door. Taryn and Demoto were almost to the door when Alicia stepped in front of them. She was crying and asking why Demoto didn't love her. Her over dramatic act was pissing Taryn off.

"WHY DON'T YOU LEAVE HER?"

"Move Alicia," Demoto moved around her headed for the door.

"Why won't you just die bitch?" she yelled at Taryn. Taryn turned around to face her.

"Because real riders never die." With that, she turned and left the house. She probably should have been worried about what Cayman had planned for them, but she wasn't. Albeit them being able to leave like that was too easy; in a weird way she trusted him. At least at that moment she did. When they were outside, Demoto was surprised to see his car there. The men that kidnapped him had obviously brought his car along as well. The ride back home was completely silent. Instead of taking Taryn home, he went straight to his house. She opened her mouth to speak, but changed her mind and followed him inside.

*****

Inside the shower, Demoto couldn't believe what had just happened. Never in a million years would he have subjected Taryn to a freak show like that. He could tell it made her feel indifferent because she still hadn't spoken. He couldn't blame her though. If he had to sit back with a gun to his head and watch another man make love to her, he would die. His life would have ended right on that sofa, the main reason being objecting to it happening. He would have gotten shot the moment the sex started. He leaned his head against the wall as the water cascaded over his body. He had just finished washing his hair when he heard the door open. When he looked up, Taryn stood there undressing. When she was completely naked, she joined him in the shower.

"You done washing that girl juices off you?" she smiled. He smirked lightly as he nodded his head yes.

"Don't worry about it Moto. You did what you had to do. If was either sleep with the desperate girl or die. I'm not tripping."

"I'm sorry you had to see that." Taryn shrugged her shoulders and began to bathe.

"Demoto I'm tired of all the crazy stuff. Can we please just have a normal relationship?"

"Yes we can, because I am too bae. I promise this is the end of the madness."

"Thank you Jesus! I'm so over it all," she said as she pressed her body against his. He held onto her tightly until the water ran cold. When they got into bed, neither of them was in the mood for sex, so he held her until the fell asleep.

*****

The next day, Demoto was up bright and early. He had things to do, and people to see. He couldn't stand the way Cayman had disrespected Taryn last night by pulling that stuff with Alicia. He had to pay. Nobody would ever choose his woman for him. There was nobody in the world that would make him leave Taryn. He didn't care what the circumstances were. Cayman was going to hate he'd ever done this. The fact that Buck had ordered a job on Cayman was just the icing on the cake. He could kill his enemy, and get paid for doing it.

He hated that Alicia was about to get caught in the crossfire, but she should have chosen the winning side. She sided with a loser, so she would suffer his fate as well. Looking across the street making sure cars weren't coming, he jogged across and stopped at the light. He had chosen to walk to handle this business. He couldn't risk anyone seeing his car. He walked a few miles before sneaking up the long sidewalk. Once he got to the back, he opened the door quietly and walked in. He stood still for a moment, listening for movement; when he heard none, he continued up the stairs. The room to the door he and Alicia had been in last night was still slightly ajar. The covers were strewn across the bed; they hadn't even bothered to clean up. Thinking about what he was made to do only motivated him more.

As he opened the door to Cayman's room, he saw him and Alicia sleeping. They were both naked, so apparently he'd finished where Demoto left off. While having sex with Alicia last night, he hadn't even given her a chance to climax. Once he'd finished, he pulled out and left her hanging. He wouldn't give her what belonged to Taryn. She was the only woman that deserved to make him come apart. She owned his body. Anything that he loved as much as sex would be paired with the love of his life. As he crept over to the bed, Cayman's eyes popped open. He smiled at Demoto as he closed them back.

"Get up," Demoto, said but he lay there and shook his head no.

"Just kill me. I've done so many bad things, I knew my time would come. I'm glad they sent a man that I respect to do the job. I've been a part of this life a long time; I know how this goes, do it and get it over with." Demoto stood dumbfounded for a moment before pulling his gun and placing two bullets into Cayman's skull.

Because he had screwed his silencer on in the hallway, Alicia hadn't heard a thing. She lay there in a peaceful slumber until he snatched her out of the bed by her neck. He squeezed until her eyes popped out of her head. She was still struggling as her face began to turn blue. She slapped at his hands wildly until her body went limp. He choked her some more before turning her body around in his arms and breaking her neck. He let her body drop to the floor before sending a text letting Bradley know it was done. He looked at her lifeless body on the floor and felt bad for a moment, but it left as fast as it came. No one would fuck with Taryn's heart or sanity on his watch. The stunt she and Cayman had pulled was enough to drive a person crazy, and he couldn't let that happen to her. His level of love and respect for her went to a totally different level last night. Anybody that could endure something like that was force. There was nobody walking this earth that could make him watch another man make love to his woman. His adrenaline started pumping at that thought. Checking to make sure everything was in order, he called the cleanup crew before exited the house. It wasn't until he was safely back across the street that he removed his gloves and walked back to the grocery store to get his car.

Chapter 19

Three months later...

Taryn had just turned in her final assignment for the quarter and was free to do what she wanted. School was not something she enjoyed, but she knew it had to be done. She packed her backpack and left the campus library. She was excited to leave because she was about to meet up with Demoto. It had been a few months, and their lives finally seemed back to normal. He and her spent every free minute they had together. Demoto had tied up every loose end and burned them, so their lives were peaceful. Two bodies had been found burned and left beneath the 10th street bridge. The bodies were found two days after their little encounter with Cayman and Alicia. Demoto hadn't outright told her, but she knew it was them, and she knew it was him. She looked up at the sun shining down on her and smiled. She liked the think when the sun shined this bright it was her parents looking down on her. *Thank you for my life Lord.* She was in the middle of her prayer when she felt her phone vibrate. Looking down, she noticed it was a text.

> **My Love Moto:** *You fed my baby?*

> **Taryn:** *an apple and some water*

> **My Love Moto:** *Ima beat your ass.*

> **Taryn:** *Sure you are. Just leaving school, I'm on my way*

She placed her phone back into her purse and looked down at her small round belly.

"Your daddy is such a meany." Taryn had found out a month ago that she was pregnant. She was even more shocked to find out she was almost six months along. She was so far when she found out she was pregnant that they were able to tell the sex as well. She had no idea how being pregnant had gotten past her. Then again, with all the drama she'd had going on she hadn't paid it any attention. Demoto was super happy and super bossy. Taryn wouldn't have it any other way. Their son was going to be spoiled. She pictured a little brown baby with blonde hair and green eyes like his daddy. She rubbed her small stomach as she got into her car. She drove to Jacko's house where she was meeting Demoto and got out. She loved Jacko's house, but hated the stairs. He had moved from his apartment and into a house. He and Kia had gotten married two weeks ago, and he wanted them to live as such. He Kia, Taryn, Buck, and Demoto had flown to Hawaii and had a private wedding on the North Shore, and flew back three days ago. The house was Kia's wedding gift.

"It's about time you got here," Kia said as she opened the door for her.

"Girl it took me forever to write that paper! What y'all in here doing?"

"I'm cooking and your man and his childish best friend are playing the game." Taryn walked into the back room that Jacko had set up as his little man cave. As soon as Demoto saw her, he paused the game and got up to kiss her lips. He kissed her mouth a few times before rubbing her belly. He rubbed all over it until he felt movement. Taryn was so glad the little boy moved for his daddy today, because Demoto wouldn't stop touching her stomach until he did. Sometimes he would touch and talk to her belly for hours. It was cute and all, but it got old quick.

"I've thought of him a name. Let's name is Ayo."

"Ayo?"

"Yeah, I want him to have an African name." Taryn thought about for a minute.

"Okay, Ayo Youngblood it is," she smiled. He kissed her again before sitting back down. They stayed at Kia and Jacko's house for another couple of hours before going home. Since Kia had moved out, Taryn had practically moved back in with Demoto. She hadn't known how scared she was to live by herself until Kia left. She had just gotten out of the shower and was brushing her hair when he walked in. She wore a sports bra and a pair of jogging shorts. He small stomach was barely poking out for her to be so far along, but she wasn't complaining. Demoto sat on the edge of the bed and watched her. He was so in love.

"I love you T."

"I love you too babe."

"I think you're beautiful."

"I think you're beautiful too," she turned and smiled at him. He laughed as he pushed his hair from his face. Before getting into bed, he pulled her to him and kissed her stomach. He talked to Ayo while she finished doing her hair. When she finished, they got into bed. The room was quiet except for their breathing. He could tell she had fallen asleep because of the subtle change in her breathing. He inhaled her scent; she was the air in his lungs, the beat to his heart, the love of his life, and the mother of his child. One day soon, she would be his wife. He basked in the thoughts of being with her until the end. He'd be with her until there was no more Taryn and Demoto.

"I want this forever," he whispered in her ear before drifting off to sleep.

Join our mailing list to get a notification when Leo Sullivan Presents has another release!

Text LEOSULLIVAN to 22828

to join!

Last release:

Luvin' A Certified Thug 3

Check out our new and upcoming releases on the next page! Click the new releases image below to read for FREE with Kindle Unlimited

To submit a manuscript for our review, email us at leosullivanpresents@gmail.com

Join our mailing list to get a notification for these upcoming releases!